The Duchess Diaries

"There is so much to love about this book. The witty dialogue and the fantastically paced writing, the characters who sparkle and come to life on every page ... a romance tale at its finest."
—Smexy Books Romance Reviews

"The reader will have a hard time putting it down."
—Fresh Fiction

"Another completely captivating combination of wonderfully madcap plotting, wickedly humorous writing, and wildly hot passion." —*Booklist*

"Fast-paced, sexy, and hilarious.... Run, don't walk, to get a copy." —*Romantic Times*

A Bride Unveiled

"Sizzling sexual chemistry and rapier wit ... a thoroughly romantic literary treat." —*Booklist*

"Hunter draws the reader in with a compelling plot and engaging characters in this smoothly written tale of love lost and found." —*Publishers Weekly*

A Duke's Temptation

"A sinfully sexy hero with a secret, a book-obsessed heroine in search of her own happy-ever-after ending, a delightfully clever plot that takes great fun in spoofing the literary world, and writing that sparkles with wicked wit and exquisite sensuality add up to an exceptionally entertaining read." —*Booklist* (starred review)

"With humor and charm, sensuality and wickedness, Hunter delights." —*Romantic Times*

continued ...

"This is the first in what looks to be a very promising, and extremely seductive, new quartet. Few can resist a novel by Jillian Hunter!" —Huntress Book Reviews

More Praise for the Novels of Jillian Hunter

"One of the funniest, most delightful romances I've had the pleasure to read." —Teresa Medeiros

"An absolutely delightful tale that's impossible to put down." —*Booklist*

"A sweet, romantic tale . . . full of humor, romance, and passion. Historical romance that is sure to please." —The Romance Readers Connection

"A lovely read." —Romance Reader at Heart

"Enchanting . . . a fabulous historical." —*Midwest Book Review*

"[It] bespells, beguiles, and bewitches. If romance, magic, great plots, and wonderful characters add spice to your reading life, don't allow this one to escape." —Crescent Blues

"Romantic and sexy. . . . Read it—you'll love it!" —The Romance Reader

"Jillian Hunter's ability to touch chords deep within readers' hearts is what sets her apart and makes her and everything she writes a keeper." —*Romantic Times*

"Ms. Hunter pens unique, fascinating stories that draw the reader right in. Impossible to put down." —*Rendezvous*

"A master at wringing emotion from every page, Ms. Hunter explodes onto the scene with an extraordinary tale that combines brilliant writing with sizzling sexual tension." —The Speaking Tree

JILLIAN HUNTER

A Boscastle Affairs Novel

The Mistress Memoirs

A SIGNET SELECT BOOK

SIGNET SELECT
Published by the Penguin Group
Penguin Group (USA) Inc., 375 Hudson Street,
New York, New York 10014, USA
Penguin Group (Canada), 90 Eglinton Avenue East, Suite 700, Toronto,
Ontario M4P 2Y3, Canada (a division of Pearson Penguin Canada Inc.)
Penguin Books Ltd., 80 Strand, London WC2R 0RL, England
Penguin Ireland, 25 St. Stephen's Green, Dublin 2,
Ireland (a division of Penguin Books Ltd.)
Penguin Group (Australia), 707 Collins Street, Melbourne, Victoria 3008,
Australia (a division of Pearson Australia Group Pty. Ltd.)
Penguin Books India Pvt. Ltd., 11 Community Centre, Panchsheel Park,
New Delhi–110 017, India
Penguin Group (NZ), 67 Apollo Drive, Rosedale, Auckland 0632,
New Zealand (a division of Pearson New Zealand Ltd.)
Penguin Books (South Africa), Rosebank Office Park, 181 Jan Smuts Avenue,
Parktown North 2193, South Africa
Penguin China, B7 Jiaming Center, 27 East Third Ring Road North,
Chaoyang District, Beijing 100020, China

Penguin Books Ltd., Registered Offices:
80 Strand, London WC2R 0RL, England

First published by Signet Select, an imprint of New American Library,
a division of Penguin Group (USA) Inc.

First Printing, March 2013
10 9 8 7 6 5 4 3 2 1

PUBLISHER'S NOTE
This is a work of fiction. Names, characters, places, and incidents either are the
product of the author's imagination or are used fictitiously, and any resemblance
to actual persons, living or dead, business establishments, events, or locales is
entirely coincidental.
   The publisher does not have any control over and does not assume any responsibility for author or third-party Web sites or their content.

ALWAYS LEARNING   **PEARSON**

To my fabulous cousin Tracy.

*I'm so happy we found each other after all these years.
I love you.*

A woman who has led a flawless life is like a book filled with empty pages.
    — Audrey Watson, celebrated
        nineteenth-century English courtesan

Chapter 1

*A*t first glance Miss Kate Walcott fancied that the shadow stretched out across the far garden wall was the estate's gray tomcat waiting for a small creature to pass in the dark. It seemed to be hiding behind the branches of the sprawling birch tree in readiness to pounce. Kate shuffled her slippered feet through the grass, hoping to give the cat's quarry a chance to escape.

"Go away," she whispered at the leafy branches. "I don't like to watch you catching things, or to hear you yowling for a mate. Cook feeds you so many table scraps that one day you'll be caught by a dog. Why you behave so badly at night, I don't understand. But I suppose on this estate, you aren't the only one."

Strange. Malvolio didn't react to her voice. Maybe it wasn't a cat at all. Maybe it was a badger. Whatever it was had been watching her since the moment she'd slipped from the manor house to meet her friend at the garden gates. Could one of the children be playing a prank on her? The young devils delighted in scaring a scream from their governess.

"Get off the wall," she said again, staring uneasily at the gates.

Mr. Stanley Wilkes, who was the village apothecary's assistant, and the young man she had an arrangement to meet, had not yet arrived. She grasped her ring of keys tightly in her palm. She counted Stanley as one in a dwindling population of villagers who defied convention to acknowledge Kate and her employer in public. Stanley treated her with respect and not the contempt she'd come to expect when she explained what she did for a living.

"Stanley?" she called uncertainly, even though she couldn't see or hear him in the driveway that led to the gates. But that shadow upon the wall *had* stirred. And the sound of its movement indicated that it was much larger than a cat.

She wondered if something had prevented Stanley from meeting her. This was the third time he'd concocted a brew to ease the chest colds that often afflicted the two youngest children in Kate's care. Stanley claimed it was a mercy that Kate hadn't taken ill yet. She explained that she couldn't afford the time to lie abed. Everyone depended on her. Moreover, Kate's employer distrusted surgeons and would not allow one in the house.

But Kate and Stanley had not openly discussed her position. He seemed to understand that just because Kate had fallen on reduced circumstances and worked as a companion to a courtesan, as well as governess to her offspring, did not mean Kate practiced the world's oldest profession herself. Often she feared it was a matter of time.

From the corner of her eye she glimpsed a long shadow on the grass. A shadow that appeared much longer and moved with more stealth than a cat or a child. Her heart missed several beats.

She listened to the night. She recognized the muted cries of male voices drifting from the stables on the edge of the estate. The stable boys and servants might be gambling or boxing again, which meant she'd be tending black eyes and bloody noses later on as well as two sick children. Splendid. There went any chance of sleep.

She stepped around the rose bower and called toward the stables, "Lovitt? Lovitt, if you and the others are fighting—"

She swung around, her ring of keys slipping to the grass. She heard footsteps, distant but definitely advancing. Lovitt was the manor house's undergroom, who hoped to be promoted when the master returned. He was a cocksure young man, but she wouldn't mind his company right now.

"Stanley!" she called in the direction of the gates. "Where are you?"

He didn't answer. But all of a sudden the gates shuddered and groaned as if a demon were demanding entrance. She fell to the grass that bordered the path, searching frantically for the keys.

"Kate!" his wary voice called through the clanking echo of iron.

"Stanley, where are you?"

"I'm hiding beside the damned gates! You were supposed to leave them unlocked for me!"

"I've lost the keys here in the garden," she answered in relief, glancing up from the lawn. She could see the pale glint of his hair. "I'll only be a moment."

"We don't have a moment!" he cried. "You have to let me in *now*. A small crowd of drunks at the pub have decided to cause trouble for your mistress tonight."

Kate turned her head, her spine prickling. It *wasn't* her imagination. There *had* been a person hiding behind the birch branches that grew onto the garden wall. Was it one of the troublemakers from the village, or merely another of Madam's would-be customers? Either way, he would not receive a warm welcome. It would have been helpful if she'd brought a lamp out to expose him.

It would have been even more helpful if her employer's new protector had waited for the ink to dry on their contract before he rushed off to business in Southampton instead of leaving his concubine and her dependents unguarded in a backward hamlet where spitting on a Sunday was considered a mortal sin.

Then again, it would have been even better if Georgette had chosen a respectable means of support. Still, Kate was dedicated to her immoral mistress and devoted to her children. Georgette had redeemed Kate from ruin when society had branded her an outcast. If not for Georgette's income, from her willingness to sleep with wealthy patrons, Kate would have landed in the poorhouse. The possibility still loomed in the future.

Still, at least in Georgette's opinion, there was no need to worry. As Kate's employer so often liked to misquote, "'Hell hath no fury like a harlot scorned.'" Then she would continue, "We shall yet have our revenge, Kate, when my memoirs are published. We will become rich and retire in luxury. The children will attend the finest schools, and those who have attacked us on moral grounds will grovel at our feet."

"And will we forgive them?" Kate would tease her. It was a game they played during lean times or low spirits— a game to motivate each other and reassert their independence from society.

"We shall have to review each gentleman on a case-by-case basis. After all, the world would be too boring without men to cause us woe."

The metal ring gleamed at Kate's foot; the keys lay tangled in a patch of clover. She reached down and froze in dead fear at the loud thump of something landing behind her.

A pleasantly deep voice whispered in her ear, "I've been waiting over a week to speak to you alone, my darling, and it seems I'm not a moment too late. You appear to have made as many enemies as you have admirers. May I come to your rescue, or will you come to mine?"

She rose slowly. She didn't recognize the voice. "Who—"

A pair of strong arms closed around her waist and drew her back against a hard torso in a hold she doubted she could escape even if she regained the ability to move. "Kiss me before I silence that idiot at the gates and inform him that you're not available to tryst tonight."

Chapter 2

Sir Colin Boscastle had been away from England for thirteen years, pursuing the man he believed had murdered his father. He appreciated the irony that his search had brought him back to the first woman he had ever loved. It had always been his intention to make amends to Georgette for abandoning her. He hadn't kept his promise, and so he should atone. He doubted she would appreciate his return, however, considering that Colin's enemy and her protector were one and the same man, and that Colin meant to confront the man even if Georgette begged him to show mercy.

Then again, the woman Georgette had become might not care about her former lover. She didn't appear to be overly concerned with the current one, either, or she wouldn't be sneaking out for a secret assignation with yet another man while Mason Earling, her protector, was away on business.

It was quite unromantic, Colin thought, even if it rang of a certain poetic justice. A courtesan sneaking out for a rendezvous while her keeper was off reaping profits he'd made on a murdered man's investments.

"Let me go right now," she whispered, bending ineffectively over his arm. "I need those blessed keys, you bas—"

"Ssh. Temper, temper. Some things haven't changed. Turn around. Do I look that different?"

She stiffened, refusing to budge. "All you drunken rascals look the same to me. You—" She broke off at the sound of running, shouting, a man cursing behind the garden wall.

"Rail at me all you like later," Colin said, tightening his grasp. "Just be quiet for a moment. Your friend will have to come back another night. I'm not going to let you go. Look at me."

She made a half turn, her face turned stubbornly to the side.

"That's better. Now—"

She kicked the inside of his knee; the way she'd lowered her head made him think she'd intended to kick him in the nutmegs. He shouldn't be surprised. Once, in the throes of their insatiable passion, Georgette had broken the bedpost to which he had tied her during their love play and then had fallen asleep. He couldn't say it was a complete shock when the local blacksmith informed him upon his arrival a few days ago that Georgette was a widowed courtesan with three children and had recently become mistress to the lord of the manor.

"I know I've taken too long to make amends." He pinned her wrists behind her back, satisfied by the warm stillness of her body. The keys slipped from her grasp. He caught the ring before it reached the grass. "You have every right to resent me."

She tossed her head. The thick knot of tawny brown hair at her nape came unraveled. "I have every right to kill you," she said, averting her face. "You must be mad, accusing me of trysts and then taking me captive. I don't know what you want—well, I can guess, and I guarantee you aren't getting it from me. Now, release me or I'll call the dogs on you."

He laughed softly. "Call the dogs. I've been nosing around this estate for four days and haven't heard as much as a 'bowwow.' How times have changed. Perhaps, instead of your hostility, I should receive preferential treatment for playing such a large role in your success."

"What role? Are you the most arrogant jackass I have ever met or simply an imbecile?"

His laughter died away. "You don't remember me yet, do you? We've changed. Perhaps you'd recognize me in the daylight." He grasped her chin in his hand to kiss her lightly on the lips. "If this doesn't awaken your memory, I'll be deeply insulted."

His mouth fastened on hers. She couldn't breathe. She parted her lips in indignation, unwillingly allowing his tongue to penetrate her mouth, to invoke sensations that set off chaos in her body. Who in the world did he think he was? What made a complete stranger imagine that he could dominate, tempt, arouse her? His free hand sculpted her shoulder blades, her backside, crushing her gently to his body. He was behaving as if she should be grateful for this impropriety.

She pulled back in panic, whispering urgently, "Take ahold of yourself this instant. I mean it."

He exhaled softly against her mouth. Moments elapsed, her heart pounding the passage of time. Her stomach fluttered as if she were falling and didn't know when or where she would land. She sensed the tension that came over him, as he slowly raised his hand to brush her hair from her face. She could feel his stare penetrate to the turmoil inside her. He shook his head.

"Why didn't you tell me?" he said, his breathing uneven.

She lifted her head. "Give me the keys," she said in a husky voice.

"You aren't Georgette."

"Of all the gall! I never said I was."

"But you sneaked out of her house."

"Yes," she said, nodding at the brilliance of his deduction. "I happen to live there. I can only assume you were hoping to reignite an old flame with my mistress. For your information, she never takes up with a lover once she's discarded him."

"An old—"

"It must have been quite a spark in its day, because I have worked as Mrs. Lawson's companion for over a decade and have *never* encountered a man so convinced of his own charm."

He shook his head. "This is quite embarrassing."

"Quite," she said, biting off the word.

"No. I am—I'm more than sorry. I feel entirely abased. You're taking this better than me, I have to say."

She held out her hand. "Give me the keys."

He sighed, reaching deep into the pocket of his black woolen greatcoat. "Who are you, please?"

"I am Miss Walcott, companion to Mrs. Lawson and governess to her children," Kate replied in the most impassive voice she could manage, the voice she used on wayward gentlemen and her disobedient wards. "I should caution you right now that Madam does not accept callers at this time of night, especially those who vault over garden walls like Visigoths invading a foreign land."

He blinked. "Visigoths?"

"That's what I said."

He studied her in dubious silence. "Are you her body-guard, too?"

"At times."

He rubbed his hand over his face. "I'm exhausted. You looked like her in the dark. In fact, you look like her now—your hair, the shape of your face, and your figure."

"My figure is none of your business," Kate retorted, too annoyed to admit that she and Georgette were often mistaken for sisters, and that, in fact, one of the reasons Georgette had taken Kate on was because it pleased her vanity to employ a companion in her own image.

Still, Kate had no intention of assuaging his guilt.

Perhaps he'd think twice before preying on another woman.

"Believe me, I came here to see Mrs. Lawson."

"Madam is not available tonight." Kate grasped the key ring and hitched up her cloak and skirts, adding as she turned to the gates, "In future you might try writing her a letter first. After she ponders it, she may or may not send you a reply stating whether she will receive you."

"Has she learned to write?"

She stopped before taking a step. How many of Georgette's past lovers knew her second-most-guarded secret? How many hours had Georgette labored to memorize entire books in order to give a "reading" to her party guests? How many times had Kate made up witty remarks for her mistress to sprinkle into her conversations at social events, only to have Georgette forget them in midrecital?

Georgette, in fact, was more ashamed of her inability to read or write than she was of how she made a living. Who but Madam's oldest friends would know what she regarded as her greatest weakness? She turned, assessing the lean face with its light growth of stubble and the devilish blue eyes, whose impact she had heard described too many times.

"It can't be," she said under her breath.

"What can't be?" he asked guardedly.

"You can't—" She gasped, glancing around the garden in disbelief.

Voices erupted in the night. Stanley had climbed the wall and jumped clumsily to the ground, muttering about a hole in his trousers. A group of servants came running into the garden from the outbuildings. Kate's heart lurched in fear. An army composed of a middle-aged butler, an aging footman, two young stable boys, an aggressive undergroom, and a single blunderbuss between them hardly posed a threat to the band of drunken rabble-rousers who had suddenly appeared jeering and shouting at the garden gates. "What do they mean to do?" she whispered in shock.

"Nothing if I can help it," the stranger said in a curt voice. "By the way, my name is Colin—"

"Boscastle," she said numbly, the mayhem breaking loose around her momentarily insignificant.

"You've heard of me?" he asked, looking puzzled as he pulled a pistol from his waistband.

"Indeed," she said in a faint voice. "Madam has devoted the entire first chapter of her memoirs to you."

"Charming. I'm honored." He grasped her arm and pulled her behind him. This time, however, she did not resent taking shelter behind the steel wall of his body. "Another thing," he said as he guided her away from the wall. "Visigoths protected their women. Hopefully, we shall be able to discuss history later tonight and not become part of it. I suggest you ask the fool who just tore his pants to take you to safety. We are under attack."

Chapter 3

A village ruffian stood atop the wall, shooting burning arrows into the garden. A second vandal knelt beside him scratching the flint of a tinderbox to supply fire as fast as his companion could take aim. Three others had scaled the wall to swing onto a branch and drop into the garden. Colin thought they might have a ladder propped on the other side.

"Lay off, you arseholes!" shouted another young male in a billowing white shirt and riding breeches as he pelted toward the wall. Five small dogs yapped at his heels. If those tiny creatures were the guard dogs the governess had mentioned, the estate would have been better protected by trained squirrels. For a moment Colin wondered whether the white shirt had mistaken *him* for an attacker. Then Colin noticed a third man grappling with an older gray-haired gent who looked as if he was dressed in servant's livery.

Colin ran across the grass, slowing to throw an intruder against the wall before planting himself in the path of yet another middle-aged man—in a cleric's collar, of all costumes. "What man of God incites a lunatic mob against women and children?" he roared. "What religion gives you the right to threaten innocents?"

"I am the Reverend Chatwin, sir," the man replied, gazing about the garden in dismay. "I'm not here to lead a moral revolt. I came only to discourage from violence those who are offended by Mrs. Lawson's profession."

"Burning a house and perhaps the people inside it isn't considered a sin?"

"Indeed, sir, it is. But my congregation will not listen to me. If Mr. Earling and the rugged footmen he employs to guard him were here, this attack would not have happened."

"Why didn't he leave them here to protect the house?"

"It is my understanding that Mr. Earling's family has been sought by a disgruntled rival for years."

"Is that right?"

"Mr. Earling's late father was forced to hide in Ireland to escape. Young Mr. Earling dares not travel alone on lonely roads to reach his ports of business. He fears this rival will kill him."

An unkempt youth carrying a bulging sack came running in their direction, a leer on his face. "Do me a favor, Reverend," Colin said tersely. "Go home and write a sermon before you are injured."

The reverend regarded Colin in vexation. "I have not seen you before. Are you one of Mrs. Lawson's customers?"

"Does it matter right now?"

Colin reached out his arm, stopping the attacker cold, and punched him in the face. The sack he had cradled in his arms, which Colin realized contained a load of stones, dropped at the reverend's feet.

"He's cracked my jaw in half," the vandal moaned, falling to his knees. "My God, the pain."

Colin stepped over his huddled form. "Perhaps the reverend will pray—" He was distracted by the sight of two figures heading furtively for the rose bower. Evidently the governess and her midnight companion had heeded his warning to stay out of sight. The Reverend Chatwin, however, still stood at Colin's side in petrified shock.

"Heed my warning, Reverend. Get out of here now. Or hide in the rose bower. Just don't pray in anybody's way."

"Where should I go?"

"In the house."

Colin didn't wait another moment. He saw a probable assailant run into the flat side of a shovel swung by the young man in the billowing shirt and breeches. As the offender staggered into a bench, the white-shirted hero proceeded to beat out the growing flames with his shovel and hold back the second intruder in alternate strikes. As strong as he appeared, he could not keep fending off attacks by himself forever.

"Hand down the buckets!" Colin bellowed in the direction of the outbuildings. He pulled off his coat and threw it over the hedge.

A burning arrow seared into his shoulder a few seconds after and fell to the ground. He stamped out the spurt of fire, straightened, and charged forward to throw his body weight at the bowman, whose taunting grin soon gave way to a deep-throated groan.

Colin clapped a hand to his shoulder, grimaced, and looked around. He saw several figures escaping over the wall. The garden was almost deserted, except for the servants, who had done their best to defend the house and stood in a cluster, watching him in cautious silence, empty buckets in hand. He nodded at them, retrieved his coat, and made a leisurely tour of the garden. When he was satisfied that all was clear except for the smoke lingering in the air, he started to walk toward the house. He assumed that by now the governess had informed her mistress that she had a visitor. Whether he would receive a warmer welcome from Georgette than he had from Miss Walcott he couldn't guess.

Chapter 4

*G*eorgette stood at the bedroom window with her son and two coughing children. The commotion in the garden had awakened the sicklings from their uneasy slumber; not one of them would heed their mother's or their nursemaid's pleas to return to bed. Why Brian, Etta, and Charlie obeyed Kate, Georgette did not know, but her hard-worked companion and governess wasn't here.

Kate appeared to be involved in the activity below, which Georgette's eldest son Brian was watching in fascination. "They're fighting. I want to go down. Look at all those men. Look at Lovitt and that shovel. Oh, it's beautiful. It's the best thing I've seen. Smack him in the chops!"

"You are *not* going out at night to risk a chest cough," Georgette said in dismay, turning to the mirror to assess her appearance. Her gold-tinged brown ringlets sat beguilingly on her shoulders. Her copper silk dress fit her curvaceous form to perfection; if there was a decent caller in the pandemonium below, she would turn him from her door, of course. But she would allow a teasing look at her in the window.

She was, after all, high-priced merchandise, a piece of ware that had been taken on lease but as yet not bought for life. She was holding out for someone—or something. She doubted it was love. Security, certainly. Respect? Impossible in her profession. Power? To do what? To stop worrying about whether her bosom would grow wrinkled, or whether she would get pregnant again despite all the precautions she urged her lovers to take.

Etta coughed again, in her face. "Mama, I want to be sick. My supper's coming up. It's the wambles."

"Do it out the window," Georgette said in panic, turning to the children's nursemaid. "No, Nan, take her back to bed. What *is* Kate doing?"

"She's with a man," Brian said in alarm. "He's pulling her by the arm. I've never seen him before. I think he's helping Bledridge."

"The butler?" Georgette peered into the garden. It was not from mere vanity that she refused to wear spectacles: not only did myopia blur her flaws in the mirror; it made many of her lovers look half-appealing. "That is the man from the apothecary's," she said in surprise. "Why doesn't she bring the medicine up here? It's not the first time Kate has seen a fireworks display. But—it isn't like Kate to fuss about when the children need her."

The nursemaid's withered mouth worked into a smile. She was still spry, in her late seventies, sharper in many aspects than Georgette had ever been. "That is not a fireworks display, madam. Those are arrows being shot aflame into the hedges to cause an inferno. The 'parade' of excitable youth is what we used to call a mob in London. Have you forgotten?"

Georgette turned paler than the water pearls threaded through her hair. "They're calling me by name," she said slowly. "Listen."

"They are calling you *names*," Nan said in disparagement. "And none of them suitable for young ears."

"Get back into the nursery, all of you," Georgette said, suddenly realizing that Nan was right. "Brian, you are going to fall out the window leaning over like that."

He didn't react. Her son was lost in another world—a man's world of danger and fighting and defending ... what didn't particularly matter as long as it roused the blood and rescued him from the nursery. "He's mowing them down like bowls," he said. "I want to go down to help him. There are men crawling back over the wall like worms and Lovitt is bashing at them for all he's worth. So is Bledridge in the flower bed. They need another man. May I go down to help him, madam?"

"Who is that other man?" asked ten-year-old Charlie, peeking around his half brother's shoulder. "Is he good or bad?"

"He's very bad," Georgette said before she could stop herself. "He has wickedness written all over his—"

She reached her arm out to her firstborn, looking down in hesitation at the stranger who had captured Brian's and now Charlie's imagination. Her heart turned over as the tall black-haired man launched himself into the fight.

"Oh, no," she whispered. "It can't be. It isn't. Maybe I do need spectacles. Maybe I have the wambles, too. Is the room spinning?"

"What's the matter?" Brian asked, drawn away from the window by the oddness of her voice.

"Go back to bed now," she whispered. "Stay there until I send Kate to bring you out."

"But what have we done?" Brian demanded.

"Just do what I tell you for once. You all be deathly ill. You need rest and medicine. I need a drink. Go! Go quickly. Everything will be all right. Kate will bring your tonic to the nursery."

Brian pulled away from her in disgust. "I am not a

baby and I will not stay in the nursery any longer. If you need me, ma'am, I will be sleeping in the stables."

"Brian—"

He swept from the room, the nursemaid he scorned and his two half siblings staring after him in shock. His outbursts of rebellion had become more frequent since Georgette had moved into Mason Earling's house, even though in all fairness Mason had done his awkward best to win the boy over.

With every year that passed, Brian had grown more to resemble his natural father, until tonight she could not even look down into the garden at the stranger without thinking that even he reminded her of the beloved rogue who had broken her heart.

Kate took the bottle from Stanley's hands as soon as they entered the house. "You are brave to risk coming here tonight with the village on a rampage."

His pale eyes regarded her in concern. "You are brave to stay in this house and serve a woman of Mrs. Lawson's disrepute. The life she leads only attracts trouble."

"Where would I go?" she asked wistfully. "Besides, this is only the second time I've encountered violence in Madam's employment. Do you think it's safe for *you* to leave here tonight?"

"I'll walk back with the reverend. Do you know where he is?"

"I assume he took refuge in the kitchen."

"The worst of the fiends have probably passed out in the woods by now. After tonight they might not return." He paused. "Who was that man who waylaid you in the garden?"

Heat stole into Kate's cheeks. "Oh. He's one of Mrs. Lawson's oldest friends, or so he claims. I have to warn her that he's here."

"Warn her?" Stanley frowned, staring across the candlelit hall to the front door. "Does he pose a danger to her?"

A danger? Kate thought guiltily of the passages in Georgette's memoirs that referred to Colin Boscastle. "He was helpful tonight."

"Is he a repeat offender?"

"I don't know what you mean."

"Is he a true friend or only one of the multitudes your mistress has entertained?"

"I think you ought to leave now," she said softly. "Watch out for yourself walking home."

She looked him in the face. Stanley was a fair-minded man, respectable and still living with his aging parents. But he didn't know all her sins. Her past. He had never, like the scoundrel in the garden, made any attempt to dishonor her. If ever in her life Kate had a chance of a future, it would be with Stanley.

"Kate—"

She drew back instinctively. He was staring at her mouth as if he knew it bore the mark of another man's kiss. "I am grateful for your friendship, Stanley."

"'Friendship' is a lukewarm word."

"Perhaps." She did not give him the chance to elaborate on whatever encouragement he might have sought.

The determined rap of the door knocker resounded only moments after Stanley had left. One of the housemaids, who had been hiding in the servants' quarters, appeared in the hall. "Shall I answer it, miss?" she asked Kate in an uncertain voice.

Kate hesitated. "Yes. Take him into the drawing room and give him refreshments."

"But who is he, miss?"

"I'm not quite sure."

"Good thing he passed by when he was needed."

"Time will tell," she said evasively. But if she had to judge based upon their first encounter, and by what she knew of his past, Kate thought Colin Boscastle was more likely to end up a heartbreaker again than a hero.

Chapter 5

The Memoirs of an English Mistress

He was the best lover I would ever have. Of course I didn't realize that then. He was gentle at times and so rough at others that the thought of what I allowed him to do still makes me quiver.

From the evening he kissed me against the casement windows of our cottage, I became his captive. I lived to give him pleasure; he knew instinctively how to starve me of his attentions until shame no longer existed. I slept with him on a beaten earth floor, in darkness, by the light of cheap lard candles.

He was the most beautiful man I had ever seen. To this day no other lover compares, except perhaps for the Duke of Preston. But even he was not the devil in bed that Boscastle was. Sometimes I dream of our sexual escapades; I am consumed by his heat, bracing myself for the first blissful thrust that was a blade to my innocent dreams. How sad to

*think I will never again experience the won-
derful degradation of that night.*

Kate paused as she heard heavy footsteps behind her.
She was halfway up the stairs when she looked back to
see Lovitt standing below. She'd no idea why he had entered the front hall. Still, this was not a night to observe
protocol. Well, what protocol one respected in a virtual
House of Venus. Kate enforced what rules she could, for
what it mattered.

Lovitt swept off his cap. "Is he a friend, Miss Kate? I
know he's a decent fighter. And I know we could use
another strong arm for defense while Mr. Earling is
away."

Kate released a sigh. "It will be up to Mrs. Lawson to
decide," she said to the row of upturned faces, which registered an understandable concern in the candlelight.

No one could predict Mrs. Lawson's reaction when it
came to affairs of the heart. In the past Georgette had
praised Colin Boscastle to the heavens, extolling his unearthly attraction in one breath, cursing him to a lesser
domicile in the next. Kate determined that she would
not play a role in influencing Georgette one way or another.

It was Kate's duty to protect the children.

But on the matter of Mason Earling's reaction to Colin Boscastle's arrival, there was no doubt in her mind.
Surely the master of the house would not welcome a
man whose mission in life had been to harass Mason's
father and now, perhaps, to take from his possession the
mistress he had paid a small fortune to acquire. It was no
secret that Mr. Earling feared Sir Colin Boscastle, and
after what Kate had witnessed of Colin's force, perhaps
Mason had good cause.

*   *   *

A door slammed in the upper hall. The staccato beat of tiny heels against the bare floorboards drew Kate from her thoughts.

"Kate?" Georgette said from the top of the stairs. "What happened? Who is here?"

Kate stared up at Georgette's elegantly sheathed figure. There was an unaccustomed urgency in Madam's voice, a quaver of excitement or fear, as if she *knew* that the man who had once meant more to her than anything was here.

Perhaps he still meant the world to Georgette, although she had sworn to Kate that all the fire and anger she'd felt for him had died down to a bittersweet regret. Kate had to wonder whether Colin Boscastle could make Georgette burn again—and how her own life would be changed if he did.

"Is it him?" Georgette asked, a catch in her voice.

"Yes, madam—wait. Don't run away!"

She followed in frustration as Georgette fled down the hall and escaped into her suite of rooms. She could hear shoes dropping on the floor, drawers pulled open, a trunk hinge creak as it was heaved open. "You aren't going to hide from him, are you?" she asked, entering the room with a stitch in her side.

"Don't be ridiculous. I'm looking for my pink-feathered fan—the one decorated with pearls. It flatters the complexion, I think. Pink is kind to— What *did* you tell him? What does he want? How dare he show up when I have finally become mistress of my own life."

With a deep sigh, Kate stared at the devastation Georgette had wrought inside her dressing closet. " 'Mistress of Your Own Mess' is what you meant to say."

Georgette raised her head. For an instant she looked to Kate more like a little girl playing dress-up with her mama's finery than she did a courtesan. Suddenly Kate wished that she could disappear before the reunion between the rogue downstairs and her employer took place.

"Oh, madam," she said, biting her lip. "What do we do?"

Georgette brushed back her hair, seemingly calmed by Kate's question. "We don't *do* anything. How has he come here? Did he say anything? Did you tell him that Brian—"

"No, madam." Kate's head started to swim, whether as a result of the perfume fumes in the closet, the thought of Colin Boscastle's eyes, or the prospect of promising to keep a secret that she knew in her heart to be inherently wrong.

"You swore you would never tell anyone about Brian," Georgette said, as if she could read Kate's mind.

Perhaps she could. Not only did they share a physical resemblance, but they also schemed alike, a necessity for two young women who survived on the outskirts of society. They had depended on each other for a decade, squabbling and pledging their mutual allegiance, often in the course of a single day. Kate and her mistress shared an unbreakable bond. The broken promises of a "gentleman" and a surprise pregnancy had spurred Georgette on to the road of disgrace. The vicious lies and abuse of another had destroyed Kate's innocent dreams and chance at a respectable life.

"I told him nothing," Kate murmured, stooping to pick up a shawl from the floor. "Haven't I always kept my word?"

"Why does your voice have that rasp? I hope you haven't caught that hideous cough, too."

Kate cleared her throat. "Perhaps I raised my voice. Perhaps it was the night air or the smoke. The villagers tried to set the estate on fire, in case you were wondering what went on in the garden."

The words seemed to deflate Georgette's panic. She bit the bottom of her painted bow-shaped lips and rose, wresting the shawl from Kate's hand. "What does he want?" she asked in a lost voice.

"I'm not sure." Kate resumed her usual role as confidante and comforter. "He mentioned Mason and said he needs to warn you." The interlude during which Colin had mistaken Kate for her mistress, she decided to omit. She believed it to have been an honest mistake, never mind how embarrassing to both parties.

"Why didn't you say I had left the parish?" Georgette said, sinking down on a stool. "Did he ask about Brian? What exactly *did* he say?"

Kate gripped Georgette by her wrist and drew her back to her feet. "I might have remembered if flaming arrows had not been aimed at my person. It was a horrid experience, madam. We cannot stay here. Even if they are only drunken youths, they will end up hurting one of us or worse, the children."

"I've never encountered hatred like this."

Kate straightened Georgette's bodice. "You have never stolen the richest landowner from a parish and had the audacity to live in sin at the scene of the crime."

"Never mind my audacity. If you want audacity, he is waiting downstairs in the hall. When I asked what I should do, I was referring to the immediate present. What am I to do about Colin Boscastle?"

Kate couldn't remember the last time Georgette had suffered a crisis of nerves at the prospect of receiving an unexpected male caller. Especially one as attractive as Sir Colin Boscastle, except perhaps for the fact that he was the man Georgette blamed for permanently putting her off love.

"I am overcome, Kate."

"I can see that, madam."

"What should I wear? What does one wear for a re-union with a man one once loved and now whose dead body one would step over in the street?"

Kate cocked her head. "What you're wearing looks fine for that."

"He mustn't see me like ... *this*," Georgette said, moving around Kate to study herself in the mirror.

Kate stifled a sigh. "Why not? Plenty of men have seen you in far less. So has he, come to think of it."

"There are children's toys all over the place. And books. I don't want him to know I'm still learning to read."

Kate looked down, afraid to admit that Sir Colin had mentioned Georgette's illiteracy. "I shall tidy up the room," she said. "Or we shall ask him to meet you in the blue parlor. It hasn't been used in months."

Georgette shook her head. "No. The children can't see him. He can't see them. If the staff asks, we'll tell them ... we won't tell them anything. He'll have to come up here. With any luck he'll be gone in another hour."

Kate nodded compliantly. "Yes, madam. I'll fetch—"

"But why is he here after all these years?" she whispered. "He must have hinted at what he wants."

"He said—well, I'm not sure I really understand why he's here." She swept around the room, scooping up books, a doll, a ball, in her arms. "Why don't I explain to him that you are indisposed for the night, if his presence is so distressing?"

"He won't take no for an answer."

Kate could well believe that. "Madam, quite a few years have passed since your ... friendship. I'm sure he understands that you haven't been standing by the gate all this time waiting for him to come home."

"I doubt he'll understand that I've become a whore and borne three children, though, one of whom is his."

"Stay calm, madam."

"Calm!" Georgette shouted.

Kate slipped out the door. "Whatever you do, keep your temper under control. If you don't want him to know Brian is his son, then the less you say, the better."

Chapter 6

"Well, well, well," Georgette said from her indolent position on the couch. "Look what my beloved companion dragged in from the garden—the prodigal rake. Kate, haven't I warned you not to talk to strangers?"

"Georgette," Colin said slowly, drawing a chair before her. "You look every bit as beautiful as the last time I saw you."

"Oh, do I really?" she asked tartly. "Do you *remember* the last time you saw me?"

"Well, I—"

"I was bawling my eyes out from the window of that miserable cottage where I was born and might have died for all you cared."

"But you were—*are*—still beautiful," he said hastily, "bawling or not. What difference does it make where we parted?"

"I don't want your flattery," she said, flinging down her fan. "It doesn't move me in the least. You can't return after all this time and expect me to be the same giddy-headed virgin I was before I met you. And you shouldn't be surprised to learn that—"

"You have made a living on your back? I'm in no

place to pass judgment on what you have done to survive."

"Thank you ever so much for the stamp of approval," she retorted. "What is this nonsense that you told my companion about Mason? He's the most placid man I have ever met."

"Why shouldn't he be?" Colin asked with a shrug. "He is sleeping with the woman who once loved me and paying her bills with the profits off the investments of the man he poisoned."

Georgette regarded him with reluctant sympathy. "Once upon a time you could have persuaded me that the moon rose in the morning. I imagined—I wished a plethora of foul fates upon you when you left me. Poor Colin. Of all the excuses I made up for your abandonment it never occurred to me that you had gone utterly mad. I hope it isn't hereditary."

His eyes narrowed. "Why?"

She should have known the wretch would catch a slip of the tongue. Why didn't clever Kate intervene or invent a plausible excuse for Georgette's careless remark?

But Kate was standing in the corner, looking as if she wanted nothing more in the world than to beat a retreat herself. And even though Georgette knew that Kate had gone through an ordeal outside, she *needed* her.

"What do you mean hereditary?" he asked her slowly. "Has anything happened to one of my brothers? Or my cousins?"

She felt a flush of apprehension warm her neck. She glanced at Kate for guidance. Kate stared back at her with an impassive expression, which Georgette knew she ought to emulate. But *calm* was not a word in her vocabulary.

She would not give him their son. It wasn't fair. Colin

had not cared whether she was with child when he left her, and now—well, he couldn't have Brian because to deny that old Mr. Lawson had fathered the boy was an admission that Brian was a bastard. And the stigma of illegitimacy would only taint Brian's future. "How can you presume to come back into my life to ruin what precious little I have built? Isn't it enough that you ruined me once? Mason loves me. He might even marry me one day." Although if Georgette had her preference, she would become rich on her memoirs and never answer to another man again.

He shook his head. "Listen to me, Georgette. Think back to the time when my father died. He had dined with Mason's father the night before. The surgeon that Nathan Earling called that morning refused to admit the possibility of arsenic. A week after the funeral, Mr. Earling senior went away on business."

She frowned. "I recall that he and your father were about to become partners with a large interest in the East India Company. Nathan traveled to secure foreign interests. He made sure your mother had money to see her through until she remarried."

"He left her a pittance," Colin said starkly. "He doctored my father's accounts and stole what should have belonged to my elder brother." He lowered his voice. "I never intended to ruin you. I wasted half of my brother Sebastien's life by taking him with me on my quest. The war gave me an excuse to release him from my obsession."

"Your brothers have done well for themselves, from what I hear."

"That is a relief to know."

"Then—"

He shook his head, his expression forbidding her to

interrupt. "What Nathan Earling confessed as he died in Ireland was what I had come to suspect too late. My father ingested arsenic the night before he died. I was in the room when Nathan unburdened his soul. It was Mason who poisoned his wine. It was Mason who plotted my father's murder for gain. Nathan tried to cover for his son."

"Mason?" Despite the disbelief in her voice, Georgette felt a chill of uncertainty burrow in her spine. Colin had always dominated his environment. He had convinced a silly country girl that her homely thatched cottage was a castle in disguise and that she was a princess who would one day become a queen.

Colin gave her a merciless smile. "Your protector served my father his last supper, a drink laced with arsenic."

"All I know for certain," she said carefully, "is that you left me and the rest of your family and that you never returned."

He exhaled, his gaze moving past her to Kate. "I swore that I wouldn't come back until I made him confess the truth. How could I have known that it would take me thirteen years? Would you have respected me if I had no honor?"

Georgette turned slightly. She didn't love the devil in the least anymore, and she wasn't sure she would ever forgive him for abandoning her. But he was still a compelling man, the father of her first child, and could hurt her again if she was not careful. "Nathan Earling is dead," she said quietly. "And you're asking me to believe that his *son* committed murder."

"Yes."

She shuddered involuntarily. A poisoner? The meek gentleman to whom she had sold her services and under whose roof her children and Kate would live? It couldn't be true.

"Mason would have been only a few years older than you at the time. I do not believe that he is capable of killing anything, not even an animal. I've never witnessed him commit a violent act."

"Why should he?" Colin said mildly. "He has everything he ever wanted. You, my father's business, a manor house, and respect."

"Respect?" Her voice broke. "Yes, he *had* respect, until he chose to be my protector."

"What kind of *protector* leaves his household of women and children vulnerable to a lunatic mob?"

She stood, nudging aside the footstool that stood between them. "In the first place, they were not a mob. They were a half dozen drunken scapegraces who for some inexplicable reason suddenly had decided it is their duty to drive me from the parish when in secret they entertain dreams of bedding me and my governess."

He folded his arms. His face drew tight. "I'll have you know that it only takes one lunatic to light a bonfire."

"Yes." She nodded, hearing her voice climb higher still. "I realize that, Colin. But do *not* lecture me. I get enough of that from Nan and Kate. They never—"

"Trusted Mason?"

She swallowed. "Do not put words in my mouth. If Mason were to come home early, I can't imagine how I would excuse or explain your presence in this house."

"I think we should continue this conversation alone," he said brusquely. "Please ask your companion to leave. She went through enough in the garden without standing witness to another battle."

Kate bolted for the door, her skirts practically shooting sparks in her apparent eagerness to be spared another confrontation. "Stay," Georgette said. "Do not leave me again with this man."

"But—"

Colin pulled out the chair that sat in front of an escritoire. "Then at least let her sit down. I have a feeling there will be more fires to put out before this conversation ends."

Chapter 7

Colin forced his gaze away from the governess, who gave a world-weary sigh and turned her attention to the papers that covered the desk. Her expression indicated that this was not the first time she had been ordered to act as a buffer on Georgette's behalf. Tonight was probably not the first time she had been kissed against her will in the line of service, either.

He glanced around the room in distaste. Marie Antoinette might have envied Georgette's taste for opulence. There was an excess of gilt ornamentation everywhere he looked—on the ceiling, the desk, the chaise, the finials sprouting from the arms of the Parisian sofa made of patterned gold brocade. The chairs and card table balanced on delicate spiral legs. The feminine gilded mirror on the wall encompassed only half his reflection. Through the door that opened onto the master bedroom, he saw an enormous bed draped in gold taffeta. The pale Chinese-silk panels on the walls added a peaceful counterpoint to a chamber that suggested sexual pleasure.

He gave Georgette a droll smile. "You have come quite far from your cottage. I might appreciate the furnishings if Mason hadn't killed my father for them. Although I'm grateful to know that you live in material comfort."

"Then why are you here to spoil it for me? Answer me, Colin. Why after all these years do you have to return?"

"I told—"

She raised her voice. He blinked. "Did you care that I had to dig myself out of a mire of disgrace to secure a marriage after you left? Did you care that my parents disowned me? Did you care that I gave—"

"Madam," Kate cautioned softly from her chair.

His mouth firmed. "I was a thoughtless rogue. I admit it. I will make amends if you allow me."

"Why didn't you write?" Georgette demanded. "If Mason is such a dangerous person, why didn't you warn me before?"

He walked a circle around her. "You aren't listening. I didn't know myself until two months ago when his father confessed on his deathbed in Ireland that Mason was the man I sought. Haven't your instincts ever suggested he is not what he pretends to be?"

"If I were a woman who could trust her instincts, I would never have slept with you."

"And you are wrong," he said. "I *did* write to you before I left England. Perhaps my letter never reached you. My mother wrote me once or twice. She said you were happily married to old Lawrence Lawson and expecting his child. I interpreted from that news that you had gotten over me and would be cared for. Was my mother wrong?"

"No," Georgette said after a long pause. "She was telling the truth. But I only married Lawrence because—"

"Oh, no!" the governess cried in chagrin. "We haven't paid the dressmaker this month."

He stopped pacing. He glanced at the figure at the desk. Except for a pinched frown on her broad forehead, she appeared completely detached from the situation.

But then—had the governess said something about Georgette's memoirs? Perhaps she'd heard it all by now. She had certainly regained her composure in the garden quickly enough. Any other woman would have gone into hysterics.

She looked up at him without warning, and he remembered how that sulky mouth had felt when he had robbed it of a kiss. He half smiled. Considering the coolness of Georgette's reception, it might have been a blessing that he had kissed her companion by mistake.

Georgette's voice interrupted his reverie. "I think you ought to sit down yourself, Colin. I must say, you look rough around the edges."

He felt it, too; anger and frustration had taken a toll on the devil-may-care boy she had once loved. And while it was true that Georgette was as beautiful as ever, she'd always had a temper, and he had wronged her. He didn't blame her for resenting him. Or for becoming a courtesan. He might have done the same thing in her place.

"For months after you left," she said unexpectedly, "I had dreams of killing you."

"Yours was not a good marriage?" he inquired in a careful voice.

Georgette stared at him. "Mr. Lawson lived long enough to saddle me with three children and a string of debts that could stretch from this village to London."

"That is unfortunate," he said.

"My life is defined by misfortune," she said without any self-pity in her voice. "My father, the old bugger, died one month after you left, and shortly after, my mother fell ill. I cared for her until she went to the grave. I'm a whore, Colin. Isn't that why you pursued me in the first place? I was an easy conquest."

"You weren't a whore when I knew you. Georgette, I am sorry. I had no crystal ball to foresee our future."

He took a breath. From the corner of his eye he saw the governess lift her hand to her face. Then he thought — no, he was *sure* he could hear footsteps outside the door, and the excited whispering of young voices.

"Do you have mice in the manor," he asked, "or do I hear children in the hall?"

The governess surged from her chair, papers scattering in every direction. "Madam, may I take my leave? As it is obvious that you and Sir Colin are not going to resolve your conflict tonight, I suggest I have a room prepared for him. No matter what stands between you, he was put through an enormous trial in the garden."

Georgette laid a hand upon her flawless bosom. "Yes. You are right as usual, Kate."

Kate bobbed both Colin and Georgette a halfhearted curtsy, so clearly glad to escape that Colin could have laughed.

"Kate." Georgette's voice intercepted her before she reached the door. "Come back for our guest after his bedchamber is ready."

"Yes, madam."

"And make sure there are no mice in the halls tonight."

Kate curtsied, not waiting for Georgette to change her mind. She had already been on the receiving end tonight of Sir Colin's masterful personality as well as the hatred of a half dozen men. She needed a little time to recover her wits.

He moved past her and opened the door, a courtesy she might have respected if he hadn't given her a heart-stopping smile at the same time.

"Thank you, sir."

"But of course."

She edged past him only to smother a gasp as she

spotted the tall boy standing in the hall, his two half siblings hiding in his shadow.

"Brian!" she said under her breath.

He stared past her to the door, which Sir Colin had closed. "Are you all right, miss?" the boy asked anxiously.

Kate's heart tightened. Heaven help the child. He looked the mirror image of his father. How could Georgette hope to hide the fact from Colin? As Brian had matured, his hard cheekbones, his chin, and above all his eyes of bewitching blue had begun to dominate his face. Georgette might be the worst mother in the world, but nevertheless she adored her children.

Still, most rakes avoided acknowledging their illegitimate offspring until goaded by conscience or a court judgment. Perhaps Colin wouldn't want to claim his son. Perhaps he enjoyed his reckless life too much to take any responsibility. At least Georgette had been married at Brian's birth, giving the boy the benefit of a last name.

"Three mice, indeed," she said, wrapping her arms around her charges and guiding them to the stairs that led to the uppermost floor. "All eavesdroppers are to be imprisoned until dawn. What on earth have you done to Nan?"

Charlie clung to her. "She drank Etta's tonic, miss, and her snoring is keeping us awake something awful."

"Why is that man in my mother's room?" Brian asked, slipping out of her grasp. "Who is he? Why did he fight to help us?"

"He's a visitor. It's nothing to do with us."

"A visitor?" he said dubiously. "Another one already? But I thought that Mr. Earling—"

"Come along, Brian. He isn't *that* sort of visitor." And if he was, Kate did not want to know about it.

The four of them walked toward the staircase, Brian

clearly not believing her. "Then what sort of visitor is he? Do you think my mother will ask him to stay?" He drew back, balking at the stairs leading to the nursery. "I'm too old to sleep in there with that crabby old woman and the babies."

"Don't be disrespectful. You adored Nan until a year ago. You also liked the nursery because it overlooks the stables."

"What if there's another fight?"

"There can't be. My nerves will unravel. I—"

She turned her head, as did the three children, diverted by the clash of raised voices coming from the main suite. In reality, it was Georgette who sounded like a raging gorgon. Obviously Sir Colin had made another remark that had set her off.

"Told you there'd be another fight," Brian said with a smug grin. "You'll have to enter the ring again, miss. No one else can soothe her temper like you do."

Kate hesitated, uncertain what to do as three pairs of innocent eyes lifted to hers. But then Georgette started to shout again, and Kate's sense of responsibility returned. These children had already suffered too much upheaval. "Upstairs! You can sleep in my room tonight, but no quarreling."

Brian scowled. "I'd rather sleep in a horse stall."

"I'd rather listen to Mama shouting," eight-year-old Etta said, sticking her nose through the railing.

Kate pursed her lips. "I've a feeling you might have a chance of that tomorrow."

After ten years it amazed Kate that life had not depleted her employer of passion. However, this wasn't an ordinary argument. And Georgette's opponent was no ordinary man.

Chapter 8

$\mathcal{K}$ate had gotten the children settled in her bed, Brian choosing the couch by the window, when she remembered her promise to Georgette. She hurried back downstairs to the floor below and made a quick inspection of the stranger's suite. To her relief the chambermaids had recently aired out the rooms and changed the bedding.

She was even more relieved to find Georgette and Sir Colin awaiting her return in a subdued mood.

"Sir," she said, standing in the door with a candle in a brass holder, "are you ready to retire for the night?"

"Yes."

Georgette flashed her a look as he rose. "Come back to me when he is settled, Kate."

She sighed inwardly as she left the room, Sir Colin following a little too closely for her liking. There would be no peace at all tonight. "Follow me please, sir. Your room is at the end of the hall."

She was so startled as his arm reached around hers that she missed a step. "Would you like me to hold the candle and lead the way?" he asked.

His voice sounded deeper now in the darkness than it had in the garden. It was also far more polite, despite an undercurrent of amusement. "I walk up and down this hall countless times every day. Why would I need you to lead the way?"

He gave her an innocent look. "I wouldn't want any of those mice to scurry past and frighten you."

She looked up at him as he took the candle from her hand. The contact of his long fingers against hers threw her into a brief panic. He smiled faintly. No doubt he understood the effect of his touch.

"It isn't that I distrust your sense of direction," he said. "I happen to be a man who needs to be in control at all times."

The candlelight flickered across the chiseled angles of his face as if paying homage to his indecent appeal. She leaned back against the railing as his large body brushed around her. "It's the second to the last room on the right," she said, still undecided whether he was purely arrogant or a little off in the head. Perhaps it had been for the best that he and Georgette had never married. He appeared to act as tinder to her flint. If tonight were any indication of their compatibility, the pair of them would never have survived their honeymoon. And yet they had produced a beautiful son who it seemed had inherited his rebellious streak from both sides of his family.

Sir Colin found the room without any difficulty. Kate remained in the doorway as he placed the candle on one of the branches of the shaving stand. He threw his black coat on the bed and shrugged off his vest.

She caught an impression of wide shoulders and a lithe body before she looked away. She retreated into the hall as he began to unbutton his shirt.

"I'll have one of the servants come up to bring you fresh water. And—" A bright stain on the right shoulder of his shirt drew her notice. "That's blood, isn't it? That's where that arrow must have struck you. All this time you've been arguing and raising a fuss when you're bleeding and don't even know it. I can't believe you didn't mention it! Is it your hope to become a martyr? Sit down on the bed this instant." Which to her surprise he did.

"It's nothing," he said.

"Do you think I want to chance finding a dead body in this room tomorrow?"

She went straight to the bed before he could reply, caution dispensed by concern. Georgette always said Kate lived for life's emergencies, to which Kate usually responded, "Yes, and it's a good thing, too, because you cause quite a few and turn quite helpless in a crisis."

He lifted his brow as she leaned over the bed.

"Do take care," he said in a low voice. "I liked kissing you tonight, and a wounded beast is always dangerous, even to those who offer help. If, indeed, I develop blood poisoning, I might not be responsible for my delirious actions."

"Were you delirious when you kissed me in the garden?" She forced herself to meet his gaze, but at a cost. He stared at her with unmasked interest, with impertinence, and while she realized that he had rescued her not two hours before, this was an entirely different predicament.

He released a deep sigh. "I cannot return to my family to confess I've spent thirteen years away from home and have nothing to show for it. Is it wrong that I crave the presence of a sweet woman to ease my worries before continuing the battle I've anticipated practically half my life?"

"I am neither your judge nor jury. Nor am I what your society would consider a 'sweet woman.' I might be a little tart, although not in the sense you desire. I have my own battles to fight."

"Alone?" he asked in curiosity.

"Do I need protection against you?" she said impatiently.

"I haven't decided yet." He scowled. "Of course not."

She narrowed her eyes to examine what she could see of his shoulder through his shirt. "It's a deeper wound than I thought. It must hurt." She laid the back of her hand across his forehead. "You're warm."

He hooked his finger in her bodice, his mouth taut with either pain or passion; she couldn't say which. She had to strain to hear the words he whispered, "Would you deny me a simple request in the event I do not survive the night?"

"Sir," she said softly, "if you do not remove your finger from my person, I guarantee that you will not survive the next hour."

"And who will I have to thank for my demise?"

"His name is Lovitt. He is our groom and he—"

"Swings a nice shovel. Sorry. You'd need another three of him to knock me out." His blue eyes glistened at her. "Perhaps I do have a fever."

She plucked his finger from her bodice.

"I will bring salve for your shoulder," she said, straightening her back.

"I don't need that type of healing," he said bluntly.

"I don't think you're in any condition to know what you need."

His gaze traveled over her. "Your company would make me feel better than any salve."

She frowned at him. "Stop making remarks to provoke me."

He leaned back on the bed, watching her closely. "Can your company be bought?"

"I am Mrs. Lawson's companion," she said, "and other than that I am not nor have I any desire to put myself on the market. You asked me as much in the garden. Do I *sound* as if I would be good company tonight?"

"I don't care what you sound like, darling. I wasn't asking for a philosophical conversation. You wouldn't have to utter a word."

"Well, I will. And the word is 'no.'"

She could feel his disconcerting stare as she cast a final glance around the room before she escaped. "You can't blame a man for trying," he said. "I'll do my best to behave myself during the rest of my stay. And quite honestly, I was only curious."

"Your stay?" She bumped against the night table. The candle flame wavered. "How long do you intend to be here?"

"It's my plan to wait until Mason returns. I'm tired of chasing the truth. Let him come to me."

"That could be weeks," she said faintly, jumping back as he swung his legs over the bed. "What are you doing now?" she asked, her body tightening in apprehension.

He hovered over her, shaking his head. "I was merely getting up to open the door for you again."

She felt blood rush to her face. "Sir, I'm only a companion and governess. To most gentlemen I am invisible."

"I doubt that. I'm having the devil's time ignoring you."

She stared at him, her mouth compressed.

"That was a compliment," he added. "It's all right for you to accept it."

Her eyes moved to the bloodstain spreading across his linen shirt. "That needs to be cleaned."

"I'll do it before bed. I do not advise you to touch me again." He glanced over her with a frown. "Perhaps you should have someone attend your needs."

"My *what*?"

"Your gown." He inclined his dark head. "Your dress is in a disgraceful state. I assume you didn't sneak out to meet your lover looking like that."

"My lover? Who are you talking about? I don't have a lover."

"You look as if you could use one."

She followed his gaze to her formerly unflawed pale silk skirt. A swag of shorn lace dangled between the muddied heels of her shoes. "Oh," she said with a groan. "It must have been the rose brambles. It's ruined."

"You and whoever he was should be grateful that you emerged from tonight's assault with only a torn skirt to show for it."

"I am grateful."

"Perhaps you should leave now," he said, looking down into her face. "If you don't, I might ask you to show me how grateful you are."

She drew a breath to break the spell that bound her. Of all the men Georgette had entertained, Sir Colin appeared the most confident of his sexuality. Kate doubted he received many refusals. In a way she held the advantage— she knew details of his past desires from working on Georgette's memoirs.

At the time, transcribing their love affair had seemed academic. Now she was tempted to return to her room and review what Georgette had made her write about him. It appeared that his allure had only grown stronger over the years.

"Go," he said. "Run. Flee while you have the chance. I'm impressed by the way you put me in my place. Not that I will stay there, mind you."

"For tonight I'll be satisfied if you simply stay in bed."

Chapter 9

*K*ate walked in dread down the hall to Georgette's room, where she found her employer and a wide-awake Nan, evidently summoned from the nursery, waiting for her.

In fact, Georgette looked animated, but then, she was trying on her rings and tiaras, and jewelry tended to lift her mood. "What do you think of him, Kate?" she said before she had even closed the door.

Kate crossed her arms. "How long will he be here? How do I explain him to the children? And what if Mr. Earling comes home earlier than expected? There will be a duel."

Georgette swiveled around on her stool. "What if he's utterly mad? What if his story is untrue?" She dropped an emerald ring into her jewel casket. "Mason cringes when he steps on a spider. He hates to kill anything. And how do we know that Nathan Earling was in his right mind when he admitted that Mason had poisoned the viscount?"

"But what if his story is true?" Nan inquired.

"Where are the witnesses? Where is the proof?" Georgette turned her head to the desk at which Kate had seated herself, leafing through a sheaf of papers. "What do you make of him, Kate?"

She glanced up guiltily. "He's exactly as you described him."

Georgette frowned. "Do you think he's cracked?"

"Do you?" Kate asked, determined to remain neutral.

"For years he was convinced that Nathan Earling killed his father." She poured out her nightly cordial as she spoke. "Now all of a sudden he's convinced that he was pursuing the wrong man. You have to present some proof before you hunt a man to the ends of the earth to accuse him of a crime."

"I know someone who might shed some light on the shadows," Nan said, reaching for her cane. "Griswold, Mr. Earling's footman. He worked for old Mr. Earling and I believe was in service at the time of the viscount's death."

"Oh." Georgette made a face. "Griswold can hardly be expected to remember something that happened thirteen years ago when it's all he can do to find the carriage. Don't you agree, Kate?"

Kate frowned. "I don't have an opinion yet."

"What is wrong with you? Did something happen to you in the garden that you forgot to mention? Did anyone hurt you?"

Kate's eyes misted over. There were times when Georgette was such a dunce that Kate was tempted to give notice. "I'm fine," she said. "I got smoke in my eyes and it still stings."

"Maybe Colin will have changed his mind by tomorrow and will leave us alone," Georgette said hopefully. "We didn't exactly roll out the carpet and give him his own set of keys."

"Yes, ma'am. Except—is it possible that he isn't mad? What if everything he said is true?"

Georgette's face darkened. "Has he already won you over?"

"On the contrary. He was rather ill-mannered earlier in the night. But then, it wasn't the sort of dilemma that brings out the best in a gentleman."

"It's difficult to remember social niceties when flaming arrows are going over your head," Nan agreed. "Some gentlemen would not have stood and fought."

"How would you know?" Georgette asked in a gentle reproach as she rose to help Nan to the door.

"I was an actress once. We used bows and arrows onstage for many a play. I'll never forget the time I shot mine into the air and straight through the Earl of Wetherby's tall black hat."

Kate laughed reluctantly. "I'd love to have seen that. You must have brought down the house."

"I brought down the earl," Nan said with an unremorseful grin. "When he realized I'd taken off his wig, he fainted in embarrassment. The audience loved me for that. They wanted to see the same act over and over. I had to take archery lessons so I wouldn't kill anyone."

Kate got up and opened the door to walk Nan up the top flight of stairs to the nursery. Georgette hung back, impulsively kissing first Kate and then Nan on the cheek. "That's what we need in this house—a good laugh. When is your new play making its debut, Kate? I've been studying my role."

Which consisted of only four or five lines, the most Georgette could memorize, although even then she'd forget and would inevitably end up improvising her role. But that was part of the fun. The audience reveled in an act gone wrong. And since this particular audience would consist of a small but elite class of freethinkers who welcomed the controversy that Georgette had brought to their boring parish, it wouldn't matter what she did on stage. It was enough to be able to brag that one had been invited to a courtesan's performance. Georgette might not have bookish skills, but she could enchant an audience with her unaffected charm.

"I know my lines," Nan boasted.

"Perhaps you'll bring down the house again," Kate said, brightening at the thought of the amateur theatricals she adored writing. She wanted to slip back into her safe world and take those she loved with her. "We have a little over a fortnight before it opens," she added. "I hope our neighbors won't be afraid to attend in light of what happened tonight."

"Those who are our true friends will come," Georgette predicted. "Who can resist a comedy?"

Kate gave her a look. "Except that this play is based on a tragedy. Good heavens. Didn't you read your part? There's even an epic battle scene to be fought onstage. I wrote it to invoke a melancholy mood."

"All the more reason it will be a comedic delight," Georgette said, winking at Nan.

They moved as one into the hall, Georgette describing her costume to Nan, and Nan pretending to listen until they passed the stranger's room. A wedge of candlelight shone beneath the door.

Georgette paused. "I shall insist he leave in the morning," she said in a soft voice. "His claim is ridiculous, isn't it, Nan? The viscount's heart could have given out. Why would Mason poison the man who was about to become his father's partner?"

"Stranger things have happened," Nan said. "Young Earling was always competing against that handsome boy in village sports. He never won. It was no secret that he considered Boscastle to be his rival."

"Yes," Georgette said, "but that was over me. It would

have made more sense for Mason to poison Colin if he wanted a clear field to engage my affections."

Nan gave a quiet laugh.

"Perhaps he tried. Perhaps Sir Colin was too strong to die after a dose or two. Ask Griswold if you're brave enough to face the truth. He might remember what happened."

Chapter 10

Colin pinched out the candle and rose to look through the window at the peaceful garden. A sliver of moon illuminated the main parterre. Shadows enveloped the swathe of turf and trees that grew against the wall.

It was easy to mistake one person for another in those places of eclipse. From a distance one might take Georgette and Miss Walcott for sisters. In the candlelight, however, they did not compare. Georgette was still beautiful and hot tempered. She had a practical side. Her companion—well, she was a complete surprise. A mystery.

He regretted his mistake perhaps more than she did. The scent and taste and feel of her had infiltrated his awareness. He would be tortured by temptation unless he could persuade her to his point of view. He thought he had a chance.

Had he imagined that during their kiss tonight there had been a moment when he felt her capitulate, submit if not invite? His instincts had prepared for her surrender . . . and warned him of her innocence.

He turned from the window, disturbed by a hesitant rap at the door. She hadn't shown the least interest in sharing his bed; in fact, all Colin had sensed in her was a panic that had doused his passion more effectively than anything she could have said.

Still, as he went to answer the door, he allowed himself a little hope. If she had returned to tend his shoulder, he would prove that he could behave when it was necessary. He could apologize again.

He opened the door. Before him stood an elderly footman, staring off at something down the hall. He held a bowl of hot water, a poultice, and clean towels on a tray. Colin waited for the man to realize he was waiting in the doorway. After a long interval in which he decided they might be standing there until the cows came home, he cleared his throat and said, "Did you knock, my good fellow?"

"Sir, my apologies. I don't know where my mind went. Miss Walcott wished me to—" He turned his head. He blinked at Colin and shrank back a step. "*You*, sir," he said, shaking his balding head. "It *can't* be you."

"Why can't it be me?" Colin asked, reaching for the tray.

"Because . . . because"—the tray listed in Colin's direction, water sloshing onto the towels—"you're dead, sir. I'm ever so sorry. I must not drink at night. I only seem to see these apparitions when I'm in my cups."

"To see what?" Colin said in irritation as the hot water started to drip on his trousers.

"Dear, dear God. I never thought— It can't be. It is impossible—" What was impossible Colin could only guess. So overcome by whatever irrational conviction had gripped his imagination, the footman appeared to forget the tray in his hands. It swayed. And then it slipped from his unsteady hold.

Colin reached out reflexively before the tray fell to the floor.

"What the deuce is wrong with you?" he demanded.

The footman retreated, mumbling an apology, and took off down the hall. Colin shook his head, closed the door with his foot, and took the tray to the dressing table. He sat, unbuttoning his shirt, and glowered at his reflection in the mirror. He was in dire need of a shave, he could take a comb to his hair, but other than that he didn't see anything of the supernatural about his appearance.

"What is it about me?" he muttered. "Do I have the mark of the beast on my forehead? Is it my breath?"

He had not anticipated a rousing welcome from Georgette tonight. He understood that his arrival disrupted the life she had struggled to make. The governess distrusted him, and she too had just cause.

But what had sent that old footman into a frenzy? Why had he taken one look at Colin's face and acted like a man confronted with a ghost? Had they ever met? That long, sallow face did seem vaguely familiar.

He slept more deeply than he had in months. For now he managed to put from his mind the fact that he had taken shelter under his enemy's roof. His shoulder throbbed, but even that discomfort did not awaken him. He needed a few hours' rest.

The time would soon come when he could not risk lowering his guard. It was unfortunate that he had no defense against his dreams or against the woman who broke the barrier of his control.

He felt her warmth, the softness of her breasts against his forearm as she bent over him. A gentle hand touched his forehead. Her low voice taunted and yet brought comfort.

"No fever, thank God. All I need is to have an ill mischief-maker on my hands. Who else would take care of him, I ask? Who else is stupid enough to pity a scoundrel?"

The rustle of the sheet pulled down off his injured shoulder wrenched him into wakeful awareness. He opened his eyes to see a dark figure standing over him.

"Stay," he said hoarsely.

"I can't stay," she whispered in vexation.

He sat up. "Then why are you here again? Is this your revenge because I kissed you?"

"I wanted to make sure that your shoulder wasn't infected. I sent Griswold up to take a look and poultice you, but apparently you gave him the fright of his life. I realize that you are accustomed to having your own way, but does that mean you have to upset everyone in the house?"

He frowned. "I didn't do a blasted thing to the man. I behaved toward him with the same civility I am showing you."

She shook her head. "Well, if you invited him to keep you company during the night, I'm surprised he didn't hit you with the tray."

"I beg your pardon. I didn't get out two words before he went off about his drunken apparitions."

It was obvious from her skeptical expression that nothing he could say would convince her. She said, "Griswold is one of the most dependable servants I have ever known, and I have known him for years."

"Griswold?" The name *did* seem familiar, but in all honesty Colin didn't give a damn about an emotional footman, except that the longer he kept this conversation going, the longer Kate would stay. "All I did was open the door, and the man went to pieces. He looked at me and dropped his tray. I've no idea why. Do you?"

"None of us have the wits to interrogate him at this hour. Besides, he's foxed again. All I know is that our butler had to put him to bed."

"You still don't believe me."

"Maybe the blood on your shirt frightened him," she speculated. "How does your shoulder feel?"

"I'm in absolute agony. I don't know that I'll be able to sleep now."

She drew herself upright with a sigh. "I might not, either. Etta's cough is worse."

"I thought I warned you that you enter this room at your own risk."

She edged to the bottom of the bed. "And I thought you were asleep."

"I was," he said moodily. "And my shoulder is fine. The fuss you're making is unnecessary."

She regarded him uncertainly. "The arrow you took could just as well have struck me as you, and if it had, I wouldn't be in pleasant mood, either. Everyone is grateful that you intervened when you did."

"Someone had to do something," he said. "Your lover was all but useless."

"My— What are you talking about?"

"The one who cowered in the roses at the first sign of trouble."

"You told me to hide him!" she exclaimed. "I'll have you know he took a chance coming here ahead of those hatemongers."

"Well, I'll have you know that if he had any guts, he would have made sure you were hidden and then come out fighting. The twit seemed more concerned about the tear in his pants."

She drew back in chagrin. "There's brandy on the corner table if you need it. Thank you again for your courage. Sweet dreams, sir. Let us hope the morning finds you in a finer temper."

He laid his head back on the pillow, watched her flit across the room in the dark. She paused at the door to curtsy, gone before he could confess that he needed more than brandy or that he might have enjoyed nothing else but her company. A quick wit. A gentle touch. He might have refrained from baiting her if he hadn't sensed that she could give as good as she got.

She had wished him sweet dreams. Not quite yet. He had a few matters to attend to before he could rest again.

Still, the woman had made sure that if he managed to catch even another hour of sleep tonight, his dreams would be more sensual than sweet.

He waited for twenty minutes after she had sneaked into the room to check his shoulder. He sat up in bed and stared around the unfamiliar room. She would be relieved that she wouldn't have to dispose of a dead body before breakfast. He was relieved to have survived the night himself.

Doubtless she would chide him if she discovered that he intended to wash, dress, and take a walk around the estate and through the woods before the sun rose. At first light he would visit her mistress to explain what course of action he had decided on during his night of broken sleep and second thoughts.

He passed through the gardens, and all was quiet. He left the estate by walking around to the stables, an area vulnerable to attack unless someone stood watch. He was both relieved and concerned that no one noticed his departure.

It took longer to walk to the smithy than he had allowed for, and his thoughts wandered. He'd been gone from England for an eternity; the rustle of a hedgehog, the flutter of moths through the wild honeysuckle that smothered the stone-walled lanes brought back a painful rush of memories.

He allowed his thoughts to wander back to his family.

He ached for what he'd abandoned. He hadn't realized until three years after leaving home that his mother had remarried. Only his youngest sibling, Gabriel, had stayed with her. Colin's eldest brother, Damien, the heir, had entered military service in Nepal before their father died. Sebastien, Colin's second-youngest brother, had done his utmost to emulate Colin's wicked deeds.

Colin had adored the beasts and recalled their earliest years with rueful affection. He wasn't proud of the fact, but he had taught Sebastien everything a young boy needed to know to survive.

One death had splintered the family.

Honor had fallen to Colin's shoulders; he believed to this day his father had been murdered by a man of high ambition. Nathan Earling had resented Joshua Boscastle for excluding him from Joshua's original foreign ventures. The night he was poisoned, Colin's father had planned to propose a partnership with Earling as a conciliatory venture.

Colin knew because he had been escaping through the conservatory to meet Georgette before his parents could stop him. It was to be the last time he saw his father alive.

"Yes, it's a risk," his father informed his wife before he trapped her between two potted ferns of prehistoric dimensions. "But Nathan has ambition."

"He is obsessed with wealth."

"Obsessed. Driven. With his ruthlessness and my connections in India, we stand to make a king's ransom."

"Nathan has always envied you," Marceline said with uncharacteristic rancor. "I wonder sometimes if he has a human heart. He didn't mourn when his wife and their unborn child died."

"Some men hide their pain."

"Others cause it."

His father said to the woman he worshiped, "I'll buy you scented fans and carved tea caddies—"

Colin could hear Maman's low, wonderful voice in his mind. "What use will scented fans be to me if my husband isn't home to take me to parties? I know you, Joshua Boscastle. You can't abide sitting still for two hours straight. You'll sail off for months and the boys and I will be alone. I hate being alone. And I'm French. I prefer coffee to tea."

"Marceline—"

"I don't even want to go tonight. Colin is carrying on with that pretty girl in the village. He's entirely wild, and his younger brothers are following under his bad influence. Unless you want us to become grandparents soon, you'll have to find another school to accept him. Colin needs a strong hand."

"Or a strong woman. Trust me, Marceline. I've even shown the statements of profit to Ramsey Hay, Nathan's solicitor, and he offered his services on the spot."

Colin had often wondered whether his mother had felt a premonition that night. And yet he'd put it from his mind in his hurry to meet Georgette.

He shook off his reverie.

"Sir?" a disembodied voice said from the flame-tinted darkness of the blacksmith's yard. "I've been expecting you. I had the farrier shoe your horse. I heard you had quite a night. Will you be leaving soon?"

"That all depends," Colin said. "Despite your warning, I was not as prepared for the young vandals as I should have been."

The blacksmith rose from his forge. "It wasn't always like this. I remember a time when I didn't know what the word 'corruption' meant. Perhaps it is good that you have come, sir. Perhaps you were brought here for a purpose other than what you intended."

Chapter 11

*K*ate trudged back upstairs, her conscience appeased, her thoughts unruly. She should have known it would take more than a poorly aimed arrow to fell a man of his physical stamina and strength of will. Any gentleman who had spent thirteen years pursuing justice was not one to be easily discounted.

But what had happened to *her* will?

A stranger's kiss in the dark, followed by his wicked flirtations, and she had come undone. It had been her first genuine kiss, too, and he had meant it for another woman.

The flaming arrows hadn't helped her nerves, of course. And how unkind of him to infer that Stanley had not stood his ground against the ruffians. In the first place, Stanley would lose his job if the apothecary found out he had brought a tonic to the house, even though it would be added to Mason's account and eventually paid.

Really, how many men were stouthearted enough to battle against a group of unknown bullies and emerge the winner?

Only two, not counting the reverend. Lovitt and Sir Colin.

She undressed in the dark, as usual. Not since her first

employer, Lord Overton, had sexually assaulted her in London had she felt comfortable looking at her naked body. There were still faint scars where he had bitten her on the breast, and underneath her upper arm stretched a scar that reached behind her shoulder from the bottle he'd used as his weapon. One of her bottom teeth had chipped when he'd hit her in the face with the sherry decanter he'd broken in his rage when she had refused to lift her skirts. Georgette promised her that nobody would ever notice the marks unless she pointed them out, but Kate knew they were there. How would she explain them to her husband if she ever married? Who would love her enough to overlook her imperfections?

Lady Overton had caught the governess in the act of seducing her husband, and so had three other servants standing in the door behind her. Kate hated to think back on the scene, but it was never far from her thoughts.

"The little slut was working her wiles on me," Lord Overton said, smoothing his neckcloth. *"When I told her she would be dismissed, she tore open her bodice and started screaming that I had assaulted her. She'd been drinking sherry. She broke the bottle to attack me and I had to wrestle it from her hands before she injured me. She reeks of drink."*

Kate had been shaking so badly she couldn't rehook her dress; three of the eyelets had been torn off, and what was she supposed to use for evidence? Show the cuts and bite marks on her breast to Lady Overton? None of the other servants would stand up for her for fear they'd lose their jobs. What could she do? A governess's word wouldn't stand against an aristocrat's. She could be sent to gaol.

She had run out of the house and into the street, not knowing where she could go or where she could hide. A small barouche had almost run her over, and when the passenger stopped the vehicle and saw the condition of her victim, she had insisted she take Kate back to her town house to hear her story.

Kate blurted out everything.

And Georgette believed every word.

"I'd wager that you weren't the only servant he has abused," Georgette said.

"I'll never know. I wasn't allowed to talk to them again. I couldn't even say good-bye to the little girl I watched. I won't be able to find work anywhere. I left all my belongings behind me."

"I am in desperate need of a governess and a companion for myself."

"You, madam?" Kate asked, dry-eyed and drained of tears.

"I want a girl who is clever, patient, and charming. I don't want my son raised by a dour-faced prune, although his governess must have the backbone to discipline him. Are you strong willed enough for a young boy who won't obey me? I will probably conceive another child before the end of the year. It appears that I have a talent for conceiving children and none at all for raising them. I know my son is young, but already I see rebellion in his ways."

Kate felt a surge of hope. At the time she hadn't understood that Brian wasn't Mr. Lawson's natural son or the nature of Georgette's profession. It wouldn't have mattered to her decision, anyway. She needed this position or she might find herself in the same position as Georgette.

"I'll teach your son to treat you with respect, Mrs. Lawson. He'll be so proper after a month with me, you won't recognize him."

Georgette smiled at her, doubtful but compassionate. "As far as serving as my companion, I've no desire to be made proper at all. It's far too late for that. I'm a fallen woman, and I have scant chance of redeeming myself in *society, which does not mean that I can't become a wealthy or popular figure."*

Kate had tried to appear composed, even though it was obvious that Georgette sensed how desperate she was. "What would my duties include as your companion, madam?"

"I am illiterate and uneducated," Georgette replied. "I know my way around a gentleman's body. I could pleasure a marble statue if I set my mind to it. But hand me a book, and an iron door slams shut in my brain. I would at least like to achieve a certain level of literacy. I need my companion to answer my letters with wit and verve."

It was a position that sounded like heaven to Kate. She could have believed that Georgette was her guardian angel in the disguise of a beautiful courtesan.

"I love reading and writing, madam. I could die happily in a library. Or at a desk."

Georgette laughed. "I doubt that I shall ever ask you to sacrifice your life to cover my deficits. But you have been truthful with me, and I will keep your confidences. Will you keep mine?"

Kate almost wept in gratitude. "You won't be sorry that you hired me."

Georgette rewarded her with one of the smiles that few gentlemen could resist. "You might be sorry one day that you have pledged your loyalty to a whore."

"I won't," she said with feeling.

"Yes. Right now you are furious at the male sex. Long after the scars on your body heal, you will lock the pain away in your heart. Perhaps one day you'll even meet a man who holds the key."

"I don't care about my heart. I don't even care about the wounds on my body. I need a roof over my head and a house in which I am safe."

Georgette nodded in understanding. "I choose my lovers with great care to their character, but even so, once in a great while, I am deceived. Woe befall the man who harms my child or my servants."

Kate lowered her head. "I'll never be able to repay you."

"Nonsense. But there is a price to your acceptance that you ought to consider."

"Madam?"

"It's unlikely that you'll ever find employment in a decent house again."

Lord Overton was killed in a duel a week before Georgette moved her household from London. By then Kate had learned from a courtesan that decency meant nothing without compassion. And though many times during her employment she'd threatened to leave, she had never gone farther than packing her bags.

What an unbelievable irony it would be if Colin Boscastle, of all Madam's lovers, would be the force that drove Kate back into the world.

Chapter 12

$\mathcal{G}$eorgette felt so groggy that at first she imagined that Mason was sitting at her bedside. "It's not even dawn yet," she said. "I must be dreaming. Leave me alone."

She dragged the pillow over her head only to feel it gently tugged away. "I'm asking a lot, I know. But we will need to set a trap for Mason, as soon as possible."

"A trap? Oh, God, this isn't a dream. It's you again. What do you want from me, Colin?"

"A little cooperation, that's all."

"What sort of trap? I'm not about to lure Mason to my carriage on a dark country road so that you can do him in. I'm not chasing him down in a disguise, either."

Colin laughed. "Not even if I buy you a black hat with a veil?"

"And I'm not meeting him in a rat-infested tavern where you can hire returned convicts to pummel him into confessing while I hide behind a dressing screen."

He scratched his cheek. "Are you finished?" She nodded. "All I want you to do, undramatically, please, is to insist he return home. Make up the most compelling excuse you can."

"So that you can take his life the instant he enters his home?"

"I've no intention of killing the man without observing formalities. What if he pulls a gun on me first?" He scowled impatiently. "He deserves a chance to be heard, and that is all I can promise. Presumably I will challenge him afterward. I do not intend to kill him in cold blood."

"Couldn't *you* meet him at another neutral spot?" Georgette suggested.

"You know as well as I do that he runs at the sound of my name."

"I might, too," she said crossly. "Do you realize it isn't even light outside yet? I'm not coherent until noon. I might not be responsible for whatever I have agreed to. I may not even remember this conversation tomorrow."

He laughed as he stood to leave. "Ask your companion for help. She appears to be a resourceful woman."

She frowned, staring at him through the shadows of her room. "Why are you all dressed up at this hour, anyway? I thought you had been wounded."

He paused at the door. "I left my horse and other clothing at the smithy. The blacksmith helped me, and I mean to repay him. When I return to the house I do not wish to be known as Sir Colin Boscastle. I will assume the name . . ."

His voice receded. Nobody kept Georgette awake at this hour unless for professional reasons. He could wait until tomorrow to repeat whatever he had said.

It was Kate's habit to arise early in the morning. Today was an exception. As he had done too often to Georgette in the past, Colin Boscastle had given Kate a restless night. There was no sign of him, however, as she walked downstairs. She could only hope that the rogue had vanished from Madam's life again.

He couldn't stay. His claim about Mason was impossible. Mason was mild-natured to a fault; Georgette had complained on countless occasions that she had to goad him to stand up for himself. His father had bullied him, and now he was a marionette in his solicitor's hands. It took practically an Act of Parliament for Georgette to get her purchases approved.

Mason would not return to the house if he discovered his enemy was here. He would die of fright before he faced Colin on a dueling field.

A housemaid, bustling past with a flannel cloth and furniture polish, paused at the sight of her. "You're up late, miss."

"Why is the house so quiet?"

"The staff is giving our new head groom a welcome breakfast, miss. If you hurry to the hall, you might find a few bites left. Or at least a drop of tea. You look like you could use it." The maid shuddered. "After all the horror last night, I'd be unsettled, too. But now we have Castle to take care of us. I'm so happy I could sing."

Kate couldn't find the words to express what she felt.

Our hero.

Our new head groom.

Castle.

She walked slowly to the servants' hall and stood in the doorway, unnoticed in the excitement. It seemed to her that everyone at the table was talking at once, until Colin started to recount how he'd lost his horse during the war.

"How, sir?" Brian asked.

"She shielded me from cannon fire."

"That's sad," Etta declared, staring down in misery at her plate of eggs.

"Soldiers don't cry, ninny," Brian said.

Kate was about to say, "Please don't call your sister

names, and finish your toast." But Colin spoke first, and she was too enrapt in his reply to interfere.

"I did cry," Colin said, addressing Brian as if he were an equal. "She laid down to cover me, and I'll never love a horse as I did her. How many people display that much loyalty?"

Kate glanced from Colin to his son, her heart gripped by apprehension. She had noticed last night that Brian resembled his father. But to see them sitting together for the first time — no, there were scores of blue-eyed, black-haired males in England. She recognized their bond only because she knew the truth. And because she was sworn to keep it secret.

"Miss," a voice whispered in her ear.

She turned, startled out of her thoughts. It was only Nan — Nan who would bring her back to earth, assure her she was being absurd. Besides, Colin hadn't come here to claim a child he didn't know was his. He had returned to fulfill a personal vendetta. Family landed in second place after his honor.

"What is it, Nan?"

Nan crooked her finger. "Come away before you are seen," she said softly.

Kate sneaked one last glance over her shoulder. Brian was teasing his younger brother, and Colin's interest had wandered from the table, though he hadn't spotted her yet. Head groom. What effrontery.

Nan pulled at her hand. "Come into the morning room. There's something you *have* to know."

Kate shook off the foreboding that clouded her reason. "If it is a plan to be rid of a certain rogue, I shall be all ears."

Nan hurried down the hall, shaking her head like a soothsayer of doom. At last they entered the musty-curtained room. It took Kate a moment to perceive the gaunt figure stretched out across the royal blue sofa. His crossed hands rested across his chest.

"Dear heaven! Is that Griswold? Is he dead or passed out again?"

He cracked open one red-rimmed eye. "Neither, miss."

"He's in shock," Nan said. "As you will be once he recounts what he told me late last night."

Kate threw up her hands. "Don't you think we have more to worry about than a tipsy footman? Our *visitor* has taken over the house—the scoundrel has inflicted another of his delusions on us—he's named himself the new groom. Mrs. Lawson will thump his thick head when she hears this."

Griswold sat up, his long face waxen. "Not when she hears what I have remembered, miss."

Kate felt her nerves prickle. "I've a feeling I might take to drink myself after I hear this."

Griswold fell back against the sofa. Nan stood over him, recounting what he had apparently revealed to her late last night. "Griswold worked at Mr. Earling Senior's house as an underfootman on the evening the viscount dined there, before he died the next day. It was the shock of seeing Sir Colin, who greatly resembles his father, that brought his memory back."

Kate wavered. "Memory of what?"

Griswold sighed. "Once I calmed down I began to remember details of the dinner."

"What reawakened your memory?"

"It was seeing the viscount's son opening the door last night. I'd had a drink. All right. I'd had several. I don't deny it. But he looks so uncannily like his father that I fancied I was standing before a ghost. Poor bereft boy never would believe the viscount died of natural causes."

Kate tried to envision Colin as a young, grieving avenger, one who had loved Georgette and his father, one whose devil-may-care life had been forever changed by the viscount's death.

"Did anybody else believe that the viscount had been murdered?" Kate asked thoughtfully.

Griswold nodded. "Plenty of those in his service did. He was a vital, healthy man."

"Did you believe it?" Kate asked slowly.

He gazed up at her, righteous anger flashing in his eyes. "It struck me as odd at the time that the younger Mr. Earling served the viscount wine at the table that night."

Kate frowned. "Mason, you mean?"

"It was my duty to pour that evening, but he took the bottle from the sideboard before I had a chance. I recall it was a special vintage to celebrate the viscount's invitation of a partnership with Mr. Earling Senior. Viscount Norwood had many business connections in India. He was willing to invest a great sum of money in their undertaking."

"Heavens," Kate murmured.

"The hell," Nan said, striding across the room to the windows. "I'll never drink a drop of wine in this house again."

Kate looked down at Griswold. "Did anyone else suspect the viscount had been poisoned?"

"There were rumors in the village," Griswold said, blinking as Nan threw open the drapes. "But it wasn't long before the viscountess remarried, and with her three older boys gone from home, what could she do?"

Kate frowned through the dust motes that floated in the air. "Why didn't you explain all this before Mrs. Lawson moved into this house?"

"It didn't all come together in my mind until I saw the viscount's son," Griswold said. "Who'd take the word of a shuffling old drunk, anyway? I have no proof and I know we're running low on funds. It seemed to me that the mistress and Mr. Earling care for each other. Perhaps I was afraid she would think me a senile fool who was more a threat to the house than an asset."

"I assume you haven't spoken to her yet, Griswold. Nan?"

"You're the only one she ever listens to," Nan said.

"Why didn't anyone else at the table fall ill?" Nan asked.

"The viscount drank most of the wine himself. Mr. Earling had a goblet, but he knocked it over as his son was filling his glass. I was sent to the pantry for two other bottles, of an inferior but still excellent vintage."

"You weren't tempted to taste this special vintage?" Nan asked, her hands clasped behind her back like a barrister in court.

"Most certainly not," he said. "The bottle was empty, even if I had wanted a sample. It must have been strong. I was helping another footman carry the stained carpet outside the next morning when the viscountess's son galloped into the courtyard begging for Mr. Earling's help. He said his father had been seized with unbearable pain. Mr. Earling expressed his distress and sent immediately for the surgeon. But it was too late."

Nan's face wrinkled in a frown. "Didn't the surgeon say his lordship's heart had given out?"

"The surgeon who worked for the Earlings," Griswold said with bitterness.

Kate stared around the study, picturing Mason playing fetch with his silly little dogs, allowing Etta and Charlie to jump on his best sofa. Was his weakness a masquerade? Was his fear of Colin Boscastle a symptom of his own guilt?

"Why?" she wondered aloud. "Why would he kill his father's partner?"

"Mason was his father's only heir. Yet there was more than money involved. Even at his young age he considered Sir Colin to be his rival."

"Over Madam?" Kate asked, knowing the answer.

Griswold sighed. "She loved young Boscastle so deeply that I doubt she knew Master Earling was alive."

"She has to be told," Nan said.

"She isn't going to take *my* word," Griswold said. "Everyone knows I'm off in the head."

"I'm too old," Nan said. "She won't heed my advice."

"Cowards," Kate whispered.

"You're the only person she doesn't throw things at in a temper," Griswold said in sympathy.

"That is not true at all. I simply happen to duck faster than the rest of you."

Chapter 13

Kate steeled her spine, left the room, lost in thought, and walked straight into the tall figure standing at the bottom of the stairs.

"Miss Walcott," he said, nodding his head in deference to her.

"Sir—Mr. Castle," she bit out, drawing a deep breath to steady herself. "How is your shoulder?"

"It bothers me less than a bee sting."

"Well, good," she said, unwillingly admiring how nicely he filled out his riding jacket. "May I congratulate you on the occasion of your self-appointed service to our house?"

"Thank you."

"I wasn't serious! How are we going to explain this to the staff?"

He shrugged. "I served in the military and I worked in a duke's stable after the war. I am an old friend of Mrs. Lawson's, and she is generously helping me earn enough money to set out on my own."

"Yes. After you kill her protector."

"I don't have to kill him if he can convince me that I am wrong about him. I am a very reasonable man once you get to know me."

She dropped her voice. "You weren't reasonable last night when I took you to your room."

His mouth curved in a thin smile. "Considering the fact that we'll be working together, I propose that we do our best to get along. Shall we start anew?"

"Will you promise to behave yourself?"

"I can try."

"Then this conversation is over," she said, lifting her skirts to mount the stairs.

He followed her a few steps. "You can't ignore me forever."

That's what he thinks.

"We shall have to act like civilized adults in front of the children."

The children! As if he cares.

"After supper tonight I will lay out the new rules the household is to obey."

She gripped the staircase railing. She would *not* respond. Rules, indeed.

"I am also setting a curfew against any further nocturnal activities in the garden."

She pivoted slowly on the landing, provoked to her last nerve. "Excuse me?"

He shook his head. "All meetings are to be conducted before dusk. This restriction, of course, will not extend to me or to any male servants whom I assign to a nightly patrol."

"A patrol?"

He frowned. "Do not be alarmed if you hear me walking the halls during the wee hours."

"You would presume to restrict *my* freedom? By what right?"

He held up his hand. "It is only for your protection, Miss Walcott. No one in this house will suffer injury or intimidation under my guard."

*   *   *

It was the first time that Mason Earling had traveled on business without his solicitor. He was forced to make his own decisions to impress accomplished gentlemen who had become wealthy beyond belief on the riches of foreign lands.

At first he had hesitated to share his opinions, his suggestions for safer travel, for expanding trade routes. He thought these hardened men would laugh at him; instead, they bought him drinks.

He didn't know how it had happened. He'd always needed his solicitor to talk for him. Perhaps it was Georgette who had given him confidence.

Suddenly his advice was sought, his business courted, his fellow tradesmen the friendliest he had met in months. It confused him. His solicitor had been warning Mason for more than a year that the company would soon go bankrupt.

He had expected other investors to avoid him. He had expected the usual excuses of uncertain markets and the hazards of putting confidence in a foreign country. But these gentlemen of Southampton encouraged him to grow bolder, to grasp a piece of the wealth they had discovered.

He was hopeful.

He would share the news with his solicitor, Hay, of course. But it was Georgette he wanted to impress. Mason had sent her a pearl choker and hadn't heard a word. Hadn't she liked it? Had it been stolen from the mail coach? Why hadn't *she* written to him?

"Earling!" A young stockholder in the East India Company wanted to show Mason a sketch of his home in Madras.

"Come to supper with us, Earling!" That was the director who thought Mason had a talent for reading maps and could be invaluable surveying a new and faster Suez route.

Mason liked these men, their energy. They appeared to trust him, when all his life his father and their solicitor, Ramsey Hay, had expressed doubts that Mason had a head for business.

"For whores, yes," Hay had announced at a party once. "But I am fond of the boy, and I will protect his business from the unscrupulous."

With his father on the run, and now dead, Mason had more on his mind than reading the fine print on his agreements or even spending the time consulting another solicitor for a second opinion.

He knew it was only a matter of time before Colin Boscastle found him. He did not want to run his entire life as his father had done. He wanted peace; he wanted his mistress to be his wife.

But one thought chilled him. What if Boscastle wanted Georgette back, just to spite Mason? Would Mason keep running if it meant he would lose her?

Chapter 14

$\mathcal{G}$eorgette was horrified by what Kate told her of Griswold's revelation. She also wasn't quite awake, drowsy from her nightly dose of laudanum. Gradually, as the opiate wore off, Georgette's sense of self-preservation came through. Her thoughts understandably turned to concerns about how this discovery would threaten her financial and physical well-being.

"To think Mason insisted on filling my wineglass when we took supper together. And the coffee in bed he brought me each morning. How many times did the deceitful swine lift a cup to my lips? Who knows what potions I might have ingested?"

Kate could only shake her head as Georgette sat down at her dressing table to enact her morning beauty ritual. "It's a good thing you've never given him reason to be rid of you, I suppose."

"Until now," Georgette said, shuddering as she dabbed a blob of white salve on her chin. "He loathes Colin Boscastle. Oh, Kate, I don't want to die by poison."

Kate picked up the jar of unguent and sniffed it. "You're more likely to be poisoned by your elixirs of eternal life than by Mr. Earling. Stanley said many of these face-whitening potions contain mercury."

"Mercury, Venus, or Mars," Georgette muttered. "If I make enough money off my memoirs, I won't have to look for another lover to support us. Have you had breakfast?"

"No," Kate said. "The head groom has taken over the table. I might never eat there again."

"Head groom?"

"Well, we didn't have one. So Sir Colin decided the position should be his."

"But Mason had promised that Lovitt would have the position when he came home. Colin will take over the estate, mark my words. Whatever will we do about him, Kate?"

"You could insist he leave."

"Do you believe for one moment that he would?"

"I don't know him as well as you, madam."

"Should we try to escape?"

"And go where?" Kate asked. "We can't abandon the household. Nor can we give up on your memoirs."

"I'll ring for coffee and pastry. I trust Nan can occupy the children for an hour."

"They are not with Nan. The last I saw of them, they were vying for 'Castle's' attention at the table."

" 'Castle'?"

"Subtle, isn't he?"

"Oh, no." Georgette turned her salve-smeared face to Kate. "I made him a promise before dawn."

"Oh?"

"Not that kind of promise. I need your help. Please take down this letter before I change my mind."

Kate drew out the chair by the drop-front desk. "Go on, madam."

"I'm betraying Mason."

"How?"

"Colin has convinced me to set a trap with a letter. Oh, Kate, just write what I say or Colin will never go away."

Kate sighed heavily. "All right, madam."

Dearest Mason,

I promised you I would not accept private engagements while you provided for me. However, it appears you forgot to pay my bills before you left. Your solicitor shows me as little respect as he does financial support. You are in arrears for my accounts with numerous merchants.

You promised to send me presents to remind me of your devotion and letters describing your ventures. I have written you three times and received no reply. I worry that your affections for me have waned.

I also worry that I might be carrying the child you have wanted.

Last night our house was vandalized by village ruffians. The children and I no longer feel safe without you here to protect us. You need to return home immediately, Mason, if only for a brief time so that these troubles are amended before it is too late.

Your languishing mistress,
Georgette

Kate put down the quill and looked at the letter Georgette had dictated to her. "Is it true?"

"Is what true?" Georgette said blankly.

"Are you pregnant, madam?"

"I doubt it. My menses have never been the same since I gave birth to Charlie."

"Another baby," Kate said, sighing. "And a trouble-maker in the house."

"It could be a girl."

"I was referring to Sir Colin."

"Oh. Oh, I see."

Kate suppressed another sigh. "I'll have Lovitt or one of the younger footmen post this, then, unless Sir Colin wishes to see it first."

"No. Have it sent before I change my mind—it *is* odd that I haven't heard from Mason yet. The three previous letters I sent him can't all have gotten lost."

"A seaport is a busy place." Although why love letters from a man Georgette now believed to be a murderer mattered, Kate didn't know. "It's all been a shock, hasn't it?"

"Do you think that this letter will bring Mason home?"

Kate nodded. "You and Sir Colin have set an effective trap. Whether it works or not, I can't say, but if Mason takes the bait, I dearly hope that the children and I will not be witness to the end result."

"I feel dreadful."

"Then let's work on your memoirs. They always put us in a hopeful mood."

Georgette's dream of publication, of making herself wealthy by revealing the sexual peculiarities of peers and well-known gentlemen, might be a debasing aspiration, but it was not one without chance of success. Moreover, Kate would much rather work for a woman who sold her secrets instead of her body.

She found the last page that Georgette had dictated to her. It had been written the night before Sir Colin arrived, and if Kate had ever suspected that Georgette exaggerated her amorous exploits, she did not now.

"Here we go. You were describing the month you spent in the Earl of Woodhaven's dungeon—"

"Woodhaven." Georgette made a face at herself in the mirror. "That Master of Perversion. Refresh my memory. Was I still shackled naked to the wall or had I managed to overpower him and escape?"

Kate peered down at her notes, her face impassive. One did not agree to collaborate on a memoir by passing judgment on the author. It was Kate's job to inspire, incite, and prompt the forbidden details of Georgette's life, many of which, to Kate's relief, she had not been in service to substantiate.

Her face cleared. "When last we left off on your escapades, you had bashed the earl on the head with a candlestick and retrieved the keys to your shackles and the dungeon."

Georgette smiled. "Oh, right. The widgeon and his whips."

"Widgeon?" Kate paused. "You ran through the castle, clad in a tablecloth, and found his wife—"

"That wasn't his wife. That was his mother," Georgette said. "And I could have escaped without informing anyone that I'd locked the earl in the dungeon, but I didn't want his death on my hands. What was it you read recently about him in the papers?"

"He is well liked in the House of Lords."

"Not after my memoirs publish. What are you frowning about now?"

"I suspect your readers will crave the details of his depravity."

"Well, then, after coffee and a bath, I'll be in a more talkative frame of mind."

They fell into a companionable silence until Kate rose to wipe the salve from Georgette's face. Her employer was flighty, selfish, generous to a fault. Kate had watched Georgette discard lovers as thoughtlessly as she did a pair of slippers; she had also seen Georgette slip a full purse to a street pauper on more than one occasion when she thought Kate could not see her from the carriage.

"Who would have guessed I could still be fooled at my age? I believed Mason when he said that he loved me and would marry me if I agreed to give him children."

"The children." Kate glanced up guiltily at the clock. "I should have brought them in for lessons a half hour ago." If she could pry them away from their new hero.

The children had followed Colin to the paddock, where Brian was riding the sullen little pony that Mason had given him before he left on business. It had been a touching act of kindness toward Brian, Kate had thought at the time. But Brian thought himself too grown-up for a pony and had asked repeatedly for a horse.

Kate sensed hostilities mounting before she even reached the paddock. Lovitt stood with his brawny arms thrown over the railing. Scorn in his eyes, he watched Colin instruct Brian on the handling of his pony. The pony took several complacent trots around the ring before she stopped.

"Use your knees," Colin said.

Brian made a bored face.

"Give her a good tap on the rump," Lovitt said, ignoring Colin's look of irritation. He glanced at Kate. "It's degrading, making a boy that size prance around on a pony."

Clearly Brian agreed. He raised his riding quirt and brought it down sharply on the pony's hindquarters. The pony stood for a few seconds, then reared up and deposited Brian on his buttocks. Colin blew out a sigh of exasperation and made no attempt to rescue Brian from his embarrassment. Etta burst into giggles. Charlie took off his cap and bashed it on the fence, laughing uncontrollably.

Kate started through the gate. Colin strode up and

caught her by the elbow. "Let him feel the sting of shame for a minute. It won't hurt him."

Lovitt glowered at Colin. "First he's the head groom. Now he's the boy's guardian. What next?"

"Would you let go of my arm, Castle?" she asked, narrowing her eyes.

"Not if you intend to mollycoddle him. You aren't doing him any favors by encouraging him to cling to your skirts."

Lovitt straightened behind her. Brian stood up and his two siblings huddled together. Kate raised her chin, no longer the tepid governess but a person not to be underestimated. "I pity you, sir, if you were raised without gentleness and with no defender."

He laughed rudely. "A boy has to learn to defend himself. The earlier the better."

"Ah. So *you*, as a baby, strangled snakes in your crib like Hercules?"

Brian's eyes sparkled in embarrassed anger. "I won't ride a pony again." He threw his crop over the fence. "Unless I can have a decent horse, I refuse to ride at all."

Colin straightened his shoulders, and Kate shivered as his face tightened. "Walk the pony back to her stall and brush her down."

Brian stared at him as if he'd gone mad. Kate was tempted to intervene, but something, perhaps the realization that Colin might be right, made her stop.

"Are you hurt?" she asked Brian in a guarded voice.

"No," Colin and Brian answered in unison.

Kate stepped back, bumping against Lovitt, who had thrown his saddle across the fence at the first sign of tension in the air. He steadied Kate and shot Colin a baleful look.

"What has he done now?" he demanded under his breath.

"He's making Brian brush his pony," Kate said. "And Brian doesn't want to."

His forehead creased in resolve, Lovitt strode up behind Colin and coughed to get his attention. "Sir?"

Colin did not turn his head. From what Kate could see, he and Brian were still engaged in a contest of wills. "What do you want?" he finally asked.

"There's no problem with Master Lawson, sir. I'll take care of the pony for him. I always do."

"Then that is the problem," Colin said, vaulting over the fence to approach Brian. "Come on."

Lovitt made a move to follow.

Colin's voice stopped him in his tracks. "I'm handling this."

"Not very well," Lovitt muttered to Kate. "Who does he think he is?"

Brian's father, she thought in rue. *If he doesn't know, the possibility must have crossed his mind.*

"Take the pony to the barn," Colin said calmly.

Brian glanced at both Kate and Lovitt for dispensation. Neither of them chose to challenge the tall man who was handing the boy the pony's reins. Brian squared his shoulders.

"Etta should be riding it," Brian said, his face dusty and red.

"Maybe after you learn to ride, she will," Colin said, his legs planted apart.

"Oh, dear," Kate whispered. "I don't think we should watch."

"Someone has to protect him," Lovitt said.

"Which him are you talking about?" Kate inquired.

"Would you mind leaving?" Colin answered without turning his head. "You are nothing but a distraction."

Kate could have smacked the arrogant devil. "It is *my* job to take care of that boy."

"Then I'll stay to take care of you," Lovitt said.

"Take the pony inside," Colin said again to Brian.

It looked for a moment as if he'd refuse and put up a fight. Instead, he grabbed the reins and, with a mutinous look, led the pony to the stables.

"I want a proper horse," he said over his shoulder to Colin. "And I'll get one, too."

Colin stared after him, an unfamiliar pain squeezing his heart. It couldn't be. The boy not only looked like him, but behaved with the same defiant arrogance that had gotten Colin and his brothers into constant trouble during their youth. Was Brian his son? It was possible, he supposed.

He needed to know.

He needed Georgette to explain whether she had been carrying his child when he had left her. She might not have realized it at the time. Was that why she had jumped at the chance to marry old Mr. Lawson? To give Brian a name instead of the label of illegitimacy, which he could never rise above?

He would wait a while for her to confess before he confronted her. He would not leave this house until he knew.

Chapter 15

A week had passed since the self-appointed head groom's arrival. It was as if the estate had fallen under his power, and Kate was afraid nothing would ever return to normal again. Not that this had ever been the epitome of the typical English home.

But she had dedicated herself to protecting the children, and someone had to reestablish their everyday routine. The burden, as usual, would fall on her shoulders, and she vowed that "Castle" would not stand in her way—which, to her frustration, he did. He seemed to be present whenever she turned.

The evening before last she had sneaked into the garden for a short walk, and he had followed her, reminding her that she had violated her curfew. A few hours later, after the household had retired for the night, she heard a noise outside her room and cracked open the door to make sure one of the children hadn't escaped the nursery.

But there stood Castle, blithely explaining that he was patrolling the hall for her own protection.

He made it impossible for her to ignore him. With the exception of Brian, the children adored him, and where her charges wandered, there she must follow. They begged to watch him exercise the horses, and when he did, she found herself staring at him from the kitchen window, transfixed by his grace and patience. She couldn't help noticing his light touch with the mare he had hidden in the smithy on the night of his arrival. One tug of the reins, a few low words whispered in her ear, and the horse obeyed, trusting his mastery. Contrary to what Kate had initially believed, he wasn't a man who lived for immediate pleasure—even if she might be a woman who secretly wanted him to kiss her again.

"What did we do without him?" one of the maids whispered over Kate's shoulder.

Kate sighed. "We went about our work. We didn't stand about gaping like carps half the day."

"Don't you like him, miss?"

"I'd like him better if he didn't distract the children from their lessons."

Or distract her.

"Brian! Etta! Charlie!" she called from the window. "It's time to come inside and rehearse your lines for the play."

She saw the children, the little traitors, gaze up at Colin as if he could counteract Kate's order. Instead, he slid off his horse, handed the reins to a sour-faced Lovitt, and herded the three children through the kitchen door. The thought crossed her mind that Colin would make a good father and that, despite his errant ways, he was a good man.

His blue eyes roved over her with his typical impudence. "Do I have a part in your play?"

"I'm sorry, Castle," she said insincerely. "I wrote it before you arrived."

He leaned his hip against the butcher block, apparently not about to concede defeat. "Why don't I help you with the scenery?"

"Because I—because you—you have mud all over your boots, that's why." And because when he looked at her with that impudent expression, she could not think clearly.

He looked down. "Heaven forbid. I must have stepped in something."

"Please go outside, sir."

She could feel the other servants watching, waiting to see who would win this battle. Kate steeled herself for a confrontation. But to her surprise, he merely blew her a kiss and backed out into the garden.

"Well, I never," Cook said. "Isn't he the bold one?"

"He's got more sauce than a Christmas goose," Charlie said, his mouth full of the biscuit he had pinched from the table.

Cook lifted her brow. "He's got his eye on Miss Kate—that's what I think."

"Oh, really." Kate glanced at one of the grinning housemaids. "Take the children upstairs now, please, and ask Nan to change their clothes."

"Trust me, Kate," Cook said the instant the children left. "There's something about that man. He's not afraid of animals or amorous women."

"Well, then," Kate said, mildly incensed, "that wouldn't affect me, would it? I'm not an animal. And I am *not*, by any flight of the imagination, an 'amorous woman.'"

Cook set down the scallions she was about to chop. "Perhaps it's time you changed."

"I beg your pardon."

"Begging is common, dear, and you were raised to better. Yes. You were brought up to marry a squire, a vicar, or a schoolteacher, so I imagine a groom is a comedown in expectations. But let's see how he ends up working out and how long he lasts. Mr. Earling might take a liking to him."

"I doubt that will happen," Kate said. She had managed not to worry about the moment when Colin would confront Mason, and now that the time was drawing nearer, she felt sick with anxiety. Wasn't it enough that she maintained a semblance of normal life in what one could consider a seraglio? But if a duel took place—well, she supposed it was a blessing that the children had never witnessed any prior acts of violence.

She glanced up to find Cook scrutinizing her like a broody hen. "Things can change, Kate. You never know. I've a sense that there's more to Castle than meets the eye."

"What meets the eye is more than enough," Kate retorted, uncorking a bottle of vinegar. "Oh, this *is* foul. Enough of this nonsense, anyway. What we should be discussing is the shopping list for the supper party."

"You aren't going into the village after what happened in the garden?" one of the scullery maids said in apprehension.

"We can't starve because a few ruffians don't approve of us. I won't go alone. I never do."

"Take Castle with you, then," Cook said.

"Lovitt and Griswold can accompany me as they always do."

Cook snorted. "Lovitt and Griswold aren't a quarter of the man Mr. Castle is."

"I heard that," an offended voice said from the kitchen door, where Lovitt stood, his brows drawn together in displeasure.

Kate shook her head. "Cook didn't mean it, Lovitt."

"Yes, I did," Cook said.

Kate went to the door, taking the young man's arm to placate him. "Would you like a cup of tea to settle you down?"

"No. I'd like to stick the new help in a well to drown."

"Lovitt!"

Cook turned white. "I didn't mean to hurt your feelings, lad. I got carried away."

He slapped his gloves on the table.

"Mr. Earling led me to believe that I would be given that position when he came home. It's an outrage, Mrs. Lawson making a total stranger the head groom. He's taken over the whole house."

"That's an exaggeration, Lovitt," Cook said, pouring him a huge mug of tea. "He's a novelty, that's all, and if the master made you a promise, then all will be well when he returns. Sit down, my pet. We all need to be appreciated from time to time."

"He's gonna bring trouble on this house," Lovitt said, looking straight at Kate. "I feel it in my bones."

Chapter 16

$\mathcal{K}$ ate spent the rest of the morning rehearsing her play in the salon with the children and servants. It was tradition to give everyone a part in her amateur productions, but Colin had arrived too late to be written in, and in all honesty, she wouldn't know whether to cast him as hero or villain.

It seemed that he wasn't sure, either. She had sent the children upstairs to wash for dinner. The servants had returned to their regular chores, which left her with a welcome moment of quiet reflection. She stared absently at the tangled blond wig that had fallen on the steps to the stage.

"Rapunzel?" Colin asked, reaching down an instant before she did.

Startled, she recovered the wig that he was examining with unconcealed amusement. "No. Helen of Troy."

"Troy?" he said in a puzzled voice, peering over her shoulder to one of two tall pillars on the stage, against which rested a rickety ladder. "Isn't that meant to be a tower?

"No. It's a column."

"I see." He stared down at the wig, which she was nervously combing through with her fingers. "I assume that you're playing Helen."

She looked up with a laugh of disbelief. "The most beautiful woman in the world? That would take some imagination."

"Not for me." His gaze drifted over her face to the décolletage of her gown as if searching for her heart. "It isn't dark at all in here."

She frowned, felt her blood quicken at the deep rasp of his voice. "What does that mean?" she asked in hesitation.

"It means I couldn't possibly mistake you for anyone else."

Her throat closed. She was certain now he had found her heart because it beat through her body with an intoxicating anticipation. She went still as he placed his hand at her hip. Mesmerized, she made no objection as he pulled her toward him. "And?" she asked faintly.

His innocent smile belied the dark intentions in his eyes. "And when I kiss you, this time, I will know full well who you are because—"

"I warned you—"

"I warned you, too. It's obvious that neither one of us is good at taking advice. Here you are again in my arms, and *you* know who I am."

"I know *what* you are—an undisciplined—"

His kiss silenced her voice but aroused such a clamor of raw feeling inside her that she couldn't begin to fight. What had happened to *her* principles? Had she forgotten how to breathe? He teased his tongue between her lips, a slow penetration that disarmed and pierced to the deepest part of her. The hard warmth of his body offered a refuge that felt too wonderful to refuse, even as her inner voice whispered that once she accepted his shelter, she would never be allowed to escape.

Unfair. Unwise.

"Sweet," he whispered as his mouth seduced hers,

sought and found the vulnerability that she had hidden away for years.

She recognized in his eyes a shadow, the playfulness deepening into desperate hunger. His—or hers? She felt his hand coaxing her into the core of his body. She swayed, molded herself to the thickness that pressed against her skirts. Pale sunlight poured in through the windows. How indecent of her to submit to him without the cover of darkness to conceal her desire.

"Even sweeter still," he said against her mouth. "Put your hand around my neck."

She obeyed because she could not trust her balance. Why did his kisses provoke excitement when another man's had filled her with panic? How could a look, a few words between them, flare into an intimacy more potent than any force she had ever known?

Her body didn't care why. It invited his decadent touch, encouraged this dangerous exhilaration. He lowered his head and kissed her throat. She shivered, breathless for endless moments before she realized that his other hand had stroked a path to her breast. Her nipples ached against her corset at his caress. It was more than she could endure. If it did not end now, she would be lost.

He knew. He lifted his head, still holding her as she recaptured her control. She felt bereft, aware of a hollowness in her belly, a wanting she wished he had never unbound. Slowly she let her hand slide from his neck. Her body throbbed in complaint as he loosened his grasp.

Still, they stood together, silent, unmoving, until she dredged up the nerve to lift her face to his again.

His beauty hurt her eyes. His sensuality endangered her heart. It was perfectly clear that sooner or later he meant to possess her and that she could not trust herself in his presence.

"Now we know," he said, his voice laced with rue.

She sighed. It took all her effort not to crumple on the steps. "What do we know? Each other? Have you mistaken intimacy for something more?"

"No." His eyes, so dark moments before, glinted with humor. "We know that we like kissing each other."

Her heart slowly returned to a normal rhythm. "Did I say that?"

He lifted his hand and traced her bottom lip with his knuckle. "You melted the moment I touched you. You clung to me when I could have taken shameless advantage of your response. You could have broken free anytime during our kiss. It is not as if I had you chained to my side."

"That is true, sir. But perhaps instead of pointing out my weaknesses, you might do better to question your own resolve."

He frowned. "I chose to kiss you. It was an act of free will."

"Was it?" she asked daringly, the chance to retaliate too delicious to resist.

His brows flew up. "Are you admitting that you enticed me?"

She turned, staring at the stage.

"I didn't admit anything of the kind."

He laughed helplessly. "All right. Then what are you telling me?"

She smiled at him over her shoulder. "That you might want to ask yourself how dallying with a governess will help you achieve a goal that has eluded you for thirteen years. If you are determined to seek justice, I doubt that you will find it in a kiss."

He watched her step down from the stage and walk calmly from the salon, not quite certain what had just happened. She had called him undisciplined. Did she have any notion of the willpower he had exerted to limit his craving for her to a mere kiss? He could have seduced her on the spot if he'd set his mind to it.

He had assumed she was innocent. She had implied otherwise.

Now he wasn't sure what to think.

She kissed like a virgin. Yet she had a mouth on her like an untamed shrew. He wanted her. That was torture enough. Had he underestimated her or overestimated himself? Had she issued him a challenge? If so, it pained him to realize that her parting words had hit their target.

He had come to this house with a clear mind; he had a plan to enact. He couldn't afford to lose his edge over a woman he had no right to pursue.

How in God's name could he hope to trap a murderer when thoughts of romancing Miss Kate Walcott replaced those of his long-awaited revenge?

Chapter 17

"Madam, it's time to start the day, or what's left of it," Kate said as she entered Georgette's room that same afternoon and placed a tray of buttered toast and steaming coffee in a silver pot on the bedside table.

"Do I have an appointment with a dressmaker?" Georgette asked listlessly.

"No. With me. I doubt the dressmaker will visit you again until you pay your bills. We agreed to work on your memoirs for an hour every afternoon before the rest of the house takes tea."

Georgette rolled across the bed in her floral silk wrapper. "I'm ill. I've caught Etta's cold. I don't want to think about sex when I have a runny nose. You write original plays. Can't you make up a chapter or two until I feel better?"

"About?" Kate asked, frowning in annoyance.

"Make up something about Sir Colin, the more wicked the better."

"I'll do nothing of the kind. Anyway, I thought we'd finished his chapters."

"I thought so, too, until he came thundering back into our lives like a crusader."

"*Your* life," Kate said absently. "I had never met him until a week ago."

"Well, you both seem to know each other now," Georgette said, blowing her nose on a lace-edged handkerchief.

"Excuse me?"

Georgette fell back miserably on her pillow. "I've seen him look at you, Kate, and I've caught you sneaking a look back. It's all right. I understand the attraction all too well."

"Attraction?" Kate said, mortified that yet another person had accused her of what she was struggling to deny.

"The housemaids melt into little puddles whenever they catch sight of him. He's a spectacular wretch."

"Is he?"

"Oh, Kate. As if you hadn't noticed. You are not made of stone. I know how deeply you've been wounded, but it is no sin to have one's feelings stirred by a man. I might admire him, too, if I didn't know better."

"I have no comment."

"His mother was French, you know. I was told she had a trace of royal Bourbon blood, and that one did not ask whether it was a legitimate association or not. Still, a blend of Bourbon intrigue and Boscastle sexuality—who was I to resist?"

"The Bourbons," Kate said, her skin tingling as she imagined dashing aristocrats, French kings, generations of those who believed they had been born to reign.

"Do you think I *could* die from this cold?" Georgette asked in alarm.

"He draws women to him like dust to venetian blinds," Kate said.

"Yes, dear. I was his piece of fluff once, if you recall."

"The spinster sisters now pass the stables in their phaeton twice a day. One of them even took out a sketching pad when Sir Colin was in the pasture training that unschooled colt who gets the better of the stable boys."

"I think Squire Billingsley's son fancies me," Georgette murmured, her arm flung over her face. "Invite him to my funeral if I pass away unexpectedly. And Squire Winchester's family."

"And I'm not sure, but I think I saw the widow who lives by the old granary riding through the woods above the house."

Georgette sat up. "I dislike that woman intensely. The little witch had her eye on Mason only a month after her husband died."

"Why are we discussing him at all?"

"It's all right, Kate," Georgette said sagely. "I am your mistress, not your mother. Colin is a prime example of the masculine ideal, cad that he might have been during our youth. He's more subdued than when I knew him, but, oh, to have loved him at his wildest."

Georgette paused, apparently lost in memories. Kate paused, too, to settle at the desk and pick up her pen. It was hard to imagine Colin any wilder than he was.

"How would *you* describe him?" Georgette asked unexpectedly.

Kate watched a blob of ink spread across the C she had just written. How would she describe him? Vital, decadent, a man a woman would desire to her detriment. What would Georgette think if she knew that Colin had kissed Kate in the salon today? Kate didn't even know what to think herself.

"These are your memoirs," she said, shrugging.

"Give me your impression."

"Handsome."

Georgette sighed. "Yes, yes. Deeper than that."

Kate wavered. "He does have lovely blue eyes."

"Yes," Georgette said dryly. "So does his son. What else?"

Kate stared across the room. "There's something about his smile."

Georgette's chin lifted. "What about it?"

"It can be cruel and tender."

"It can? Hmmm. I must have forgotten."

"His mouth hardens when he talks about avenging his father. He looks quite forbidding. But when he's teasing or—" Kate blinked, catching herself from making a confession that she would never live down.

"Teasing who?" Georgette asked, intrigued.

"The children, of course. Good heavens. What does it matter what your companion thinks of your past lover's mouth?"

"We were discussing his smile," Georgette said slyly. "I suppose he does have a mouth designed for inflicting pleasures that could be described as cruel. I doubt that every woman's first lover is her best."

"I doubt that most women have a list as long as yours to make the comparison."

"True." Georgette sniffed. "That is why my story shall fetch a fortune on the market. If I can find a publisher who is more interested in making money off my past sins than ones he wishes to commit with me."

"You aren't crying, are you?" Kate asked suddenly, staring back at Georgette in surprise.

"Over Boscastle? Never again. It's this blasted cold. Did I ever mention the time that he and I made—"

Kate feigned a coughing fit, cutting off Georgette's confession. "Oh, my. I think I've caught it, too." Her face averted, she pretended to search the desk for a handkerchief. She could feel Georgette's skeptical glance, and she coughed again for emphasis. Let Georgette think she'd lost her head. It was better than hearing her relive the details of Sir Colin's carnal skills, the faithful recording of which hadn't bothered Kate a bit until she had encountered the man.

"He could be uncouth at times," Georgette said, dabbing again at her nose. "So could I."

"Yes, madam. I do remember what you did to Lord Darlington's hip."

"No one has ever explained the use of a cane as proudly as Darlington did in his club. When a man his age can boast he was injured in a woman's bed, he incites more envy than censure from his peers."

"Be that as it may, we should perhaps leave a few episodes to the reader's imagination. It wouldn't hurt your reputation to confess that desperation drove you to your life of sin. Why don't we describe how you worked as a milliner's assistant when you were between lovers?"

Georgette stared at her in exasperation. "You might be one of the few people in England who would pay to read about my unsuccessful attempts at collecting feathers for horrid little hats. I didn't make enough to feed a sparrow from that affair. It was an indignity to my profession. Can you imagine any of the great harlots in history wasting their talents in menial labor? I'm fairly certain Caesar didn't expect Cleopatra to clean fish bones for supper on her barge. That miserable milliner cheated his customers and he cheated me. If he is mentioned in my memoirs it will only be to publicize his deceit."

"We shall be lucky if we aren't sued for criminal libel and put in a penitentiary," Kate murmured.

"Nonsense. I have proof of every arrangement I have conducted. You've read through my correspondences. I have three trunks stuffed with letters that you haven't seen yet and I still can't decipher. Who will bring a suit against me for telling the truth? We can even expose your lecherous Lord Overton if you like."

Kate shook her head. "I don't like. He's dead."

"Well, dead or not, he deserves it," Georgette said, thumping one of her cushions with her foot. "It might make other men consider their abuse if they realized their crimes could become public knowledge."

"The aristocracy rarely pays for its crimes," Kate said. "Anyway, I'd rather forget the damage he inflicted on me than inform the world about it."

"You look ill," Georgette said in concern. "Go and have a sit-down. We'll carry on tomorrow."

"We can't keep putting everything off, madam. We must be prepared to face what might be. What if Mr. Earling comes home early? What if—"

"I've wondered the same thing myself," Georgette said, closing her eyes. "I've . . ."

Kate waited. "Are you falling asleep again?" she whispered.

Georgette didn't answer, escaping into dreams that Kate could only envy.

She stood. She had dreams of her own. The time had come to tell Georgette that she thought Stanley *might* propose to her and that she *might* accept. She wasn't passionately in love with him. She wasn't convinced she loved him at all. But her chances of ever making her own life grew daily more remote.

"We'll try again tomorrow," Georgette whispered as Kate tiptoed to the door.

"Perhaps the day after," Kate replied. "I have to market in the morning."

Chapter 18

*K*ate usually enjoyed the drive through the winding roads and lanes of cheery thatched cottages that led to the village. But the day had dawned with purple-gray clouds that hovered over the small carriage like an omen. The air turned still and oppressive, with a storm lurking above the hills. Nevertheless Kate would be grateful if ill weather was the only threat that came their way.

Brian had asked to come with her, but Kate had thought it safer for him to stay home. Sir Colin insisted that he and the coachman drive together, two footmen at the rear, leaving Kate in the carriage with only Nan for company.

With his high black hat pulled down to hide his watchful expression, a musket balanced between his long legs, it seemed doubtful that anyone would cross him or even dare to cross his path.

"Nobody's given us a second look yet," Nan observed as the carriage rattled past the village green.

"That's fine," Kate said. "Perhaps we'll be able to finish our shopping before it rains."

"Usually there's a crowd gathered, hoping for a peek of the harlot."

"Well, don't wish trouble on us."

Nan stared through the window as the carriage slowed. "I take that back. The village hens have noticed Castle in the box. I'll bet he'll go to the top of their shopping list, well above candles and linens."

"Good," Kate said irritably. "Let them notice him and leave us to our errands."

Nan drew back from the window with a scowl. "He doesn't want to be noticed, does he?"

"No." Kate stared up into his shadowed face as he opened the carriage door for her. Her pelisse felt heavy and overwarm, and, blast it, but Nan was right. His appearance had already drawn the notice of a young housewife riding pillion who craned her head to gaze back at him. So brazen was her curious stare that Colin tipped his black hat, ignoring Kate long enough so that when he turned around to help her down the steps, she was already standing in the street.

His mirthful eyes met hers. "I'll stand outside the shops unless you indicate I'm needed inside."

She lifted her pale green wool pelisse from the curb. "I'm sure there will be plenty to please your eye while you wait."

"*My* eye?"

"Yes. The eye that gawked at the woman who just rode past us."

"I did not gawk. I was merely being polite by acknowledging her. It would have seemed rude if I had ignored her, wouldn't it?"

Kate clasped her empty basket to her side. "Rude? You are employed by a fallen woman. No one expects you to mince about with the false manners of a footman at high tea."

He grinned, slouched up against the carriage. "Well, since I take some fault for her fall, I don't think it's appropriate to be rude. I—"

"Turn your head," she said quietly. "Examine the horses. Search the gutter for a lost coin. Try to hide your face."

He obeyed her without question, joining the footmen at the carriage's rear to comment that a passerby had dropped a shilling in the street. Kate forced herself to behave normally, although her heart thundered in her ears. Advancing in her direction was Mason Earling's solicitor, a man who made no secret that he disapproved of his client's relationship with a courtesan. Kate had unsuccessfully urged Georgette to hire her own solicitor to ensure she was protected in case she conceived a child or Mason tired of her. Ramsey Hay rarely missed a chance to mutter some lowering imprecation about Georgette under his breath when he visited the house.

He was slightly more civil to Kate. "Miss Walcott," he said, drawing her into the doorway of the bookseller's shop. "Do you think this is wise, for you to be seen in public?"

He looked at her closely, although what he imagined lay underneath her dull muslin dress and buttoned pelisse she did not want to know. "Wise, Mr. Hay?"

"I heard there was an incident at the house. I can't say I am surprised. I have suggested that a cottage in the next village would be safer and certainly more discreet."

"Less expensive, too."

He frowned, glancing around at the carriage parked behind them. If he had looked back a second earlier, he would have caught Colin standing with his legs braced apart and his arms folded in contempt. Perhaps Colin knew who he was; Hay had worked for Mr. Earling at the time of Joshua Boscastle's death.

"I don't think you should visit the village again," he said bluntly. "If there is anything you need, contact me personally. And please tell Mrs. Lawson that I will not fund her frivolous tastes. I suggest she start trimming her expenses by letting some of the staff go. That doddering old drunk of a footman should be the first dismissed. Tell her also that her credit will be suspended at the end of the month."

Her face stung as if she had rubbed nettles on her cheeks. "I'm shopping for Mrs. Lawson right now, sir."

"Mrs. Lawson could live on one casket of her jewels for the next ten years, I've no doubt."

Nan approached the shop, giving Hay a glare. "I think I just felt a raindrop. Don't want to be caught in a storm, do we?"

Hay ignored her. "It is inappropriate for a gentleman to lavish his money on baubles for a woman who will not become his wife."

"He might marry her," Nan said. "You never know. He's loved her all his life."

"Pardon us, sir," Kate said. "I need a few simple items—a bonnet for madam, a treat for the adorable pony Mr. Earling bought for Mrs. Lawson's son, and I"—she lowered her gaze demurely—"I am desperate for a new pair of silk stockings."

He stared at her, his mouth flat with anger, his eyes dark with unpleasant interest. "You had better mind yourself, Miss Walcott. There aren't many desirable positions for a young woman of your background."

He nodded, casting another look at the carriage, and walked off. Kate felt herself trembling inside, insulted, more convinced than ever that he would do everything in his power to sabotage Georgette's affair with Mason.

Then she looked up. In the shop window she saw Colin's reflection as he returned to the door of the carriage. His eyes followed Hay's retreat with palpable contempt. She sighed. There went the hope for an untroubled day. It was all she could do to concentrate on making her purchases.

In fact, because Mr. Hay had spoken so contemptuously of Georgette, Kate decided to buy her mistress not only a charming pink bonnet but lace gloves to match.

When she exited the last shop, she spotted Stanley, hurrying from the apothecary's shop. He gave her a passing glance that made her throat tighten. Was he now going to pretend in public that they weren't friends? She knew she shouldn't blame him; he was timid and respectful of his father's reputation, but still, she could not respect a hypocrite. But then he stopped, regarding her with surprised pleasure, and she suffered a pang of guilt for her misjudgment. "Kate—I mean, Miss Walcott. What a treat to see you today! Everyone is out to do their shopping before the storm. But is it safe to be here unescorted after what just happened? Wouldn't it have been better to stay in the house until the furor died down?"

"You are a kind man, Stanley."

"I regret I can't stay to talk. I've a delivery to make for an old lady who has fallen down her stairs and is in considerable pain. Perhaps I can stop by tonight . . . ?"

She glanced involuntarily toward the carriage. She assumed that Colin had been watching this exchange. The thought pleased her. She hoped he would conclude that there were some gentlemen in the world who still considered Kate to be a wholesome young woman and not one to be kissed and invited to bed on the basis of mistaken identity or her employer's profession.

But Colin wasn't watching her attempt at flirtation at all. He was engaged in one of his own with the young widow whose sea captain husband had died two years ago. How dare the woman with her thick red hair and lily-white skin appeal to Colin's lower instincts? No wonder Georgette disliked her. True, the widow had to raise two little boys on a meager pension, but she had virtually thrown herself at the feet of every eligible man in the village. Would Colin be the one to succumb?

"Kate," Stanley said. "What is it?"

From what Kate could see, the widow's helplessness was appealing to the village's latest and most eligible newcomer—Colin was helping her and a store clerk load her supplies into her simple cart.

Her two sons stared at Colin.

The clerk stared at Colin.

The widow stared up at him in blushing gratitude.

And Kate knew why.

"I have to go now, Kate," Stanley said with a touch of impatience. "Do finish your errands before the storm breaks."

Chapter 19

The widow was as persistent as she was pretty. At another time her unsubtle overture might have aroused Colin's interest. But it was damned awkward to wear his hat pulled low, keep an eye on the governess, and assist the widow in collecting the lace and cabbages she had deliberately dropped in the street.

"I am so clumsy," she said, moistening her lips. She glanced back nervously at the two little boys chasing each other around her cart. "Please don't trouble yourself. I'll manage."

She bent, offering him a tentative smile and a glimpse of her full breasts straining against a worn bodice.

"It's no trouble, ma'am," he said as he gathered her fallen goods. "There. A good wash and all will be well."

She blushed. "Are you new to the parish?"

He glanced at Kate from the corner of his eye. She met his gaze in faint disdain and looked away. "Yes—what—I'm sorry—you were saying?"

She followed the direction of his stare. "Do you work for Mr. Earling?"

From the corner of his eye he spotted a young man swaggering up behind Kate. "No," he said briskly. "I don't work for Earling. Mrs. Lawson has employed me, ma'am."

One of her boys pushed her against Colin's arm as she spoke. "My name is Rachel Pleasance. It's difficult to make friends in the parish, but your master has been kind to my family."

His master? Hadn't she listened to what he'd said?

He didn't bother to correct her this time. He was more concerned that the young man on the sidewalk was practically breathing down Kate's neck. He saw her shoulders tighten. She seemed intent on refusing to acknowledge his existence.

The widow sighed. He forced his attention back to her. What was her name? Had she admitted it was hard for her to make friends? "Yes," he said. "I imagine it is. Perhaps time will help."

"It can be lonely," she answered in a clear effort to prolong the conversation. "But perhaps when one lives and works in a large house with others, there isn't much time for longings."

Longings. The woman had just told him that she had longings. If that wasn't an emblazoned invitation to her bed, he didn't know what was.

"Do you have a name, sir?"

He looked at her then. "My name is Castle," he said distractedly.

"Castle," she said, her eyes searching his shadowed face. "The name suits you. No one builds strong fortresses anymore."

"I wouldn't want to live in a castle," he said to be polite.

"I live off the lane up the hill from the old granary."

He turned his head, manners now the last thing on his mind. The man harassing Kate had drawn a group of supporters, who crowded on the corner to cheer him on.

"Damn them to hell. That swine stepped on her cloak on purpose."

The widow retreated from his fury, one hand reaching out to grasp her wriggling son by the collar. A spool of black lace fell from her basket beneath the carriage wheel. Neither she nor Colin retrieved it this time. "I suggest you go to her rescue," she said in resignation. "A woman alone is easy prey for a young man's wrath."

Kate might have pulled her pelisse free and escaped without further intimidation had Colin not jumped onto the sidewalk and strode up behind the man in palpable anger.

She made a half turn, forcing an unfriendly smile at her offender. "I would remove your foot from my person before you regret your actions. The gentleman behind me doesn't quite know his own strength."

The pedestrian appeared to be about nineteen; his friends gathered closer to leer at Kate. She was aware the oaf hadn't stepped on her cloak from clumsiness. He meant to humiliate her in public.

"Take your shoe off me this instant," she said in a louder voice, tugging at her pelisse to no avail.

He stepped down all the harder. "If a whore sells herself in this village, I say it's only fair that we view her wares."

She wrenched herself free. The hem of her pelisse bore a filthy footprint. "Hurry into the carriage, Nan. Take the basket."

But Nan stood frozen, a smile breaking across her creased face. Colin touched his hat in taunting respect to the man trapped in his shadow. "You've dirtied the lady's cloak. That isn't nice."

"Lady?" The younger man glanced over his shoulder, seeking another show of support from the group, which had begun to disappear into the street. "She's a harlot. Perhaps you are new to the parish, coachman. Perhaps you do not understand polite society."

"I'm not the coachman," Colin said, gently inserting himself between Kate and the aggressor.

"Are you the village idiot, then? Our last one drowned in the stream. We were too late to pull him out. It happened on a day like this, right before a storm."

Kate felt a sick fascination grip her. It was like watching a wolf toy with a wounded rabbit. She knew what would happen. She knew she ought to intervene. But the primal anger on Colin's face kept her at a distance.

"That was good of you to try," Colin said as if he were too dense to understand he was being threatened.

"Wasn't it? We could take you to the place where he fell."

"Could you? Perhaps we should join hands and pray for the poor fellow."

"Join hands? Like we was ladies?"

Colin made a show of flexing his black-gloved fingers. "Or I could save time and just crack your heads together in his memory."

"I can take care of this," she whispered, thinking not of herself but of Colin, his desire to hide his true identity.

Colin gave no indication that he had heard her. "You will apologize to the lady, and we will send the bill to your house for the replacement of the garment you have ruined."

"Come, Kate," Nan said in a worried whisper. "Into the carriage now."

The young aggressor looked down at Kate's tattered hem. "She'll be naked on her back tonight. Why waste good cloth, coachman? Tumble her and let us know if she rivals her employer's reputation. If the price is reasonable, we can all have a turn at her."

Colin's fist flew through the air. At first Kate thought he had controlled his punch merely to glance a blow. In the next instant she saw blood gushing from the other man's mouth, splattering on her sleeve. "Oh," she exclaimed as Colin hit him again. Nan dragged her to the carriage, the footman fumbling to lower the steps.

The man reeled back against the shop-front window, tears of fury and pain in his eyes. Colin touched the tip of his hat again. "I trust you will be lying incapacitated on your back tonight. It was a pleasure breaking your acquaintance. Good afternoon to you."

Colin's gaze cut toward her. How much he reminded her of Brian. She had always blamed her young ward's temper on Georgette. But that fire in Brian's blood clearly flowed from both his parents. It was rather enough to send a beleaguered governess to the couch.

"I think it's time to go home, don't you?" Colin asked, recovering his aplomb so easily she could have hit him. "We've had a full day."

"Indeed, we have," she said, and gave the footman her hand. "I enjoy humiliation as my daily fare. Mockery and insult add spice to life, I always say."

She clambered into the carriage, not looking back even as Nan spoke behind her. "Am I seeing things?"

Kate dropped onto the seat and closed her eyes.

"Kate, who is that walking up to the solicitor's office?"

"I don't know," she said with a deep sigh, "and I don't care. I have blood on my sleeve. I want to go home and wash until this stain disappears."

Nan subsided into thoughtful silence. Kate knew she would have to apologize later. But not now. Not with Colin Boscastle's furious face emblazoned across her mind as he had come to her defense.

No. Not now.

She wanted to savor in private the wicked pleasure of his protection for as long as she could. He acted as if he owned her, as if he would allow no one to mistreat her.

There were definitely advantages to accepting a dangerous man as an escort.

"It couldn't have been him," Nan muttered a half hour later as the carriage approached the manor's drive and Lovitt sprinted forth to unlock the gates. "He's right there. My vision is going bad from witnessing all this sin."

Kate shook her head. She'd no idea what Nan was blithering about. She kept picturing Colin flirting with that pretty widow and then flying off the handle to punch the bully in the face. Not that a man who accosted a woman did not deserve it. Kate decided the heavy-footed oaf might even have been one of the garden marauders. Who could say how far their hatred would go? Perhaps they *should* take a cottage in another village.

The clouds broke to flood the hills and wash out the road to the manor house with waves of mud. Kate wished the rain would dilute the bloodstains on her attire before she went inside so that the children wouldn't ask her what had happened. She had never *lied* to them before, although she had evaded the truth about their mother's profession, their status in society, and what they could expect once they left the dubious security of their childhood. Not arsonists and vengeful lovers if she had any influence on their future. It would be a blessing for the children if Georgette could settle down and lead a stable life.

Etta and Charlie waited inside the front door for the cakes she had brought home. Brian, for some irrational reason, stood outside on the step in the lashing rain and stared at Colin helping her down from the carriage. The boy's empty look struck an unfamiliar fear in her heart.

"Brian." She jumped over the puddles on the steps to guide him back into the house, "why are you standing here in this deluge?"

He stared past her to watch Colin and the coachman drive the carriage around the house. Brian's expression suggested that he had been expecting something.

"Go inside now," she said firmly. "Etta is sick and you will fall next if you linger in the damp."

He wavered, more an angry boy on the verge of adolescence than a child. "I thought Lovitt would bring it home today."

She frowned down at her basket. "Lovitt didn't come with us today. But I bought the fresh muffins that you like."

He backed away from her. "But I wanted a horse. I told you and Castle that I wasn't going to ride a pony again. Lovitt promised me he would get a horse from the gypsies."

"And how would Lovitt, who doesn't have a guinea to his name, manage to buy your horse?"

"He said that Mr. Earling's solicitor managed all his and my mother's money. I overheard Mr. Earling ask her not to buy anything on credit. Lovitt said he knew how to make a deal."

Rain blew through the door into the hall. "Lovitt has no right to pry or make promises he can't possibly keep."

"But the head groom my mother hired because he's handsome has the right?"

"Do not speak of your mother as if—"

"—she were a whore?"

She stared at him in unflinching anger. Some of his defiance receded, but she did not fool herself into believing this was the end of the matter.

"Please, miss, if I had my own horse, I would be happy to teach Etta and Charlie to ride it when they're old enough." At that, he stomped upstairs, pausing once to call over the railing. "If you don't say yes, I'll run away."

"Another problem?" Colin asked as he sauntered up behind her.

"Everything is fine, Mr. Castle."

"Is it?" He peered over her head to the empty staircase. "Where do you want me to take this basket?"

"You—if you expect to pass as a servant, then deliver it to the servants' door behind the house."

"Ah." He nodded as if they were sharing a private joke. "It's a good thing you reminded me of my place. If we were alone I'd explain where you belong."

"Mr. Castle?" she called when he was halfway down the hall.

"Did you need me for something, miss?"

She could see only his profile until he turned his head toward her. The sultry heat in his eyes could have turned every drop of falling rain outdoors to steam. "Please change your clothes before dinner. And be aware that no one is allowed to discuss upsetting events at the table. It hinders good digestion."

He looked away with a laugh. "There's not much else left to talk about, is there? The only pleasant thing I've experienced since I came here is you."

"Me?"

"Sorry. That just slipped out." He tapped his temple. "It goes to show what's on my mind, doesn't it?"

"I can't say that your motives are exactly a mystery. However, as long as you keep those thoughts to yourself and dress appropriately, you will be welcomed at the table."

Chapter 20

*H*er words would soon come back to haunt her. When Colin appeared for dinner at seven, he looked so vital and crisp in his muslin shirt and gray trousers that even the butler complimented his appearance. "Now, that is how one should present oneself at the table. Very well turned out, Mr. Castle. The rest of the staff could learn a lesson or two from you."

"Oh, couldn't we, though?" one of the housemaids whispered, but dropped her gaze when Kate gave her an exasperated look.

"Are you going to eat your pudding, dear?" Cook asked. "I made it especially for the mistress. She fancied something sweet to settle her stomach."

"She's got the worst of Etta's cough," Nan said. "It's a miracle we all aren't dropping like flies. Good thing we've got Castle here to guard the house. Didn't he draw the cork this afternoon? I hope that bloodstain comes out of your sleeve, Kate."

"Nan." Kate gave her a tight smile. "Why don't we talk about current events?"

"It only happened today," Nan said, buttering her peas.

"I was thinking more of Queen Caroline's affair."

"Nobody gives a toss about Queen Caroline's woes," Nan said. "We've enough trouble of our own."

Kate nodded in agreement. "Which we can discuss at another—"

"What happened in the village today, Castle?" asked the butler, who had made no secret of the fact that he appreciated another man about the house in the master's absence.

"It was nothing," Kate said, rising to push in her chair. "We will not talk of it."

"She was accosted," Colin explained. "One of the little badgers who attacked this house last week dirtied her cloak."

"Pelisse," Kate said through her teeth.

Colin looked at her. "Please, what, miss?"

"What did you do to the badger?" asked Tom, who as a stable boy had to keep rodents from the feed.

The five dachshunds shot up from the hearth in a barking frenzy. Colin grabbed a knife from the table.

"Why are they barking?" he asked, rising to stare around the kitchen.

"It's the breed. They were trained to hunt badgers," Kate said in exasperation. "And if you repeat the word, you'll have to take them for a walk until they're tired out."

"I'm not walking five dogs in this—"

The kitchen door swung open. An unrecognizable man appeared with a blanket hooding his head and driving rain at his back. Cook gave a shriek and clasped her hands to her face. The butler rose and crossed the floor to snatch a poker from the hearth.

"Don't hit me, any of you!" Lovitt threw off his dripping horse blanket. "I might deserve it later, but we've a bigger problem on our hands for now."

Colin put down the knife and came to his feet. "What's wrong now?"

Lovitt wiped his streaming face with the towel that Cook brought him. "The pony is gone, sir."

"Well, she couldn't have gone far in this weather, and—how could she escape her stall by herself?"

Lovitt swallowed, meeting Kate's eyes. "She wasn't by herself," he said. "I'm guessing Brian took her."

Colin strode forward and gripped him by the shoulder. "He took her where? Give me your best guess."

"To the gypsies, sir. It's all my fault. I put the idea in his head. I was only half-serious. I told him he could trade in that pony and one of his mother's diamond necklaces for a horse. I said—I bragged I knew how to make a deal. I didn't think he'd act on it."

"Then why did you do it, you great useless thing?" the head chambermaid asked.

Lovitt swallowed, casting a shamed look at Colin's face. "I was jealous of him. Here I've worked for two years, and he comes prancing in the garden and all of a sudden, he's ordering me about."

"Where is the encampment?" Colin demanded, bending to pick up the boots he'd left drying by the fire.

"There isn't one," Cook said in a distraught voice. "The gypsies left days ago because they couldn't find work in the village. I packed up a sack of food for a family who came begging at the door."

"I've saddled two horses for us, sir," Lovitt said, and drank the glass of porter that a housemaid brought him. "He probably took the path—"

Kate didn't want to hear another word. She ran in to her small office, Nan advising her that the mistress should not be alerted yet. No one in the house was brave enough to bring Georgette unwelcome news.

"Go and make sure the other children are still in bed,

Nan." She took the time to lace on a pair of half boots and grab from a chair the satin-lined opera cloak that Georgette had bought her when they had spent a summer in Brighton.

"Why didn't I pay attention to his threat this afternoon?" she said to herself on her rush through the kitchen and out the door.

The answer sat astride the mare Tom had saddled and walked from the stable. Kate ran through the mud to stop him.

"You aren't coming with us," Colin said in a merciless voice as he looked back over his shoulder.

Kate grasped hold of Colin's trouser leg and held on for dear life. "You will either take me with you, or Lovitt and I will go alone."

"Lovitt is in enough trouble tonight without your assistance."

"I can help," she said, lifting her hand to his. "Brian trusts me. Please, sir. Let me come with you."

He relented.

A small party that consisted of two stable boys, the gardener, and the coachman followed Lovitt, Colin, and Kate from the estate. The other servants broke apart to scour the grounds, the sheds, the wagons, the places where a runaway boy might hide if he lacked the courage to stray too far.

Either it was the foulest storm Kate could remember or her anxiety made it seem so. Her fashionable cloak seemed to absorb every drop of rain that fell. She grasped the pommel in one hand, shivering in silence until the horse carried them between the dark wooded hills. "I told you not to come," Colin said. He unbuttoned his black wool coat and drew her tight against his chest and thighs. She reveled in his warmth. His strength. She found a haven in the hard contours of his body. She rested her arm upon his. His chin brushed the back of her head. Or had he kissed her? For once she wouldn't object.

"If anyone can find him, it's you," she said, uncertain he could hear her through the rain and hoofbeats cutting heavily through the muddy undergrowth.

"Why do you say that?"

His gloved hand gripped her tighter as the horse took a curving path. *Guard yourself,* Kate thought.

"You understand horses. You ran away yourself. I just thought—"

You swore you would never tell. Although, she did wonder whether it would make a difference if she did. Would he search harder knowing Brian was his son?

He called up to Lovitt, who had taken a narrow path into the hills. "Are there any quagmires near?"

"I'm not sure, sir. The smugglers' bridge is where the gypsies were last encamped. It washes out in a good rain."

"Why would he do this?" Kate said, staring into the dense tangle of trees.

"Because he's a rebel who hasn't learned that he can't have everything he wants when he wants it."

"What if we're going the wrong way? What if he got lost or one of those village boys took him? No one would hear him in the rain."

"He'll be all right," Colin said. "With any luck this will make him think twice about running away in the future. Hang on. We're on an incline."

She felt herself slide against his arm. "Would it have turned you into a cautious boy?"

"Am I a cautious man?"

From the fast-flowing river below the hill a cry rose above the rushing water. "Down here!" the servants shouted.

"There beside the bridge, sir, miss!" Lovitt called in relief, jumping off his horse. "I see something moving about."

"Shall we dismount here?" Kate turned to ask, her dress, her hair saturated, heavy with rain.

"Yes, slide off carefully. Wait. Hold my—"

She didn't wait. She appeared too eager to see Brian for herself. She started to slip the instant her feet met the ground, mud gushing around her ankles.

"Your hand, Kate!"

He reached down, missed her by a moment. He felt the mare lose her footing, then regain it as he dismounted to lighten her back. Kate wasn't as fortunate. She dropped into a slow slide through mud and loose stones until a birch tree stopped her descent. She pulled herself up before Colin could help her.

"I'm fine," she said quickly, a sight if ever he'd seen one.

He guided his horse to a steady ledge and tethered her loosely to a branch. "I knew I shouldn't have brought you," he said, stepping down sideways to grasp Kate by the forearm before she took another step.

The yapping dogs and Lovitt's cry of relief brought tears to her eyes. "They're down here, sir! Both of 'em under the bridge! Looking very graciously alive, may God be thanked."

Kate flung herself into Colin's arms; he couldn't decide whether she looked more like an orphan in that preposterous cloak or a creature that had clawed through the bowels of the earth to attach herself to the first mortal man she met.

"Dear, dear me, Miss Walcott," he chided softly. "I do so wish to take advantage of you."

She sniffed, lifting her head. "What did you say?"

"You have a talent for dispelling the dark moods that

often besiege me. When you cling to me like this, I quite forget myself. It's an effort to remember why I returned to England." He stared down into her face. "Do not let go of my hand until I say so."

She nodded. She even managed to remain upright as Colin ascended the hill into the tufts of cattails that grew along the embankment. Brian looked up at Colin with unflinching acceptance. For an instant Colin was thrown back into the past, to a memory of catching his younger brother Sebastien in a misdeed. He released Kate's arm.

"Are you hurt?" he demanded of the boy.

Brian shook his head. "No, sir. I was trying to come back home, but the bridge looked unsturdy, and then she slipped in the mud and wouldn't get up."

"Where did you intend to go before you changed your mind?"

"I thought I could trade her to the gypsies for a proper horse."

"Did you?" Colin wondered how many times he'd ever done anything this stupid and potentially tragic when he was younger. He knew what his father would have done for punishment. "What were you going to barter with? Your mother's stolen jewelry?"

"No, sir." A note of hurt pride crept into Brian's voice. "I meant to ask for a loan."

Colin grunted. "Well, someone needs to lend you some common sense. Get out of the way."

Lovitt had already waded into the water. "She's petrified, sir, but she isn't acting as if she's in pain."

Colin glanced back briefly as Brian ran into Kate's arms. Seeing the pair of them console each other softened his anger. "Brian, take your governess and stand with her under the trees with my horse."

The boy was safe. So, it appeared, was the terrified pony, which had to be unsaddled and pulled from the stream in a sling of straps and ropes by the coachman and the two stable boys. At first the animal resisted in panic, sinking deeper in the rising stream with her front legs tucked beneath her belly. Colin kept talking to her until she calmed. The instant the men lifted her from the mud churning over the flooded bed, she clambered to solid ground.

Lovitt sloshed up after her and crouched. "Her knees are sound. It looks like she's bruised an ankle and will be in bad temper for some time. Other than that, I can't see any injuries."

Colin ran his hand through his hair. "Then take her and Brian home."

Lovitt hung his head. "Sir, this is my fault. I've been a damn fool."

"I don't disagree."

"I've done more damage than anyone knows," he muttered.

"Crime and punishment will have to wait until tomorrow. We'll all be washed away if the storm worsens."

He trudged up through the mud to Kate and Brian, who lifted his head from Kate's shoulder as if her comfort made him look childish. "Kate, you will return with me. No one can ride that pony with her bruised ankle."

"Sir," Brian said, his voice breaking in misery, "I didn't mean to hurt her. It was a stupid act. You were right. I don't deserve a horse."

Colin placed his hand on Brian's arm. "You aren't the only boy in the world who thinks he knows better than everyone else. Did you break any bones?"

Brian swallowed. "No, sir."

"Then go home with the other men and don't let your mother see you until you've washed and changed."

Chapter 21

$\mathcal{K}$ate knew that Colin was guiding the horse along a different path than the one they had followed to the bridge. The woods grew denser on this questionable detour, and the interlocked branches provided some shelter from the driving rain.

"Why aren't we following the others home?" she asked through her chattering teeth.

"There is a hunting lodge a quarter mile from the estate. I thought we could talk in private in front of a fire."

"I ought to be home with the children. And how do you know about the lodge?"

"I stayed there for a week watching the house before I thought it an opportune time to announce myself."

She shuddered, burying her hands in the folds of his coat. "Talk? About what? You certainly picked an eventful night to do so. Why can't we wait to talk until the morning? I need to see that Brian is—"

"The storm is worsening by the moment. I would like to rest my horse. She slipped back there on the hill, and I'm afraid she is favoring her right leg. I guarantee that Brian will recover from this incident faster than either of us. Are you afraid to be alone with me?"

"Don't be ridiculous. I am chilled to the bone, although I'd prefer to change my clothes and sit in front of a fire at home than to take refuge in that lodge."

"What is wrong with the lodge?"

"It's where Mrs. Lawson and Mr. Earling became lovers. They often went there to indulge their passion for each other without fear of the children interrupting them."

His lips curled. "We can only hope that the rain has washed their sins away."

So that they could commit their own? she wondered.

The lodge had last been used for a small hunting party when Mason had invited a few friends for the weekend. Georgette had been one of those guests, and it was during this affair that he had suggested their current arrangement. For once Kate had not disapproved. Georgette's bank accounts had dwindled to almost nothing. Her household could not survive the winter without funds.

While Colin tended to his horse in the small adjoining stable, Kate moved through the musty hall. At least she didn't hear any mice scurrying to hide. She walked toward the pitch-black fireplace. She detected the acrid scent of a recent fire, mildew, and burnt food.

"Go upstairs and take off your clothes," Colin said behind her.

She spun around in astonishment. "*This* is your opening to conversation, 'Go upstairs and take off your clothes'? What a master of subtlety you are. You're worse than the wheelwright's sons, who bang their hammers on the forge whenever a woman passes by."

He grinned. "Georgette kept a small wardrobe upstairs, didn't she?"

She stared at him. "I feel warmer now."

"So do I," he said as his gaze traveled over her. "But not warm enough to ride through the rain quite yet."

"I've never met a man who has made as many heroic

gestures as you, and in such a short time. I have also never felt as cold and miserable in my life."

"Then stop arguing with me and find something dry to wear."

He tried several times to light a small fire while Kate rummaged upstairs through the selection of gowns Georgette had left in the closet. Once, twice, a flame leapt to life only to die in the damp, cobwebbed wood that had been ruined from rain dripping down the chimney. He had stripped down to his birthday suit before he realized that he would either have to wait naked for his own clothes to dry or put on Mason's trousers.

He couldn't do it. It was demeaning. It was like asking Mason to give him a cuddle. He'd rather stride about in the nude than degrade himself by putting on that murderer's clothes. He would have to cover himself with one of the blankets he had noticed on the corner chair.

Kate, unfortunately, misread his reasoning and gasped when she returned to the hall to find him standing bare-arsed before the hearth, the blanket he'd been about to use grasped in his fist.

"Good heavens, man! Where is your modesty?"

"What modesty?"

"It's a good thing for you that it's dark in here, or I might never have recovered from your display of—of *everything*."

"I wanted to give you a fire."

"Well, you gave me a shock."

She put one hand over her eyes. The other held an unfastened gown to her shoulders. "I was going to ask you to hook the back of this dress, but in view of your natural state, I think I'll just go back upstairs and lock the door until daylight."

"Kate, don't. I'll put my clothes back on."

"I knew this would be a mistake."

"Please. I feel unmanned, if you must know the truth."

She peeked at him through her fingers. "From an impartial glance, you don't look it."

"I can't wear Mason's trousers. They'll be too tight in the balls for one thing, and—" He glanced around. "Where the hell did I put my clothes?"

"For the love of all that is holy, Sir Colin, I swear this has been a diabolical strategy on your part to lure me to a lonely spot and render me helpless by the removal of our clothing."

He let several moments elapse before he answered her accusation. "Do you really believe that I am that devious?"

She lowered her hand from her face. "Yes. Absolutely, and I should have known better."

He knotted the blanket around his hips and picked up another that had slipped off the chair. "Are you accusing me of provoking Brian to run away with that poor animal and staging a dramatic rescue in the rain?"

"Did you?"

"By damn, I've been accused of many sins in my life, but none of this magnitude. Yes, you've caught me out. What a production that was. You can't believe how much effort it took to have people hurling buckets of water from the rooftops and the trees as we passed beneath."

"Yes or no?" she asked, turning the instant he brushed toward her to find his shirt.

He let the second blanket drop to the floor so that he could place his hands on her bare shoulders. "That would make me the most devious man on earth, and you the most desirable woman, which I am afraid you are—" He lowered his head to hers. "Yes, I wanted you alone. I crave you like a wild animal chained inside a cave craves freedom. You're the only woman who can release me."

He dragged his mouth down her neck. "Or is it you that needs to be set free?"

"Animal," she whispered with a resigned smile, and he realized that she hadn't made any attempt to move. "So there was nothing that had to be said between us in private?"

"No. Yes." He placed one hand on the small of her back. "Sometimes you look so lonely that I know it would be easy to slip past your guard. I wanted to bring you out of the cold. I wanted a chance to make you warm."

She was frozen on the surface but felt molten beneath her skin, rivulets of blood unthawing in her veins, emotions seething, seeking a vent, escape from a pond so overcoated with ice that one could skate upon her in midsummer without fear she would crack. Suspended. Half-alive. Her needs submerged. She shrank from his touch, afraid of what would happen when he exposed her to his warmth. He kissed the corners of her mouth, his hand rising to her shoulder, where she grasped the gown to conceal the scars another man had left upon her body. How grateful she was for the darkness.

"Come upstairs," he coaxed her.

She felt a flicker of panic. "I won't lie on that bed. I don't know how many people have used it, and for what purpose."

"Then lie with me in front of the—on the floor. The carpet at least is dry."

He led her forward. To her disbelief she let him draw her down beside him. "Are you warmer now?" he whispered, rubbing his hand down her arm.

She nodded. His strong fingers sent shocks of heat through her skin. She refused to lower the gown still draped over her shoulders, even though it provided a negligible defense in a situation like this. If he had pursued revenge for thirteen years, would he allow a flimsy barrier of old silk to stop his pursuit of pleasure? Could she summon the resolve to deny him?

He leaned over her. She stared up in fascination at his strongly sculpted face and shoulders. Darkness became him. But then, he had nothing to hide. "I could make you warmer," he whispered, his eyes inviting her to play.

His hand slipped from her elbow, descending indecently to slip beneath the gown to the smooth skin of her belly. Her muscles tightened in suspense. She inhaled to calm the rapid pounding of her heart. His fingers stroked in slow persuasion over her wet curls, parting the swollen lips of her sex for his exploration. She could not see properly, but she could feel. Oh, how she wanted to know, to experience just once the passion he offered. Her blood sang in readiness. But for what? How far did he intend to take her? He tempted her with so little effort on his part; he touched her where she was still innocent and throbbed for a merciful relief.

She lifted her head. "What are you doing?"

He glanced up at her in undisguised arousal. "Pleasuring you. Am I the first to have the privilege?"

She couldn't answer. She wasn't ashamed to admit she was a virgin, but the impulses she felt bewildered her. Why did she bask in his sweet humiliation?

"Answer me," he said, inserting only the tip of his finger inside her. "Are you a virgin?"

He waited, allowing her to understand, accept his invitation, submit to his sexual power. He could wait a century, she thought. He could seduce her body, demand she respond. But he couldn't break the bonds of shame that she carried every moment of her existence.

"I am," she said. "And I would like to give myself to the man I will marry."

He bent his head to her neck, his voice heavy with

desire. "I envy the man who takes your virtue and shares your bed. I envy the man who marries you."

She quivered. His mouth abraded her throat, her neck, the tops of her breasts. His tongue circled the outline of her nipples through her gown. With each caress her craving for him grew. Her hips moved helplessly against his hand. She needed him to fill the hollow ache she felt inside. She couldn't control the moisture that gathered between her thighs and dampened his hand. She was so embarrassed by her body's response to his petting that she reached down blindly to make sure the gown covered her scars. Inadvertently she touched the hard bulge beneath the blanket. His body jerked in reaction or she might have stroked the shape of him once more.

"Do that again, and we'll both be in trouble," he said softly, his instincts sharp. "You like what I'm doing, don't you?"

She moaned, silently begging him to break the tension that was mounting inside her by the moment.

"Is there a man you plan to marry?" he asked, his thumb stroking the sensitive knot above her cleft. She went tight in every muscle, suspended in a deep pulse of impending pleasure.

"There might be one," she whispered, stretching her spine to encourage or elude him, she wasn't sure. She was enslaved to the frantic desire that consumed, confused her.

A moment later he sank his middle finger high inside her until he found the membrane of her hymen. She gasped, her eyes searching his in shock and uncertainty.

"Intact," he whispered. "I can't believe you have guarded your purity for this long, not when Georgette's suitors must have wished you were available as a side course. I want you quite desperately. I hope you're not wasted on that boy who cowered with you in the flowers instead of defending you like a man."

He rolled away from her and to his feet, snatching the shirt he had hung on the fireguard to dry. Her body felt unfulfilled, flushed and eager for the decadent pleasure he had tendered and taken away. "I dislike you very much right now," she said to his shadow. "Stanley is not a coward."

"If you say so."

"He's a man."

"I shall have to take your word on that."

She braced her weight on her elbow only to fall back as he turned without warning and looked down at her. The beguiling darkness of his gaze made her think of coal before it becomes diamonds. She stood slowly; she was afraid she'd sink once more into the drugged spell he had cast.

"He's the most decent man I've ever met."

He laughed. "Well, no one will make that claim about me."

"He took a risk coming to the house to bring the medicine for Etta."

He let her struggle for a full minute with the hooks at the back of her gown before he stepped over to her and completed the task. Her hands were shaking, clumsy.

"I'll never trust you again."

"I don't blame you."

"You've mucked up everyone's life," she whispered, the words catching in her throat.

He hesitated. "Not on purpose."

She spun around. "Can't you control yourself?"

He stared at her with unflinching calm. "Obviously not."

Shame and longing crossed swords in her heart. "Go to hell."

"It's only a matter of time."

"I will not get back on that horse with you," she said.

"Yes, you will."

"I'd rather swim in a sea of mud."

His voice deepened. "If anyone asks, and they will, why we are late returning to the house, you can say I insisted we wait out the worst of the storm. With any luck, Brian's return will have provided enough of a distraction."

She swallowed. "I was convinced Georgette was exaggerating when she said you were shameless. If you're so desperate for a woman, why didn't you visit the widow you met today in the village? It was obvious you were flirting with each other."

He bent and felt around the floor for his pants, shaking his head as if the answer were obvious. "If I'd felt the slightest twinge of desire for her, I would be in her bed right now." He picked up the half boots and stockings she had discarded. "I can't even remember what the woman looks like. Yet tonight when I am unable to sleep, I will think of how beautiful you are and how badly I fought not to wield every secret I know to make you mine."

She blinked back tears as he knelt to help her put on her boots. "Could I be any more gullible?" she said in self-contempt. "I believed you when you told me you needed to *talk* to me alone."

"That was the truth, although I don't fault you for distrusting me. I know that you love Brian and that you and he share a special bond. Perhaps I don't deserve an honest answer. I will demand it all the same. Is he my son, Kate? Is it coincidence I see myself whenever I look at that boy?"

She lifted her head and met his searching gaze. Was that why he had brought her here, to weaken her defenses so that she would betray Georgette? No. He had not caused the storm or made Brian run away. He had merely taken advantage of a woman who yearned for what she had never known.

"I wasn't working for Madam at the time of Brian's birth," she said evenly. "I know he was born at full term after she married Mr. Lawson, and Brian was brought up as his son."

"Have you seen his certificate of birth? A marriage document?"

"I most certainly have not. It isn't my business to read my employer's personal records."

He glanced away.

"Perhaps you should ask her yourself."

"Perhaps I should."

Georgette had married the old gentleman two weeks after she realized she was pregnant. Her husband was delighted with his son. In gratitude for giving her his name, she had produced Charlie a few years after their marriage and was dismayed when after only a year Etta was conceived.

Mr. Lawson loved them and passed away in his sleep before Etta's first birthday.

Kate felt it was wrong of her to withhold the entire truth. But she had pledged her loyalty to Georgette, and not even Colin would provoke her to break her promise. Still, she believed he had a right to know and that one day he would find out.

Chapter 22

Georgette woke up to the sight of rain slashing against the windows. It was a rare night when anything disturbed her laudanum-laced dreams. Why had Kate forgotten to draw the curtains and recount how she and the children had passed the day? Perhaps Kate had caught this nasty cold that had given Georgette a throbbing headache and broken her sleep.

She shoved off the bedcovers and walked in reluctance to the window. Then she remembered. Brian had run away in this miserable rain and had been brought home. Nan had come flying into the room after the fact to inform Georgette. Or had it been Lovitt? She couldn't sort out the sequence of events. She was a dreadful mother, and now, because Colin had reappeared in her life, she would lose the only man who was fool enough to claim he had loved her since she was a young girl.

Mason, a murderer. She would have wagered her soul that he was incapable of a criminal act. He was the most generous lover she had ever taken. But then, it was easy to spend the riches that one had stolen. Perhaps his generosity appeased his guilt. It was disturbing to realize she had grown fond of a man who could one day slip poison in her wine to be rid of her.

And yet she believed Colin. She believed him even though he had caused her unforgettable pain. She believed—

She reached up to draw the curtains and froze at the sound of light footsteps in the hall, the familiar creak of a door opened and closed. That was Kate's door. Surely she hadn't spent half the night with the children. Where had she been? Not out in this rain alone.

She placed her hand on her heart. "Oh, no." It couldn't be.

But she knew it was.

Her innocent companion was falling in love with Colin. It was probably too late to be undone. Georgette should have intervened earlier. Now there was only one way to spare Kate a broken heart. Kate would have to beat the master at the game of seduction.

It would be a challenge, but Kate had a backbone. Even better, she could receive lessons in passion from a woman who was writing a book on the subject.

Kate had just reached her room, washed with cold water in her hip bath, and changed into a warm night rail when she heard the urgent knock on her door.

She decided to ignore it. The children were asleep; Brian was penitent and quiet. How much strain could she take before she collapsed? Hadn't she been through enough tonight? The past week? The last decade?

"Miss Kate, please, open the door. It's me, Lovitt. This is urgent."

"Is anyone ill?"

"No," he said. "Well, I feel sick."

"Oh, for heaven's sake." She went to the door and unbolted it. Lovitt entered her room without hesitation.

"I've something to confess, miss. It's bad."

She sighed. "Why does everyone have to confide in

me? Why don't you go to Mrs. Lawson if this matter is so important?"

"I did," he said, his sandy brown hair still damp from the rain. "She said I should come to you for advice."

"Did you explain how important it is?"

"No. She kept falling asleep whenever I tried to explain what I'd done. I doubt she'll even remember I was in her room when she wakes up."

"Fine." She sat at the edge of her bed, her braided hair draped over her shoulder, and sighed. "Confess. And then let me sleep. I'm frazzled."

"You won't hate me forever?"

"What have you done, Lovitt?"

"It's pretty bad."

She made a fist at him. "Out with it, or I just might punch you in the nose."

He blinked. "Criminy. Maybe I should face him myself. If I'm going to be brutalized, it might as well all be at once."

"What did you do?"

"I visited Mr. Earling's solicitor today."

"That's what Nan was talking about," she said with a frown. "She saw you."

He hung his head. "I thought I'd be out of there before you reached the village, but Hay wasn't in when I arrived, and I had to wait and then dash home before you all returned."

She was wide-awake now. "Why would *you* go to a solicitor?"

"I went there to complain about Castle, to tell Hay that I didn't trust him—"

"Oh, dear God."

"—and that I thought he had some ill motive in mind, but then halfway through our talk, something happened to change my mind. I stopped making it sound as if Castle was dangerous."

Kate stared at him. "What are you saying?"

"I made it seem as if he were merely eccentric instead."

"*What?* You're the one who sounds off."

"I figured he wouldn't link an eccentric groom to Sir Colin Boscastle."

"You *knew* all along?"

He met her gaze. "I heard you and Madam talking, and I figured it out. I didn't tell Mr. Hay, though."

"What stopped you?" she asked, shaking her head at his foolishness.

"When I was in the waiting room, I saw another man come out of the clerk's office with a purse. I thought at first he'd gotten an inheritance. Then I realized I'd seen his face before. In the pub."

"And?"

"And in the garden the night we were attacked. It took me a while to put it together. Mr. Hay paid those men to attack the house."

"What—"

"I know Hay never approved of Mrs. Lawson. And he'd approve of her even less if he knew she'd given his client's enemy sanctuary in his house."

She took a breath. "Is that all, Lovitt?"

He sighed. "Not quite. Hay's coming the night of the play to inspect the house for Mr. Earling and to meet the new head groom for himself. But what if Hay decides to pay a sneak visit beforehand? It wouldn't be the first time."

Kate almost fell back on the bed. "Oh, no."

"You'll have to warn Castle, Kate. Or hide him. If it's true that Mr. Hay is behind those attacks, he won't hesitate to use force on Sir Colin."

"Why don't you warn him?"

He swallowed. "I'm afraid of him."

"So am I."

"Yes, but he likes you. Everyone in the house can see that."

Kate's robe kept snagging on the ladder to the loft. Her hair came unbraided. She couldn't see well. She hadn't dared carry a candle through the straw. Colin was stretched out on his stomach on a pallet that he'd drawn up to a dormer window.

He didn't move. It appeared he was asleep. Perhaps she would wait until morning. *No.* This couldn't wait. He had to be warned.

"Colin," she whispered. "I need to talk to you."

He swung over, his arm capturing her before she could even cry out. "Listen to me," she said impatiently. "I'm not here to play games."

He forced her onto her back. "I'm glad you've come to your senses—or lost them, whatever the case may be. I haven't stopped thinking about you since you went into the house."

His dark face hovered over hers. She had time to take a breath, to deny him, and then his mouth descended. He kissed her hard and deep, into a daze. He stroked his knuckles over the contours of her breasts until her nipples puckered against her night rail. His kisses wandered lower.

"Nice," he said, wetting the tender peaks through the thin cotton with his tongue until two dusky tips protruded. "I wish you'd been in the mood for me when I had you to myself in the lodge. I knew you'd come to me sooner or later."

She laughed quietly. "Don't be so sure of yourself. You don't know why I'm here yet. We have another problem to confront."

"The problem will have to wait." He raised her robe and night rail up around her bottom. His fingers stole across her bare hip. His voice immobilized her. "I wonder if you're still wet for me. I could play with your quim for hours." He slid between her thighs, braced on his arms above her. "And this," he said, rubbing his prick against her mound. "If I could shed these trousers and evict the other grooms below, we would soon be better acquainted."

"I'm surprised you sleep with your clothes on at all," she whispered, breathless from climbing the ladder and from him. "Can't they hear us?"

"Not likely. They sleep at the other end of the stable block."

"Well, keep your voice down, anyway. I'm in no mood to explain our situation."

He laughed softly. The weight of his body held her captive, unsure of surrendering her will. She waited for the familiar panic to intrude, for the ugly memory to forbid her to feel any pleasure. But all she felt was a gentle power that would possess her as soon as she gave her permission.

It was all she could do not to protest as briefly he lifted himself from her. Damp air rushed over her to counteract the heat he had provided. "What are you doing?"

He hovered over her. The rigid column of his penis pressed between her thighs. "What would you like me to do?"

She lifted her hand to his shoulder. His muscles contracted, and she slid her hand down his chest in helpless desire, following the ridges of ribs and sinew to the light sprinkling of hair at his waistband.

"Touch it," he said, his voice beguiling.

She did. Her fingers felt the length and thickness of his cock in a caress that provoked a soft growl from his throat. "I came here because—"

She closed her eyes, heard him shift again. She should have waited until morning. She gasped in surprise as he used his elbows to push her knees apart. He pressed his finger inside her sheath. She lifted her hips in restless uncertainty.

"More?" he whispered roughly.

She bit the inside of her cheek to smother a cry. "Please."

Another finger stretched her wide, slipping out and back inside before she could move. Faster, then harder. Her nerves knotted. His thumb probed the seam of her bottom. She opened her eyes only long enough to see his face disappear, dip between her thighs.

"You aren't—"

His illicit mouth fastened on the bud of her sex. His fingers worked her without mercy. Her temperature rose. Her breasts felt heavy. And the pressure in her belly crested, infusing her with a hot rush of relief as he removed his fingers and stabbed his tongue between her folds.

Long moments ticked by before she stirred, listening to the tapering rain, the horses shuffling in the stalls below. She could have fallen asleep. She felt him shift position. She forced her eyes open, shivered at his possessive stare. His breathing sounded uneven and deep.

"I forgot to tell you why I came here," she murmured.

He drew her robe and night rail down to her ankles. "I think we know why."

"You're wrong."

He gave her a knowing smile. "You don't have to admit anything. I'm here whenever you need me."

She laughed in reluctance, wishing she could hide her face. "What a consolation that is."

He leaned over her. "Day or night." He kissed her on the mouth. "Rain or shine."

"In sickness and in health?"

He stared at her.

"That's what I thought." She rose to her knees. "Lovitt wanted me to talk to you. He was afraid to tell you himself."

He shrugged and sat back on his heels, his shirt hanging over his trousers, his face curious. "If it's about Brian running away, Lovitt can redeem himself with a week's extra work. The storm will leave a mess."

"It isn't." She swept her hair back from her face. "You know he's been jealous of your 'position' since you gave it to yourself."

He nodded. "I should have thought ahead to that, but if it's any consolation, I don't plan to spend the rest of my life as a groom."

She wondered if he'd made any plans at all beyond making Mason pay for his crime. "That's not the problem," she said in an undertone. "Lovitt was so enraged, so certain that he'd been cheated out of his due, that he told Ramsey Hay today that you are a suspicious character and he doesn't trust your motives."

"Why didn't Lovitt come to me first?"

"Probably because you *are* a suspicious character and—"

"—he doesn't trust my motives. Damn fool."

"How well did Ramsey Hay know you?"

"He knows of me. He knows enough about me, I would guess, to wonder who I am. He must have seen me years ago. But I don't suppose it's common for men to drop in on Georgette and ask for a hand in hard times."

"Oh, it's very common," Kate said with a sigh. "But I would say that none of them have been as forceful in asserting their authority as you."

"Well, perhaps Georgette is still more attached to me than I realized. For reasons she has not explained."

"Perhaps." And if he thought to trap Kate into admitting Brian was one of those reasons, he would be disappointed. "Mr. Hay said he would pay a visit soon to the house on his client's behalf. He usually attends the theatricals that I perform."

"Yet another reason to dislike him."

"Do you think that if he met you in person, he would guess who you were?"

Colin stretched forward to kiss her again. "You guessed who I was, didn't you?"

Her lips tingled. "That's different. I have heard about you ever since I started to work for Georgette. I have written chapters in her memoirs extolling your sexual prowess—"

"You haven't."

"Oh, yes. And she described your physical person so well that *I* should have recognized you in the garden." Not to mention that she was also raising the son who resembled Colin more every month. "Hay is dangerous. He hates Georgette. He looks at me like—"

His eyes narrowed. "Does he, indeed?"

"Well, that's not the point. How *are* we going to explain you? How do we throw him off your scent?"

"You're the playwright," he said with a wry smile. "What do you suggest?"

"Perhaps a disguise. Nothing too dramatic. A few subtle changes to your appearance. But most of all it is your manner that gives you away."

"What about my manners?"

"Your *manner*. Your demeanor. You have an arrogance that is so deeply inbred that I don't know we can hide it."

"Perhaps, then, I shouldn't bother to try." He glanced at the window, rising to his feet. "The rain is lighter. I'll walk you back to the house."

"There's no need for both of us to get wet again."

"I insist."

"There you go." She stood unsteadily.

He took her hand and carefully guided her to the ladder. "Are you committed to the chemist?"

"Am I committed to the—who?"

"Apothecary. Chemist. Charlatan." He watched her as she extended her leg to begin the climb from the loft. "You know who I mean."

Her bare feet curled around the ladder's wooden rung. "You'll have to be more explicit."

"All right." He pulled his coat from the peg on the wall. "Have you promised yourself to him? Has he promised himself to you? Has he pleasured you as I just did? Do dreams of him awaken you throughout the night?"

She dropped to the straw floor below. "Why should I tell you?"

"Have you made each other any promises?" He slid down and landed deftly at her side. "Yes or no?"

"That's none of your affair."

He nodded. "Good. He hasn't. Not that my conscience would keep me up at night in this situation. But I would like to know who I have to knock down to clear the field."

"How romantic. Do you enjoy physical violence?"

"It may not always be necessary, but I've found it efficient when hoping to make a point."

One of the stable boys emerged from a stall, glancing at them in astonishment before continuing outside to scrub the water trough, which Colin insisted had to be clean before morning.

"Wonderful," Kate muttered.

"Well, it isn't as if you're living in a convent."

He led her out into the kitchen yard, holding his coat above their heads as protection from the wet gusts of wind that blew across the meadow. Colin frowned. He opened the kitchen door for her but didn't come inside.

"I'm only trying to understand," he said. "All I want to know is if you and your friend have been as *friendly* as we were tonight."

"Would you like me to make you a mug of chocolate?"

"No. I don't want to wake anybody up and have to explain myself."

She nodded, resisting the impulse to wipe the rain sliding down his cheek. "If Hay suspects, we've got to be careful. I've never liked that man."

"The best thing to do is follow your usual routine. I'll stay in the background as much as I can."

She shook her head at that. "Excuse me, Castle, but you're the one who's thrown our routine into shambles. The children need a regular schedule, and I do, too."

"What is the point of life if we can't look forward to a few surprises?"

"A few?" She laughed.

"'The play's the thing,'" he mused.

"Well, let's just hope that nothing more than your guilty conscience is caught before it's over."

"I told you I should be given a part."

"That would only make you more noticeable," she said in astonishment. "It is not as if you are a man who disappears in a crowd. Perhaps you could act as an usher or help in the wings."

They broke apart at the sound of footsteps coming from the servants' quarters. "Go," she said, pushing him out into the rain. "I can't think anymore tonight. I may never be able to think again. In fact, I may have to avoid you completely after tonight."

She closed the door.

*   *   *

He lifted his face to the rain, letting it run down his neck. Usher. He liked that idea. He could watch people come and go, keep his eye on the house and, during intermission, on the garden. Better still, he could keep an eye on Kate onstage and not offer any excuses for taking a personal interest in her performance. Perhaps it would be easy to fool Hay. After all, he had almost managed to fool himself.

Chapter 23

*E*arly the next evening Griswold brought Kate a message in the salon as she and the chambermaids were stitching sheets together for the play. She had not seen Colin all day and she could not imagine what they would say to each other when she did. But when Griswold stooped, his knees popping, and whispered in her ear, "A certain gentleman wishes to see you at the old fountain in the garden, miss," she knew it was Stanley.

The chambermaids glanced at one another, brows lifting in speculation.

"Does this gentleman have a name, Griswold?"

He frowned, unfolding his body one loose-hinged joint at a time. "I expect that he does."

Kate looked up. "Well, what is it?"

He frowned. "I don't believe he said."

"Is he known to us?" she inquired in an exasperated voice that gave the chambermaids another reason to eye one another in amusement.

"I've seen him," Griswold said thoughtfully. "I can't remember where or when, but he has brought you flowers."

"Flowers?" one of the maids said with a wink at Kate. "Fancy that."

"Did he explain what he wanted?"

Griswold shrugged. "I assumed he wanted to give you the flowers. He didn't offer them to me."

Irene, the head chambermaid, stood, carefully edging around the sheets that rippled down the salon steps. "Shall I fetch Lovitt or Castle to escort you, miss?"

"No." Kate shook her head resolutely. "It has to be Mr. Wilkes. I'd like him to leave tonight without missing any teeth."

"Have a nice time!" Irene called out to her. "We'll never tell!"

She smiled, taking a breath. "We don't know if there's anything to tell yet, do we?"

She reached the front door and ran down the steps into the garden. She was amazed that no one had stopped her for some emergency or other. She hesitated, unaccountably apprehensive to face her friend. Had she betrayed him last night? Surely he would never speak to her again if he knew what she had done. She could not explain it. She could not excuse it except to say that her distress over Brian's disappearance had caused her to behave as the wanton most people assumed her to be.

Stanley must have seen or at least heard about the violent encounter in the village. Even his parents must know by now that Mrs. Lawson's groom had knocked a man to his knees for insulting the governess. No doubt it was the scandal of the year. No doubt Kate would be accused of exaggerating what had merely been an accident.

Then she saw him, waiting for her with a bouquet of wilted red roses that she guessed he'd picked from other gardens on his way here. It was as skillfully arranged as one of Etta's posies, half-denuded dandelions and foxtail grass wrapped in drooping ivy.

"What is it, Stanley?"

He grasped her hand and pulled her into the old fruit orchard, where the scent of humus and fallen blossoms hung in the stillness. The grass that brushed against her skirts felt heavy with yesterday's rain.

"Sit with me," he said, motioning to the edge of the stone pond.

"This sounds serious."

Colin had seen two figures skulking around the garden as he was beginning his nightly patrol. He moved silently between the hedges until he recognized the man and woman sitting on the edge of the stone pond.

He had no intention of spying on Kate and her— whatever he was. On the other hand, he didn't want to come clumping out of the bushes and interrupt a private moment. He could hear every word they said. He'd simply have to wait out their rendezvous before he could return to the stables.

He could only hope they would keep their conversation brief and part before he was spotted. Kate would never believe him if he explained he was innocently patroling the garden. As for what had happened in the lodge and the loft, he couldn't guess how she felt. He was sure that she was attracted to him, and yet he had the sense that he might have moved too fast and frightened her.

She would never have let him take such liberties if she didn't like it. He believed he was her first, the only one to touch her and ask for intimacy. Then what was she doing in the dark with the little curly-haired cherub of hers? He shouldn't listen. It was impolite. Bad. An invasion of her privacy.

He crept closer to the end of the hedge to hear.

"We've talked about marriage, Kate," Stanley said, still holding her hand.

"We've talked around it," she murmured. Good heavens. Was he going to propose to her? If he'd given her a hint that tonight was the night, she wouldn't have come out to meet him wearing Georgette's pink tissue ball gown—at least she'd have thrown a wrapper over her shoulders so she didn't feel so bare. She looked up suddenly. "Do you hear that?"

"All I can hear is the pounding of my heart."

"Well, it wasn't a pounding noise. It sounded more like twigs rattling."

"Oh, that. I chased the cat away when I was waiting for you. It's on the prowl again."

"Oh," she murmured, glancing into the dark shrubbery.

"I talked to my parents about you tonight." He lifted her hand to his mouth and pressed his lips to her knuckles. It didn't feel like a kiss or a romantic overture. It felt as if he knew he should make a gesture, but he didn't know how or what. If he was about to propose, and she accepted, she would let him kiss her. But quite frankly she wasn't looking forward to it. Not to being his wife or trying to please his parents. What did that say about her?

What had changed her mind? She had been working up the courage to tell Georgette that she might leave her position. But then last night had happened.

"Is everything all right, Kate?" Stanley whispered.

She looked back at the house. "I don't know."

"Are you ill?"

"Pardon me?"

"Your face is flushed."

"Oh, well, I was sewing. Stitching sheets to use as props. Hard work, you know." She turned her head back to his. "Do I look feverish? I was out in the rain."

He touched his other hand to her forehead. "No. You feel cool." He cleared his throat. "I picked the flowers myself. I've never told you that the soap you use reminds me of attar of roses. My great aunt used to dab its oil between her—well."

"How moving, Stanley. That I remind you of your great aunt."

"Moving," he said. "Yes."

This was how a proper gentleman went about courting a woman. She couldn't imagine Stanley pouncing on her in the dark like a wolf and demanding more than a kiss. Not a polite peck at the knuckles, but a ravenous kiss that would make her feel as if she were falling from cloud to cloud. Falling, she thought. She hadn't hit the ground yet, but it would be difficult to stop her complete descent.

"You talked to your parents," she said, prompting Stanley to continue. "What did you say? What did they say?"

He looked past her to the pond. "They don't approve of you."

"Are you surprised?" She drew her hand back to her side.

"They don't believe that it's possible for a young woman to work for a—a ladybird and not become tainted herself."

"That sounds like a lovely conversation." Her shoulders tightened. "It's a wonder my ears weren't burning. Aren't you the wicked one for defying their advice to come here tonight? They do have a point." She kicked off her slippers. She'd grabbed them thinking she would only be in the salon tonight. None of Georgette's off-cast shoes really fit. The heels wobbled. The toes pinched and made it difficult to chase after the children. Or to walk to the stables to watch a swaggering groom teaching his son how to ride.

"*Kate.*" Stanley's voice startled her. "Do you understand what I'm trying to say?"

She picked up one of the slippers she had removed. "I understand exactly what you said. You don't want to marry me because I might turn out to be a whore. Or be one now."

He sucked in his breath. "That *word*."

"What word? Oh. Whore. Prostitute. Abbess. Mistress. Concubine. Courtesan. Jade. Jezebel—" She broke off to examine her discarded slipper. It was beautiful, really, with pink bows and seed pearls stitched to the tiny heel. "Oh—where was I? Baggage. Strumpet." She took a loud breath. "Did I say harlot?"

His face had turned so white during her tirade that she thought he was going to faint. She fanned his cheeks briefly with her shoe. "Listen to you," he said, aghast. "Is that the vocabulary you would teach our children were we to marry?"

"As it appears we are *not* to be married, what words would you prefer our nonexisting children learn? Intolerance, bigotry, judgment, hypocrisy, shallow—"

He grasped her by her shoulders and planted a hard, unpracticed kiss on her mouth. "Perhaps we can run away together. I don't have much money, but if you could find a few pounds lying about—"

"Get away from me." She pushed him, turning her face from his. "Wouldn't you have to ask your parents for permission first?"

His fingers dug into her shoulders. "They want me to propose to a young lady from Devon. She isn't pretty at all and I have no feeling for her, but she's well-bred. And well-off. If I marry her, there's no reason that you and I can't find a way to see each other in secret as we do now."

She closed her fingers around the instep of her slipper. "Meet? Us? In secret?"

"Why not?" he whispered, burying his face in her neck. "My parents might not approve of what you have learned from your mistress, but I would be an eager pupil in your arms. You know about passion, don't you? You know what a man needs. You understand those things."

"Stanley?" His mouth moved down her throat. She shivered, but not in pleasure. His lips reminded her of a grub crawling over a stone. *"Stanley."*

He drew back, his eyes glazed. "What?"

"I have your answer."

She raised her arm. He looked up briefly, uncomprehending, as she banged the heel of the slipper on his head. "Leave this garden now, and don't ever return."

"Oh, my God! My head. Look at my *head.*"

She did. "It's still there. Not that it contains a single thought that your parents haven't put inside it."

She raised her arm, but she didn't have to hit him again. He leapt up and ran across the garden without another word. The footman on guard unlocked the gates and stared after him. Kate dipped her hand in the fountain and lifted it to her mouth to erase the lingering feel of his kiss. What a paper-skull she had been. Stanley had never considered her worthy of being his wife. What decent man ever would?

He stepped out from the hedge, waiting for her to notice him on her own. But then she jumped up like a bird about to take flight and he went back into hiding. Perhaps it wasn't the best idea to admit he'd been eavesdropping. She would be doubly humiliated once she realized he had overheard that degrading rejection. She wouldn't believe he hadn't followed her outside.

She was crying—no, she wasn't. She was swearing and plucking the petals off the red roses Stanley had given her as a token of his insulting offer. She seemed to be arranging them in a circle around the pond. Colin poked a peephole through the hedge. He had a feeling he was about to witness one of those female rituals that were meant to be enacted in private. It looked like a pagan ceremony.

She pulled up her skirts and yanked off the other slipper. He stared, his blood stirring at the sight of her well-shaped calf. So far . . . so good.

"You son of a weasel's mother! Take this as a symbol of *my* affection."

She raised her slipper to her shoulder. Colin reared back. The heel of the slipper descended. Once, twice . . . too many times to count. It pulverized the delicate petals. It shredded them into a potpourri of bleeding mush.

"Attar of roses, my . . . arse!" she burst out. "Every man I have ever met is a . . . a—contemptible—"

Colin couldn't make out the rest over the hammering of the slipper. This was Cinderella on a rampage. He was afraid to breathe, to step on a twig. He was afraid Lovitt would let the trained squirrels out on their nightly tinkle and his presence would be revealed. He would never be able to convince her that he wasn't a contemptible man.

The best he could hope for was that she wouldn't notice him at all. He knew now what he had to do. This was the opening he had waited for without realizing it. Later, when she and her slipper had calmed down, he would find a way back into her favor by proving that not every man she had ever met was unworthy of her heart. And he didn't deceive himself into thinking that he had a long road to travel.

"Kate?" a young woman's voice called from the salon window. "Is everything all right? We heard something banging out there."

"I shall be right in." She sniffed. "Just let me put my slippers on."

Chapter 24

For a moment Colin debated chasing after the apothecary's boy to give him a few choice words, if not another thump on the head. But he didn't want Kate to be alone. He wanted to distract her from her humiliation, help her forget the jackass and his bouquet of battered flowers.

He wanted to convince her that no man in his right mind would let a woman like her go. She was strong and warmhearted, and what did it matter that she worked for a whore? *She* wasn't one, though Colin didn't doubt she would command a fortune if she ever chose—

He waited for her to return to the house. She couldn't really have loved the unappreciative sod, or she would not have given Colin the chance to pleasure her. She wouldn't have come to the loft if she wasn't concerned about, drawn to, Colin despite herself. But he didn't know her secret feelings, her dreams.

He knew nothing about her.

She knew too much about him, or at least about the selfish pleasure-seeker who had thoughtlessly ruined Georgette's life.

He looked up and saw a light behind Kate's window curtains. How could he console her without revealing that he'd been peeping through the bushes to invade her privacy? How could he make her believe in her own worth, that her sexual appeal was only a small part of it, when he had consistently let his penis do the thinking during the short time he had known her?

He walked back to the house, amire in his thoughts, and let himself in through the front door. Instead of the usual bevy of household servants fussing over him, he was met by a band of staff members whose cold stares could have turned him to stone.

"What's the matter?" he asked carefully, not about to reveal Kate's secret rejection even to those who loved her. He would protect her pride, dammit.

No one answered. Not even his staunchest ally, Bledridge, the butler.

"I know," Colin said, sighing. "A servant is supposed to enter by the back door. And"—he looked down—"I didn't scrape off my boots. But—"

To his amazement the small band swept from him as one and proceeded to file out of the lobby and into the servants' hall.

"What did I do now?" he said into the void of silence that enveloped him.

"As if you didn't know," a scathing voice said from the floor above.

He recognized Georgette standing at the top of the stairs like a queen about to order an execution. He ran up to meet her, two steps at a time. By the hostile look on her face, she must have an idea what latest sin he had committed to turn everyone against him.

He hadn't sneaked into Kate's room early this morning, as he'd often imagined doing. He hadn't talked to her at length since the rainstorm, and the kitchen help hadn't caught him staring at her across the table because she had taken her meals upstairs.

So what had he done?

"What is it?" he demanded as he reached Georgette's side.

"Follow me," she said in an icy voice. "And please do not speak until we are alone."

He heard whispering from above. He glanced at the upper floor and saw three faces watching through the staircase railing. "Where are we going and why?" he asked Georgette.

"She ought to put you in the dungeon and lose the key like the earl did," Brian said.

Georgette scowled up at her children. "Go to bed this instant."

"Why should we?" Brian asked.

"Because you were told to," Colin said.

"So?"

Etta and Charlie gasped, turning to each other in gleeful horror. "You've had it now, Brian," Etta said. "After all Castle did to save you when you ran away in your stupid temper."

"I don't care. He made one of our allies cry. You know the rules. An enemy to one of us is an enemy to all."

Colin glowered up at the older boy. "I'll deal with your insolence tomorrow in the stables," he said as he reached the second floor.

Georgette motioned him into the open door to her suite. "You'll deal with him after I have dealt with you."

He looked down into her face. Whatever offense he'd committed had to be serious. She hadn't brushed out her hair, powdered her face, or rouged her lips. He had to tread carefully before he found an uncluttered spot to stand. The bedchamber looked like a battlefield that had been bombed with fans, stockings, and furbelows.

"What is it?"

She walked up to him and slapped him across the

face. She didn't pack enough strength in the blow to break anything. But she'd made a point. He was still a scoundrel in her eyes.

"What has come over everyone?" He strode to the mirror, catching his foot on a plumed turban, and stared at the welt that covered half his face.

"As if you didn't know!"

He turned, staying clear of her reach. "I *don't* know."

"She ran into the house crying and locked herself in her room before anyone could ask her what was wrong."

Colin lowered his head. Kate hadn't been crying when she'd run through the garden, and if she hadn't wanted to explain to Georgette what had happened, then why should he?

"What the devil does this have to do with me?"

"I heard a noise below in the garden, and I peeked through the curtains. What do you think I saw?"

"Grass? Trees? A prowler—"

She shook her head. "I might not be able to understand great literature, but I do know a few things about love."

He folded his arms, keeping her in his view. "What exactly have I done to merit a crack across the chops like that? I accept responsibility for my old sins. But what did I do tonight?"

She picked a path to the window. "That's what everyone wants to know. What did you do to my companion to make her cry? I haven't seen her weep like that since the day I employed her. And she's had plenty of cause since that day to cry."

He tucked away that comment to mull over at another time. Kate knew more of Colin's embarrassing secrets than any other woman but Georgette. And Georgette had gone out of her way to hide who and what she was.

But Kate—Colin didn't have any idea who she had been before he'd met her. She had never mentioned her past. No parents. No siblings. She had to have come from somewhere. She had to have learned from someone how to read and write, how to comfort and take care of others, the most important person being the boy he suspected was his son. Who was she? Why was he so drawn to a woman who was such an enigma?

"What did I do?" he asked again, irritated that he'd been so intent on himself he hadn't been paying close enough attention to what was happening under his very nose.

"I've forgiven you for the past, Colin, but I won't allow you to plot designs of an amorous nature against my companion."

"Designs—"

"She went out into the garden alone. As you had a few moments earlier. Less than a half hour afterward, you both returned, separately. Katie came flying upstairs as though her heart had been broken."

"That wasn't my fault. All I did was stand behind a bush and behave with some discretion."

"How utterly disgusting! Anyone could have seen you from the windows. Some acts are meant to be private."

He blinked. "It wasn't that kind of behavior. I was hiding so that I wouldn't embarrass her."

"Oh, Colin, don't expect me to believe that. I've known you for too long."

"It's true," he said in frustration.

"You didn't touch her?"

"No." Well, not tonight, except in his thoughts. "Your companion is an attractive young woman. Perhaps you should interrogate her."

"I'm questioning *you*, Colin, and I have the strongest sense that you are evading a truthful answer."

"Perhaps one of your former clients came to the house and—"

"My clients know better than that," she said, turning in a swish of her skirts from the window.

"It never occurred to you that one of your clients would proposition her or seek her company?" Hadn't anyone else seen Kate's caller? Had he come to the door?

"My staff and my children are untouchable."

"Well, I'm not one of your clients, and I didn't make her cry tonight." But he knew what had, and he could keep a secret as well as anyone else in this house. He turned. "Good night."

"Are you finding the stables comfortable, Colin?"

He paused at the door. "I'll say one thing for sleeping in the loft. I don't have to listen to a damn drama unfolding every few hours."

"Drama," she said, scoffing at him. "Listen to the original player."

Chapter 25

*W*ithout another word to Georgette, he opened the door and turned to leave. Kate stood before him, smiling in curiosity, not a tear in her eye.

"Oh, excuse me, madam, sir," she said brightly. "I didn't realize you were entertaining."

"She isn't," Colin said before Georgette could reply.

Georgette glanced up at him appraisingly. "Castle thought he saw a prowler in the garden."

Kate edged into the room between them, a notebook and pen in hand. "I'm afraid that might have been me. I went outside for a breath of air and broke the heel of one of my favorite slippers. I was so upset I ran into the house weeping like one of the children."

"A broken heel," Georgette said slowly. "That isn't like you at all, Kate."

Kate gave a little sniffle. "Maybe I have caught a cold."

"Then why aren't you in bed?" Colin asked.

"I have a few questions to ask Madam before we retire," she said, narrowing her eyes at him in a way that suggested he was not invited to stay.

"Well, then, I'll leave you to your scandals."

*   *   *

Kate seated herself at the escritoire, purposefully evading Georgette's stare. "I know it's late, but I've found several chapters that need to be revised. We've jumped back and forth in time so often that I'm confused."

"What happened tonight?"

Kate looked up. "When?"

"When you ran into the house weeping like a fountain."

"It was nothing."

Georgette pulled a chair up to the desk and clasped Kate's face in her hands. "Griswold said you had a message, but he couldn't remember who it was from. All he could recall was that you hurried out into the garden to meet whoever sent it."

"I did."

"And?"

"And what?"

"Who did you meet in the garden?" Georgette asked coolly.

"Stanley."

Georgette gasped in comprehension. "The one who works for the apothecary?"

Kate smiled at her. "Don't you ever listen to me, madam?"

"What did he want? Have we run out of Etta's tonic? I think I might have taken the last dose."

Kate looked down at the desk, suddenly not trusting herself to speak.

"Wait," Georgette said, her eyes glassy with realization. "Now I see. You mentioned that you thought he was on the verge of proposing to you." Georgette put her hand across the papers Kate was pretending to read. "Is that what happened, Kate? He asked you to marry him and you've accepted. What about me? Our memoirs? The children? This house will collapse without you. You—you refused him, I hope?"

Kate shook her head, laughing in reluctant admiration. There was something inspirational about a woman who always put her own needs above others. "He didn't ask me to marry him."

"He didn't?" In an instant Georgette the Hedonist became Madam the Champion for her beloved companion.

"Then what is wrong with you? Who made you cry? I've never had the sense that you truly cared for him. Are you sure this doesn't concern Colin? Did that scoundrel embarrass you in any way? Would you like—"

"No. Don't do anything. It wasn't Colin, or Castle. I broke the heel of my slipper. The pink one you gave me."

"Do not lie to me, Kate Walcott. Your eyes are rimmed red like a rabbit's. You look a little unhinged. I've never seen you cry over a shoe. I have a closet of them at your disposal."

"Fine." Kate sat up straighter, her elbow poised on the desk. "I shall tell you the truth. Stanley did not propose marriage to me tonight. He proposed that I become his mistress after he weds the well-bred young lady his parents have chosen for him."

"The pig!" Georgette laid her hand over Kate's. "As if I'd allow you to sell yourself to a mere apprentice!"

Kate had to smile. "I don't intend to sell myself to anybody."

Georgette lifted her hand away, clearly relieved. "I wish I could say that I'm sorry, but I know it's for the best."

"So do I," Kate said ruefully.

"Did he attempt—"

"I took care of him, madam. With your shoe."

"Oh, dear. I was afraid when Colin came in right after you that he had caused some of his old mischief. All of us in the house did."

Kate stared at her. "He came in right after I did?"

"Yes. We all assumed that he had done something to upset you."

"He was in the garden?" Kate asked slowly.

"Nightly patrol, and all that."

"Oh." Kate swallowed. She and Stanley had not heard the cat in the hedge. The rustling had been made by a larger predator. Which meant that Colin had listened to all or a good part of her debasing rejection.

"Where are you going?"

"To my room."

"Not to cry?"

Kate smiled. "Oh, no. I've a few lines to study for the play."

She left the room, so engrossed in thought she was startled by the firm hand that reached out of the shadows to draw her against the wall. "Kate. Shh. It's only me."

"You," she whispered, turning her face from his. "I'm quite disgusted with you for eavesdropping in the bushes. If you make fun of me, I swear you'll be sorry."

"I wouldn't dare. I witnessed how dangerous a shoe can become in your hands."

"That's exactly what I meant, you busybody. Let me go."

"Not yet."

He turned, stepping into her until she stood pinned between the wall and his hard torso. At her left stood a long table on which were displayed a collection of Chinese figurines. She saw him follow her gaze in concern.

"Kate, are you all right?"

She shrank against the wall. She wanted to escape, to hide, to become invisible, to busy herself until she was too tired to think. Colin did not remind her in the least of Lord Overton, but this scenario did.

"Kate, don't shy away from me. Please. I won't touch

you or do anything that you don't like. Give me a moment. Trust me?"

She wanted to. Of all the men she'd met, he was the one she *wanted* to trust, and yet she knew she could not. "Why did you have to hear everything?" she said. "Stanley was right. You're wrong. I'm not as innocent as you think."

"Yes, you are."

"How do you know?" she said, defiance in her eyes.

"You showed me last night. I'm a threat to your innocence."

"My heart hasn't been innocent for a long time."

"Neither has mine."

She stared up into his drawn face. "You saw what I did to him. Was that something a well-behaved woman would do?"

His eyes darkened in contemplation. "My female cousins did that sort of thing all the time when we teased them. I have to admit, though, in all my years I have never seen a slipper put to better use. He'll have a hard time explaining the mark on his head to his parents."

"I was mortified," she said in a lost voice. "I didn't know I still had that much anger left inside me."

"Left inside you from what, Kate?" he asked cautiously.

"From—it must have been from the night we were attacked in the garden."

"I'm not convinced," he said, catching the hand she raised to push him away. "I noticed that you weren't wearing any slippers when you left Georgette's room. Unless—should I check you for hairpins or other concealed weapons?"

"You impudent—"

His mouth came down on hers, stealing her unspoken words, her breath. She reached back clumsily for balance, knocking over one of the figurines on the table beside her. Breaking their kiss, Colin reached down to clasp the porcelain lady from her fall. "I've got her," he said. "She's safe now."

She laced her free arm around his neck, whispering, "No, she isn't."

She stroked her hand through the hair at his nape. She caressed his shoulder, the muscles of his back, until he lifted his head and looked into her eyes with a black desire that made her forget she had sworn she would never forgive or talk to him again.

His smile was strained. "I think that's enough. You're entering dangerous territory—for a virgin."

A heady feeling of freedom swept through her. "You're showing remarkable restraint—for a Visigoth."

"I'm not going to tup you up against the wall in a hallway for your first time. Perhaps once we are better acquainted. You see, I really don't know anything about you. I don't know when or where you were born."

"Perhaps I don't want you to know."

"But you know so much about me," he said wryly. "Is that fair?"

"Nothing in life is fair, sir."

"Now you sound like a whore, and I do not like it."

"What is it to you?"

"You are not one."

"Who's to say?"

"I am."

She traced her fingertips across his lips. He closed his eyes momentarily, his expression indefinable.

"May I go now, sir?" she whispered.

"No." He opened his eyes to stare at her. "He doesn't deserve you."

"Why not?" she whispered, shrugging her pale shoulder. "If you heard anything of our conversation, then you know that what he said is true. No proper gentleman would want me as his wife."

"I have no patience for hypocrites," he said quietly.

She laughed in rue. "I have no patience for men who hide in hedges or squander their lives seeking honor."

He combed his fingers through her hair. "What other kind of man is there?"

"I've no idea," she answered. "Nor do I have the curiosity or the freedom to find out."

"Would you have married him?" he asked, his voice as rough as gravel.

She stared up at his face. "We'll never know, will we?"

"What did you see in him? What do you want?"

"I want love, with all the trimmings," she said, surprising even herself. "And if I can't have that, then I'm not about to bother with the rest. I'm sorry if you don't understand. Georgette doesn't, either. Everything in between doesn't interest me. I don't have the time for frivolous pleasures."

"The time?"

"Yes, sir. That is what I said."

"You do know that I want you."

"What was it that you said about Brian? Something to the effect of 'He can't have everything he wants when he wants it.'" She turned. "I wouldn't expect you to understand. I live in a world of shadows. Sometimes I despair of the darkness I see—of what the children know. Ours isn't a perfect life. But there are few options in our place. It is my job to keep them safe."

He could have thrown himself at her feet. "And who is to watch over you?"

"Good night, sir." She slipped around him with an elusive smile. "Don't waste your worry on me. I'll be fine."

*   *   *

It wasn't until Kate had reached the top of the staircase that Colin noticed Georgette standing in her doorway.

He straightened. "How long have you been listening?"

"Long enough to know that my concerns about you and Kate are justified. You must have been very engrossed in each other not to have seen me."

He waited until he was certain that Kate was inside her room. "Splendid. Now you and I are *both* guilty of eavesdropping. Shall we call it even between us?"

She walked across the hall toward him. "We're guilty of more than that. However, Kate isn't. Do you really intend to pursue her?"

"I never intended to become involved with her at all."

"But you have," Georgette said, no trace of temper, only resignation in her voice. "Can you let her go?"

"She isn't mine to hold or release."

"I love her," she said, "as the younger sister I always wanted. I am a whore, Colin. She is not."

He didn't bother to deny his desire for Kate. He had known it ran deeper than the physical. "I don't understand her. One moment she is warm to me, inviting. In the next she seems afraid to even look at me. There's nothing more between her and me than flirtation. I think it was obvious after tonight that her heart had just been broken by that little boy who's ashamed to defend her to his parents."

Her face reflected a bitter darkness. For a harrowing moment he swore she had ripped his chest open and peered inside as if looking for something he doubted she would find.

"I'm not the same man I was thirteen years ago."

"I can see that. You carry far more potential for heartbreak."

He exhaled slowly. "No. No, I won't be here long enough to cause her the pain that I caused you."

"But in that brief interval, you might as well seduce her?"

"That's a hypocritical warning coming from a woman who makes her living bleeding dry the romantic dreams of foolish men. Help me, Georgette. I don't understand her. Is she innocent or not?"

"If she wasn't, would you consider her fair game?"

"I don't consider a desirable woman to be a conquest. But—"

"—you can't stop yourself?" She considered him in silence. "Perhaps I should tell you something that will influence your behavior once and for all."

"Please do."

She walked down the stairs and through a dark corridor to a small settee wedged between a pair of long lead-paned windows, to a place where the wall sconces were never lit and secret confessions encouraged. He followed and sat beside her. "I am breaking her confidence, and she will not forgive me for doing so. I will forgive myself because to keep a grudge is an utter waste of one's vital energy."

"What confidence?"

"Do you care?"

He lowered his eyes. "God help me, Georgette. I have never cared so much."

She sighed. "I know her heart, Colin. I have entrusted her with not only my scandalous secrets, you being one of them, but with the upbringing of my children. And I promise that if you mistreat her, I will make it my life's mission to destroy you, as you have made it yours to ruin Mason."

"There's a vast difference between demanding honor and pursuing a woman." He broke off. "What have you told her to make her afraid of me?"

"Nothing. She was afraid of love the day she came to

my door, and now I am going to betray her and tell you why."

"While you're at it," he said, "you might as well admit that Brian is my son."

"You bastard," she said, her voice deepening. "Brian is mine."

"He is ours, Georgette."

Chapter 26

 $\mathcal{K}$ ate's first experience with passion had broken her trust and scarred her body. And from that violation she had emerged as a caring woman, one still vulnerable to abuse.

Everything began to make sense to Colin, and he wished he could start over from the night he had met her in the garden. No wonder she thought him arrogant. How had he not seen that she occupied the throne of power in the house? Her fear that he would usurp her authority was groundless, though. He questioned whether even his nemesis, Mason Earling, had ever dared to stand against Kate.

She ruled the roost with a quiet voice, a stern eye, and the most formidable weapon a man would ever have to fight—a pure heart. She was cynical and innocent, self-righteous and unselfish. Sultry one moment, as sour as lemons the next. She fascinated and frustrated his private demons.

It even made sense why, on the night of their initial encounter, he had assumed she was the mistress of the estate. In a practical sense she was. The servants sought her advice before taking action. The children obeyed her, when they obeyed anyone. Georgette consulted Kate before she took a lover.

Colin felt the invisible strength of her influence. She was quietly intimidating. He could feel her study his every move. Did she realize that he was studying her?

They had come to an impasse.

He didn't know how to proceed. Should he give her time to come around? She seemed to have drawn away from him since he'd found out her secret. He wasn't sure if she was ashamed or angry, or if she even knew that Georgette had betrayed her.

He would have to regain her trust.

He would also have to convince the rest of the household that he wasn't the reason she had run in from the garden after Stanley's disastrous visit. Lovitt was the only servant who had openly defected to Colin's camp, grateful that Colin hadn't throttled him for sneaking to Ramsey Hay.

Colin knew this because he had walked into the kitchen yesterday morning in the midst of a conversation about his standing among the servants.

"He's got my full support," Lovitt had asserted, banging his fist down on the table with such force that the spoons played a lively game of leapfrog and hit the floor.

"He's got to redeem himself to Kate for whatever he did to upset her," Cook replied with a dark glare in his direction. "And those were clean spoons, young man."

Redeem himself.

To Kate Walcott. Governess and companion. History no longer unknown.

She brought out every feral Boscastle battle instinct that flowed through his veins. It wasn't in his nature to let her go without a fight.

She had barely spoken to him in three days. She took her tea and meals only after everyone else, children included, had theirs. Almost daily he invited her to come riding with her charges, but she refused to ride. She watched only out of concern that he might encourage Brian to imitate skills he hadn't practiced.

"He has to learn eventually," Colin said forcefully when she questioned him in the paddock. "If he'd been raised by a proper father, this wouldn't be a problem."

"If his father couldn't stay long enough to guide—" She trailed off, and Colin pretended not to notice. He knew now that Brian was his son, and so did Kate. But he was still working up the courage to talk with the boy. And he and Georgette had yet to work out a solution that would be best for Brian.

Kate spoke quietly again. "It wasn't Mr. Lawson's fault that he died when the children were young. It wasn't Mr. Lawson's fault that Brian grew up to be a rebel who questioned rules."

A Boscastle trait that.

"I'd prefer it if you and the children stayed as close to me as possible, considering the attacks on the manor."

She raised her brow. "I'm afraid that would disrupt our reading and history lessons. It's difficult to compete for their attention when you are forever present to distract them. You are an exciting character, sir, and children crave excitement."

He smiled inwardly. It was not the time to tease her when she was beginning to open up to him again. "All three of them should learn to sit a horse."

"As governess, I insist that academics come first."

"Then perhaps Brian should be sent to a proper university."

"Excuse me?"

He tried not to smile. "What I meant is that growing up in a freethinking environment does not provide the discipline he needs."

She frowned. "On the other hand, it does offer the

children a variety of experiences that open the eye to the unoriginality of a common life."

He glanced at her. Her cheeks glowed with passion. He decided that her cool disdain defied not him as much as it did society. Nor did it fool him for a minute. She knew as well as he did that the children deserved better, but the choices offered them had never been hers to make.

"How do you think he'll fare if he's plucked right from your gentle instruction into university and hasn't learned how to defend himself from attack?"

"Attack," she said, paling. "I can understand that it's best for him to go to—"

"—Eton. And, oh, what a charming time he'll have there. Bullying, overcrowding, food you'd hesitate to throw to hogs. He'll be beaten until the day comes that he's big enough to beat other boys."

She looked shaken. "I've spoken to Madam about fencing instructions. We have been waiting for—"

"—Mason to come home. Yes, yes, yes. Murderer and epitome of English masculinity. We're all waiting for the elusive Mr. Earling."

She shook her head in what he surmised was a refusal to admit his remark had upset her. Clearly it was one thing for them to engage in a skirmish over Brian's education or Colin's sneaking up behind her on the stairs and whispering, "Boo!" while the children went into hysterics. But the subject of a murder plot and its potential consequences was, unsurprisingly, not the fastest method of regaining a woman's favor.

It would merely make life easier all the way around if she would simply capitulate, because he swore on his life that she could not resist him any more than he could her.

"—and furthermore, I think you're more a rogue now than you were when you ruined Madam."

He blinked. "Were you talking to me?"

"Do you see any other rogues in the vicinity?"

"No." But the Coldsteam Guards could have marched by and he wouldn't have paid much notice. Kate had a talent for taking over his thoughts. And that mouth of hers. Sensual, soft, inviting—until she opened it and toads jumped out.

Now she was wagging her finger at his chin. "So, your way of not answering a question is to pretend you didn't hear it?"

"What question?"

She went out of her way to avoid him. He did everything he could to make her aware of his presence.

He challenged her to acknowledge him. He might as well have been the ghost Griswold sometimes still thought he was.

He slept in the loft.

And he wanted to sleep with her.

She was warm and affectionate and trusting with the other servants and the children. But if they met each other alone in the course of an errand, she drew into her shell, she shrank from him, and yet in her eyes he swore he saw a lonely plea that he wished he could answer. At least now he understood what had caused her pain. It made a difference. It made him more determined that she would soon be his to protect.

Chapter 27

$\mathcal{K}$ate finished her lessons with the children at fifteen minutes past noon every day for their luncheon and play hour. Typically she spent the afternoon with Georgette, who often was too sleepy to talk and asked her to come back in a few hours. On other days Georgette gave her a list of requests for her tea, asked Kate to write letters to old friends or to jot down an episode for her memoirs that she had recalled during the night.

Kate's plans for an evening off so that she could put the polishing touches on her play and go through a rehearsal were dashed when Georgette rang for her after supper.

Kate hastened up the stairs to Madam's room, ignoring the shrieks of laughter from the candlelit hall below. Given time and opportunity, Sir Colin, the great tyrant, would take over the world. It was an hour past bedtime, but did he care? He wouldn't have to tend to and teach three irritable children in the morning.

She knocked at Georgette's room. "Who is it now and what do you want?" was the encouraging reply.

She opened the door. She paused for a moment before complaining that Colin was undermining her authority again. Georgette had obviously taken her nightly cordial; she lounged on her couch in her robe, a plate of sweetmeats and piles of unopened letters in her lap. Griswold had just stirred the fire into a frenzy worthy of Hephaestus.

"Oh, good, Kate, you're here. Read me these letters from London. I think I've been invited—"

Kate launched into her oration before Georgette could squeeze in another word. "His presence is deplorable. I won't take another minute of it. Of him."

"Madam?" Griswold said cautiously.

Georgette motioned him toward the door.

He escaped into the dressing closet, realized his mistake, and exited through the door into the hall. Kate resisted the impulse to fling herself to the floor in frustration and flay her fists and feet. But that would be undignified. Instead, she darted to the corner and swept down a cobweb that one of the chambermaids had missed.

"What has he done now?" Georgette asked carefully.

"Nothing."

"Ah."

"'Ah' what?"

"Bring me the face powder. I could use your nose to find a keg of brandy in a smugglers' cave."

"I demand you put a stop to it."

"Maybe you should chew garlic after every meal."

"Has that ever worked for you?"

"I've never had reason to try it," Georgette said, her brows drawn in a frown. "Attracting a gentleman's interest is my specialty."

She curtsied in Georgette's direction. "Thank you ever so for the absolutely unhelpful advice. With your leave I'll try again to get the children into their beds."

Georgette's eyes widened. "They're still up? At this hour? My goodness. Take this plate on your way out, won't you? And come back as soon as the children are settled. I'm always here to lend an ear."

Kate swooped down, took possession of the tray, and checked for burning candles before she left the room. She would have to summon one of the chambermaids to bank that hideous fire and help Georgette to bed. For now she had to lure the children away from their hero Castle and act as the villainess who spoiled all their fun.

A masterful voice whispered over her shoulder. "Here. Allow me to take that for you."

She would have dropped the platter in fright had he not deftly rescued it from her hands. Her heart pounded double time in her ears. She felt dizzy, looking past him for the children. "Where are they hiding?"

"Who?" he asked, peering around the dark, silent hall. "Are we under assault again? Has someone broken into the house?"

"I do not find these bedtime games amusing."

The faintest smile appeared on his face. "Are we playing a bedtime game? If so, may I have a moment to put down this platter? Half-eaten food isn't conducive to creating a romantic mood."

"Where did you put the children?" she asked without any pretense of patience.

"The children? Good heavens, at this hour they've gone to bed. I had to take them up to the nursery and awaken Nan to make sure they were tucked in for the night. None of us knew where you had gone. You weren't walking alone in the garden again, were you?"

She looked up into his face, catching herself before he could unbalance her again. "How unfair," she said without thinking, "that you and Georgette were both gifted at birth with such angelic beauty and cunning hearts."

His eyes warmed. "Don't you realize how beautiful you are?"

"Your tongue forms lies as smoothly as a serpent's."

"Your tongue is sharper than a gypsy dagger." He hesitated. He gave her the impression that he was waiting for her to make the next move. Georgette was right. She couldn't avoid him. "You still don't trust me, do you?" he said with a frown.

"Not for the blink of an eye."

He nodded slowly. "Well, good for you. I wouldn't trust me, either, in your place."

"And another thing," she said, winding up again like a pocket watch. "Why should we send Brian to school when abuse is a certainty? How is he going to learn the elements of Latin when he's afraid to walk down the hall?"

"You've been living in your own world too long, Miss Walcott. His spine needs strengthening. Young gentlemen cannot rely on iron-boned corsets for their courage."

She drew in a breath. "If I had weapons available right now, I would challenge you to the death, the difference in our gender be damned."

"But you do have weapons," he said, sounding faintly surprised that he should have to point this out. "You could disarm, disrobe, or destroy me if you felt the urge."

She shook her head, retreating from the sudden intensity in his eyes. "What's the point?" she asked herself. "It's useless. You're right. I'll never win. I don't even want to—"

She heard the forks and plate rattle. From the corner of her eye she watched the graceful arch of his body as he bent to put down the platter, stood, and reached for her in one supple move. His blue-black hair fell across his cheek. She went still.

He caught her fingers. "If you ever change your mind—I won't approach you again."

"Yes, you will," she said with certainty.

He nodded gravely. "All right. I can't take an oath to it. But there is one thing that I need to say in my defense."

She glanced at the upper floor. She could hear the children jumping up and down on the beds and Nan begging them to stop.

"What defense?" she said, diverted, tempted, and thoroughly out of sorts.

"This."

Something—a glass, a vase, a mug of milk—crashed to the nursery floor. Kate still didn't move. She was too entranced by the warm grasp of his hand to bestir a muscle. She was sorry she'd let him lure her into this conversation.

He lowered his head. His lips skimmed her cheek. "If you insist on making me out to be a villain, then I shall have to prove myself thoroughly unprincipled. Your iron corset won't stop me if you give me an opening. Now, do run upstairs like a good governess and stop that ungodly racket. And if you decide you'd like me to walk with you in the garden at night, you know where you can find me."

Chapter 28

"Kate, you *are* all right, aren't you?" Georgette inquired with a consternation that was genuine, for all that it would dissipate in a moment or two.

"I'm well, madam," she said, plopping down in her chair.

"You don't look it. I suggest you take a day off and stay in bed. I shall manage on my own for a few hours."

Kate nodded, determined not to justify Georgette's concern with a yawn. Or by admitting that she was afraid of what would happen in a single day without her on watch.

Georgette rose from the couch, her eyes tender. "Oh, foolish, foolish girl. It's happened, hasn't it? You're following in my footsteps."

Kate stiffened in her chair. "I beg your pardon."

Georgette smiled at her with empathy. "That was an insulting comment. I should never judge you on the basis of my behavior. But you have to be honest with me, if I'm going to help you. What do you want?"

"A pot of tea, a hot bath, and a good book."

"What do you want for the *future*?"

Kate sighed. It was a little late for Georgette to be asking that now, when what Kate had thought she wanted had turned out to be an illusion. "I suppose I want children, madam, a home, a husband who will protect me. I don't want to—"

"—end up a whore?"

Kate didn't respond.

"It's a bitter word to say at first. But I admit it becomes sweet on the tongue. I apologize for offending you."

"It's all right, madam. I'm used to it by now." Kate turned to the desk, regaining her composure only to lose it completely at Georgette's next startling command.

"Come to the couch for a moment and pretend I am Colin Boscastle."

How Kate kept her wits about her at that instant she didn't know.

"Kate." Georgette returned to the chaise, gesturing to the carpet that covered the floor. "Sit down, dear, at my feet."

Kate folded her arms across her chest and glanced at the table behind the couch for evidence that Georgette had been drinking.

"You're not fooling me, Kate. I see that smirk on your face. Sit beside the couch and pretend that I am Colin."

"I can't. I refuse. It's impossible."

"Why?"

"Because—I obviously don't have the penchant for imagining these scenarios as you do."

"Nonsense. You write plays and act out the roles you've written. Why can't you regard me as a fellow actor? Why can't you view this as another performance?"

"Why?" Kate asked, her voice as reedy as one of Pan's pipes. "*Why?* I shall tell you why. You, in all your beauty, do not pierce my heart with blue eyes that evoke in me an inappropriate and mutinous sympathy—"

"Ah." Georgette released what could have been her dying breath for the drama it contained. "I knew. I knew it."

Kate felt as if the top of her head had flown off. "And

I don't stumble about in a daze hoping that I shall walk into your arms, which, in fact, are plump and white, while Sir Colin's are corded with lovely sinew—"

Georgette closed her eyes, murmuring. "Oh, mercy. My memory returns. Sit down, Kate, before I swoon."

"I wish *somebody* would listen to me for once in my life," Kate bit off. "I'm certain that the children are." She stood, turning to address the door. "Go back upstairs, you little wretches, or I'll put all three of you over my knee and paddle the disobedience out of you!"

Georgette's eyes fluttered open. "How I admire you, Kate, when you assert yourself like a man. I couldn't live without you. Now, be a good girl and sit to take instructions. I am not sending you out without a few kernels of knowledge. You have been hurt before. I promised you it would not happen again."

Kate folded to her knees in resignation, feeling like a ninny. "I would rather that you had been seized by inspiration and wished me to take down your thoughts for the book."

"And so I do. Do you need pen and paper or will you remember enough to write this down later?"

"Why in the world do I have to pose in this irksome position?"

Georgette smiled. During the rare moments when she managed to bring her thoughts into focus, she could concentrate with the intensity of a hawk that had spotted a mouse to hunt. "That is a position of submission."

Kate made to rise. "I'm returning to the children now. Heaven only knows what they must think if they're listening."

"Stay."

"Then explain to me what this has to do with your memoirs."

"I have been thinking that adding a few instructive chapters might enhance the appeal of my experiences."

Kate's nerves tingled in apprehension. "How instructive do you intend to be?"

"Stop asking questions. I am Colin. You are Kate. You desire me."

"I—"

"Loosen your bodice—no, leave it tightly laced. Moisten your lips. And your hair—why is it always pinned back to the sides of your head like a helmet?" She leaned down to tousle the heavy knot of hair at Kate's neck. "That's better."

"Nothing like looking slovenly to end the day."

"Think of Colin's inscrutable blue eyes when he favors you with a glance. He gives nothing away. Who would ever guess that he could make a woman smolder like a volcano with only a look?"

"Who would guess that you have ever entertained a scientific thought in your life? I'd no idea you even knew what a volcano was."

Georgette laughed. "I might have never known if not for Baron Fallbrook. He frequently excused his deficiencies in bed due to the hailstone that hit him in the head after the Laki volcano of 1783."

"The what of when?"

"The volcanic eruption in Iceland that devastated Europe. Oh, do pay attention, Kate."

Kate stared up at Georgette in consideration. "The world underestimates you."

"As it undervalues every woman." Georgette's gaze wandered to the door. "Last chance—do you wish to make him yours?"

"Madam."

"Good. Look down at the floor. Now slowly lift your

eyes to mine. No, no, don't stiffen like a wooden soldier.
Very gently put your hand on my boot."

What was the point in arguing? When one of these
moods overcame Georgette, the best one could do was
to humor her. Even though Kate *knew* that eavesdroppers lurked behind the door.

"You are a beautiful young woman, Kate. Why are you
kneeling at my feet? Do you want something of me?"

Kate stared, ashamed to admit that when she imagined Colin asking the question, a flame caught in her
belly. "All I wish is to—"

"To?" Georgette prompted, waving her hand.

Kate sighed. It was no wonder that the combination
of Georgette's beauty and Colin's charisma had created
a boy like Brian. Perhaps Georgette provided for her
family in an immoral fashion. Perhaps Colin would ruin
lives in his quest for honor. But where did Kate stand on
the chessboard between these forces? Was she always to
be a pawn?

"To what?" Georgette said.

Kate thought of some of the explicit scenes in Georgette's book. "All I want is to be yours. I'll do anything
you ask. I'll make all your desires come true."

"Will you?"

"I just said so, didn't I?"

"That isn't an enticing voice, Kate. You can't speak to
the man you are trying to seduce as if you were a turnip
vendor."

"*I'm* going to seduce *him*?"

"Not if you can't keep your mind from wandering."

"Other women do it and don't take lessons."

"Well, it really comes down to following your instincts. Unfortunately in your case, you received a brutal
blow before you discovered what your instincts were."

"It wasn't my instincts that turned Lord Overton into a depraved beast who ambushed women."

"Yes, dear. He was an aberration. Now, let us move to the specifics of how to please a man. Your intention is to convince Colin that he is the greatest lover on the Continent." She paused. "This should not be a difficult feat, as it is quite possibly true."

Kate's lips opened, but she hadn't a notion how to respond. How did one react to such a statement? "I wouldn't know, madam, having no true experience to use as a comparison."

"I've compared. Believe me. You cannot go to his bed a complete ignoramus."

"Thank you."

"Do you recall some of the positions and techniques I described when I lived in the Champagne?"

"Champagne sounds like a good idea," Kate said, seizing on any excuse to avoid this instruction. "I'll send Bledridge to the cellar—"

"Kate, you don't have to be a harlot. Just act like one. It's all illusion, imagination. Do you, for instance, know how to remove your clothes to tease him?"

Kate rose and went to the mirror, her fingers lifting to the buttons of her bodice.

"Finally," Georgette said. "Begin to undress— slowly—one lacing, one button at a time. Moisten your lips. Send him an uncertain smile. When you expose your breasts, cup them in your hands. Hopefully your garments will drop in a delicate mound at your feet."

Kate turned abruptly.

This time there was no doubt that she heard the groan of footsteps receding in the hall.

"That does it," she muttered, striding to the door.

"It was probably only the maid with our beverages."

Kate opened the door. "Wouldn't the maid have knocked and left a tray?"

"You don't have a notion what you're in for, Kate," Georgette said in resignation.

Georgette crumpled back against the cushions of her chaise, wondering when Kate would find out that Georgette had broken her vow never to reveal the details of Kate's past. Obviously Colin had not yet told her. Would he hold his tongue forever? He had not found the words to tell the boy that he was Brian's father, either.

She didn't know what he was waiting for. Georgette could not keep up this false show much longer. She could only hope that she had done the right thing, and that Colin had become a man who deserved Kate's and Brian's love.

Chapter 29

$\mathscr{A}$ t last the night of Kate's amateur theatrical arrived. Colin was surprised at the number of guests he escorted to seats in the salon. There were two neighboring squires who brought at least seven relatives apiece. He recognized the two spinsters who rode their phaeton across the meadow on misty mornings. They nodded at him as if he were a coconspirator in whatever plots they might be hatching beneath their white satin turbans. The bookseller and his wife attended, as did a dozen other local merchants. It gratified him to realize that not every person in the village had passed judgment on Georgette's household.

He did not, however, see Mason's solicitor, Ramsey Hay, in the audience, and he remained close to the doors, where he could keep an eye on whoever came and went. He was grateful that Kate had suggested he serve as an usher instead of playing a part in her performance.

With any luck *The Abduction of Helen* would proceed as Kate had written it, and Colin would pretend to watch and clap in the right places, wherever they might occur.

The lamps in the salon dimmed. The candles that lit the stage were extinguished. The curtains groaned open to reveal the darkened figure of the narrator, whose ap-

pearance quieted the house. Her voice carried across the
room, giving Colin a start.

"At a wedding begins our tale of woe—"

Squire Billingsley, sitting in the first row, burst into
raucous laughter. "Don't they all?"

"Be quiet, you fool," his wife said, glaring down her nose
at him, "or I shall teach you the true meaning of tragedy
when we return home." She glanced up at the stage, waving
her fan at Kate. "Go on, dear. He won't interrupt again."

The squire slouched in his seat, receiving a congenial
pat on the back from the gentleman behind him. Colin
looked at Kate. For an instant he thought she was going
to laugh herself. But then she cleared her throat and
started again.

> "At a wedding begins our tale of woe.
> Only one deity was not invited to go.
> She was called Eris, goddess of strife.
> Her Apple of Discord ruined many a life."

As she made her exit, one of the footmen, wearing an
evergreen wreath on his head and what might have been
a flour sack below, dashed from urn to urn to relight the
candles. Another footman was dragging furniture across
the stage until the curtain closed in his face.

Several indistinguishable players had appeared when
the curtain opened on the next part of Kate's narration.

> "Eris threw the Apple into the party just for spite.
> She knew the words inscribed on it would start a
>   fight.
> To the fairest—but who would have to choose?
> Between Hera, Athena, Aphrodite—
> Two goddesses had to lose.

Zeus asked Paris to take that dare.
The Prince of Troy must pick the goddess most
   fair."

Colin glanced out the window, wondering what Mason would do if he returned right now to find his enemy ensconced, entertained in his home. What would Colin do for that matter? Take his revenge in front of spinsters and country squires? He could picture the horror on their faces and in Kate's eyes. Why had he involved her and Georgette at all? He had no right to drag innocents into his private battle.

He pushed off the wall as a murmur of approval rose from the audience. Good God. Every pair of eyes in the salon was riveted to the stage. Candlelight blazed on what he assumed was the scene of the wedding party.

"Oh!" a lady in the third row gasped. "Mrs. Lawson is playing Aphrodite. Isn't she made for the role? How naughty of her. I am so inspired by her spirit."

Colin grinned. He should have known that Georgette wouldn't be content to portray the most beautiful woman in the world—she wouldn't represent anyone less than the goddess of love and beauty. She looked quite at home in a flowing blue gown and golden girdle. He couldn't say the same for the two other goddesses. Cook, not even five feet tall, was barely recognizable as herself, let alone as Hera, the queen of heaven. The crown perched on her gray-brown hair refused to stay on straight. Her golden robes might have made a more regal impression if he hadn't recognized her scepter as the toasting fork from the kitchen.

And if he wasn't mistaken, Irene, the upper chambermaid, was playing the part of Athena, in a white silk robe, sandals, and a helmet whose plumage bore a remarkable resemblance to a feather duster.

There was a long silence. Colin detected movement

behind one of the pillars in the background. Where was Kate? Was that her making frantic hand signals to the adjacent pillar?

Suddenly a small girl in ivory silk popped out from behind the first pillar and threw an apple on the table. Colin couldn't see if the fruit was of a yellow or green variety. Etta had pitched it so fast that she hit Aphrodite on the chin.

Aphrodite shrieked, "You could have broken one of Mama's teeth! It's a piece of fruit, darling, not a football!" Colin was fairly sure that those lines hadn't been written in the play.

But at least Etta stayed in character. As the apple bounced back onto the table, Eris ran to the front of the stage and announced: "This is what you get for not inviting me today! Read the inscription! It says: 'The Apple is for the Fairest.'"

The three goddesses lunged across the table, which to Colin's amazement didn't collapse under their combined weight. The apple, however, rolled offstage and down the center aisle. That, too, he doubted was in the script.

"I've got it," one of the spinsters in the second row shouted. "Does this mean I'm the fairest by default?"

"Toss it this way, fair maiden!" Bledridge replied, appearing from behind a silk dressing screen on which mountains had been painted above the sea and a grassy slope.

Colin recognized Kate's voice from under the tapestry. "Throw it back on the table. *Carefully* this time."

Georgette, Cook, and the upper chambermaid had started circling the table as if they were boxers fighting a match and not goddesses competing in a beauty contest. Etta had crawled under the table for a close-up view, entranced by the improvised action even though Kate gestured to her repeatedly to move offstage.

"Stop poking me with your scepter," Aphrodite said, chasing Cook around a chair. "Those prongs are sharp, I'll have you know."

"Enough!" a voice boomed from the middle balcony, and everyone in the house looked up in awe at Zeus— because from a distance, the coachman, with his curly white hair and beard, a gold-edged sheet tossed over his brawny shoulder, looked convincingly fed up with the goddesses squabbling below Olympus.

But where had Kate gone?

Colin scanned the stage only to jump out of his skin as Zeus flung up his arm and bellowed out his next lines with enough force to loosen tiny bits of plaster from the ceiling. "Paris of Troy, the goddesses await your judgment! Put an end to this bickering and decide!" Behind him the scullions banged together frying pans in an unearthly din.

"Where is Paris?" one guest in the back asked as Zeus stormed from the balcony, his hands clamped over his ears.

"It was still in France the last time I visited," the bookseller's wife said to a general swell of laughter, which died down only when a slim figure sauntered onto the stage.

Complete silence gripped the salon. Every pair of eyes in the room trailed the beguiling narrator to the table.

> "Fight no more, goddesses
> But convince Paris to decide
> For what reason he should take your side."

Colin didn't give a damn who won the beauty contest. He was more engrossed in the "handsome Prince of Troy" strutting across the stage in a belted tunic and leather sandals that laced across her bare legs. The pewter helmet that hid her hair didn't disguise her femininity at all. Nor did the kettle lid she carried as a shield.

"Let's award the apple to Paris," somebody suggested. "He's pretty enough to compete himself!"

Kate pivoted, bowed to acknowledge the compliment paid, and knelt before the three goddesses.

> "What do you offer as my prize
> To make it easier to decide?"

Colin glanced around at the guests. Every male present appeared more interested in stealing a look under Kate's tunic or at her legs than in the answer to her challenge. His burning stare followed her across the stage. If anyone made a lewd remark or improper proposal to her — well, it was none of his business. He wasn't supposed to be caught up in the play. He edged across the back wall and slipped through the door to the garden. If he wasn't mistaken, the footman had admitted a man through the gates. That was Colin's cue to make a quiet exit.

Athena had just offered Paris wisdom. Hera's bribe was one of military power. But it was Georgette — Aphrodite — whose promise ultimately won the prince's vote.

"Choose me, goddess of love and beauty," Georgette said, staring with her luminous eyes into the rows of guests, who without her spectacles must all look the same. "The apple should — should — oh, just give it to me, and stop tossing it back and forth."

"Aphrodite," Paris prompted when Georgette's mind seem to have gone missing, "repeat what it is that you have promised in return."

Aphrodite looked uncertainly at Paris. "I promise to

give you—look, I don't remember. I asked you to keep it to a few lines."

"You promise to give him the most beautiful mortal woman in the world," Etta whispered to her mother from under the wedding table.

"Do I? Just for an apple? Well, that's generous of me. Let's get on with it, then." Raising one white arm in a graceful arc, she slipped back into character. "I, Aphrodite, do promise to give you the most beautiful mortal woman in the world. She is known as—a hell of a toy."

"*The* Helen of Troy?" Paris asked in a loud voice. "The Greek queen of legend?"

Aphrodite sent the audience a come-hither smile. "How many legendary Greek queens do you think I have to give away?"

Paris raised his shield as if he expected a blow from the balcony. "But Helen is married."

"So I've heard," Aphrodite said, tugging up her golden girdle. "But we can't hold that against her any more than we can blame her for being mortal. It wouldn't be fair to offer you her immortal equivalent because that would be me, and quite frankly I'm spread a little thin these days."

Paris sighed, vowing that this would be the last part Georgette improvised. For better or worse, the first act was over. The curtains closed to enthusiastic applause. The audience had been invited to the anteroom for coffee trifle and champagne.

Kate had a hundred things to do before the next act or she might take a glass of champagne herself and discretely ask if anyone knew where Mr. Castle had gone.

Chapter 30

*C*olin had enough temptation to overcome without witnessing the effect Kate had on other men. The more he thought about what had happened to her in London, the less certain he was about how to approach her. Could he help her forget? Or was he only proving that he was no different from any other man who wanted to bed her? She had hidden her true self behind rules, behind serving others and putting on plays. He had trusted her with his motives. But he wasn't sure he'd given her any reason to trust him. He had lured her to the lodge and taken advantage. But then she'd come to warn him in the loft.

There was still hope. Should he wait for her again? *Could* he wait? He wasn't the wild boy he had been thirteen years ago. He had a son who was being raised by the woman he was trying to impress.

He wanted to explain that he desired her all the more for knowing who she really was.

He walked deeper into the garden, pausing at the crunch of receding steps on a hidden path. The senior footman stood sentry at the gates, nodding to him in recognition.

"A late-arriving guest?" he asked the footman.

"Yes, sir. That was Mr. Ramsey Hay, Mr. Earling's solicitor. He manages every halfpenny that falls into the master's hands. I daresay he would manage every move Mr. Earling makes if it were possible."

"Would he?" Colin said, staring back at the brightly lit windows. "How trustworthy he must be."

Trustworthy was not the word that came to mind when Colin found Mr. Hay pretending to examine the piano that stood in the chamber that served as a greenroom behind the salon. It was obvious when Colin entered through a side door that the solicitor would rather examine the Prince of Troy's nicely shaped posterior.

Not that Kate held still long enough to satisfy either man's curiosity. She flitted about the room like a warrior fairy, buckling on Charlie's armor and reminding him he couldn't stab his older brother after Brian had been officially killed. She stared right past Colin to the servants who had become a Spartan army, inspecting their white knobby knees and friendly faces with a sigh.

"Please," she said, "one of you, make certain the sheets are secured to the steps below the stage. I don't want Nan to slip into the Aegean Sea. Her balance isn't what it used to be. And try to look intimidating."

She turned, walking right into Colin. "Is there anything I can do to help?" he said, putting his hand out briefly to steady her. He had a feeling she barely noticed or cared whom she had stumbled into.

"Find our hammer and keep it in sight. Our props are already collapsing. Athena was supposed to calm the seas, but it didn't work."

"Perhaps these productions are not worth the time or the expense," Mr. Hay muttered. "I hear that the theatre is only half-full. For what purpose do we serve trifle and champagne to the local gentry while the master is away?"

Colin lowered his voice. "Does he always come and go as if he owns the place?"

"Yes," she whispered back. "And so do you. Where have you been, anyway?"

"On the prowl for intruders."

"Well, don't tell me until after the play whether you found any. I have to keep my mind on what I'm doing. Do you have any idea how badly Georgette butchered her lines?"

"No one will remember a few days from now."

"But all that hard work, and she doesn't even bother. I should look for new position."

"No, you shouldn't. I couldn't stop looking at you. That costume is scandalous. I don't care for it at all."

She looked a little insulted. "Don't you?"

He stared at her. "I want you to stay away from Hay."

She tilted her head back to frown at him. "I thought *you* were the one who was supposed to avoid recognition."

"He's up to something, and I'm not standing in a corner until I know what it is."

She glanced in the solicitor's direction. "He's upset that Mason bought a piano for Georgette and the children," she whispered.

"Why?"

"Well, it's a costly piece."

"It's not his money. Musical skill is invaluable."

She sighed. "Except that no one in the house can play a single note. Mason bought it because *he* thought the children should have lessons."

Mr. Hay walked toward them, his hat and cane in hand. "I'm surprised to find the new groom inside the master's music room. Are you playing for us tonight as part of the performance?"

Colin gave a sheepish smile. "Aw. No one'd pay to hear the racket I make."

"Then perhaps you should return to your duty. Whichever it is, I doubt it requires you to be here. When the master returns, I shall suggest he consider hiring a smaller and more efficient staff."

Colin stiffened. "Yes, sir." He flashed Kate a glance, muttering, "Avoid him."

"There's only one place I will be in the next two hours, and that is onstage," she whispered. "Aren't you going to watch?"

"Watch what?" he asked morosely. "Other men watching you?"

"Lift up your mind, sir. *The Abduction of Helen* is a classic tale."

"Not if it gives other men ideas of abducting you. Go on. I'll be there in a moment, and, Kate—"

"Yes?"

"I remember enough of ancient history to know that Paris plays an active role in the next act. But does he have to bend with his backside facing the audience so often?"

Colin had no intention of leaving Ramsey Hay alone in the house until he discovered what the man intended. He hadn't recognized Colin. He hadn't come to the house to watch a play. What did he want?

He waited a minute before he went outside, then walked through the rhododendrons until he reached the library window, behind which a candle flickered. He leaned against the wall. Mr. Hay had reached into the long bookshelf closest to the window. Colin frowned.

It was deuced hard to figure out what the man had in mind. Hay hadn't even glanced at the decanter of port on the sideboard. Perhaps he was borrowing a book to take home—or perhaps he wasn't looking for good literature at all.

Hay took off one glove to pull out a book and reach into the space on the shelf. What did he want that was hidden behind a book? But then Hay's hand emerged empty, and an entire shelf swung open to reveal a dark hole furnished with a small desk.

Colin edged nearer the window. He could see Hay slip inside the space, withdrawing several documents from the drawers of the desk.

"Dammit," Colin muttered. "Someone needs to clean these windows."

It looked as if Hay had placed these papers and several other bundles of what appeared to be receipts or invoices inside his heavy woolen coat.

A loud cheer from the salon immobilized both men for a moment. Colin flattened himself to the wall as Hay closed the hidden panel, looked briefly around the room, and left.

Whatever Hay had taken from the desk had to be valuable if it was hidden in the wall. However, Colin would have to wait to investigate.

If Nan slipped into the Aegean Sea because Colin hadn't secured the sheets, the old girl might injure herself. Strange, he thought as he reentered the house. All the good female parts had been taken, except, of course, for Helen of Troy. Perhaps Nan was playing her handmaiden. God forbid that she appeared onstage as a Spartan soldier.

"Mr. Castle," a breathless voice said behind him.

He swore under his breath and pivoted outside the door to the salon. He recognized the comely widow from the village and sighed. "Yes, ma'am? May I escort you back to your seat?"

She smiled ruefully. "I left my seat because you left the theatre and I wanted—"

He put his finger to his lips, opening the door with his

other hand. He knew what she wanted, but she wasn't getting it from him. "The act has started," he said somberly. "You don't want to miss a minute of it."

She gripped the cuff of his jacket. "I didn't come here to see a play. I came to see you. My name is Rachel Pleasance, don't you remember?"

"No. I've a terrible memory. That's why I'm an usher tonight, not an actor."

A burst of laughter from the theatre gave Colin the opportunity to whisk her through the door before she could object or wriggle back into the hall to continue the conversation.

"Mr. Castle," she whispered in chagrin, "why is there a hammer protruding from your pocket?"

"A hammer?"

"Well, I assume that's what it is," she said coyly. "When are you going to put it to use?"

He glanced at the stage in astonishment. The upper balcony had been transformed into the palace of ancient Troy; the tapestries that draped from the railings depicted the town's plains.

"Right now," he said, and ran down the aisle toward the silk sheets that billowed over the semicircular steps from center stage. He banged a few nails into place and escaped as the ship carrying Paris and his stolen Helen plowed toward the waves. Actually, it was Kate commanding a legless settee with three broomsticks serving as masts.

And Helen was—good grief. Even in sleeveless gold-trimmed chiffon and a flowing blond wig, it challenged the imagination to believe that Nan's face had launched a single settee, let alone a thousand ships. He grimaced as she sprang out of Kate's grasp to bellow at the audience. "Save your beautiful queen! Odysseus! Achilles! Save me from this wicked prince! Who wants to ravish me!"

Colin smiled in admiration. He'd take on that wicked prince whenever she would agree to a private war. By the disgusted expression on her face as she glanced his way, she had noticed the widow and drawn the wrong conclusion.

He looked to his right.

Lovitt, in Grecian-soldier garb, was showing Mrs. Pleasance to her seat. Colin sensed a compatibility between them. That would be one problem solved.

The doors behind him banged against his elbow and swung open; he turned in annoyance to behold Brian mounted on his pony.

"I assume this is part of the play?"

Brian nodded gravely. "I'm Achilles, and this—"

"Don't tell me. The Trojan horse." Colin moved aside. "Do your worst."

"I'll be dead in a few minutes," Brian said in disappointment.

Colin suppressed a smile. "My condolences."

"It wouldn't be so bad if Charlie weren't the one to do me in."

"That's better than your sister, isn't it?"

"I suppose."

Colin stared at the sharp-boned face beneath a plumed pewter bowl. This was his son, and Kate had raised him. He would not be denied either of them.

"Sir?" Brian whispered.

"What?"

"I think you'd best make use of that hammer. The walls of Troy aren't supposed to fall this soon."

He looked up as a tapestry from the balcony collapsed on the prow of the settee from which Kate and Nan had by a hairsbreadth just disembarked. It was a tragedy, all right. Women and children struggling to survive without a single champion in sight.

He knew what his role would be after tonight. Let the curtains close on Kate as the hero for the last time.

He hadn't even reached the bookshelf to open the secret panel Hay had accessed when a figure appeared behind him. The windows were all closed. No one had opened the door. He swung around, reaching inside his waistband for his pistol.

"God above, Kate! What are you doing here this time of night?"

"That's what I was about to ask you." She cast a suspicious look around the room. "Are you expecting company?"

"Company?" He pulled his hand back to his side, studying her in astonishment. Her long hair cascaded around the shoulders of the cream silk robe she was wearing over her night rail. She looked so soft and vulnerable that he felt his senses kindle, his gaze hungrily consuming the sight of her.

She frowned at him. "Yes, company. I noticed you and Mrs. Pleasance having a chat during the performance. If Nan and I had been knocked senseless by the fallen tapestry, I would have held you responsible."

He laughed unwillingly. "I only spoke with Mrs. Pleasance for a few moments before Lovitt took her to her seat. She was persistent. I was polite."

Kate shrugged. "You have the right to be a rake."

"Well, you do not have the right to accuse me when you are wrong. I followed Mr. Hay after you and I parted. He came in here and—" He paused. "How did you enter this room?"

He stared past her and at once knew the answer when he noticed the gaping hole where another panel should have been. The marble fireplace that stood between the two bookshelves separated each hidden recess from the other. Kate must have emerged from an unseen passageway.

He nodded toward the opening. "What's in there?"

She moved to block his way. "It's a secret passageway."

"To where?" he asked, intrigued.

"It wouldn't be secret if I told you."

"Who'll stop me if I decide to investigate for myself?" he asked her in a determined voice.

She sighed in exasperation. "It leads up to my bedchamber."

"It doesn't. Do you lead a double life as a highwayman?"

"How did you guess? Did my robe give me away?" She sighed. "The house was built by a gentleman smuggler who—"

He looked down at her face, no longer playing. "Keeping secrets incurs a heavy burden."

She bit her lip, backing away. "Disclosing a secret to a person who breaks your trust is worse."

"Sometimes a secret has to be exposed to lose its power. Sometimes it has to be shared. I know Brian is my son. And I know what happened to you in London."

She drew back, her eyes darkening in disbelief. "She told you," she said softly. "She swore on her soul that no one would ever know. Well, that's the end of it. I'm leaving this house tomorrow. I don't care if I do end up on the streets. I won't live with a thankless lot of traitors."

He caught her arm as she turned, the tears of shame and betrayal in her eyes more than he could bear. "Don't blame her. I wanted the truth. She thought I ought to be told."

"I don't blame her," she said in a low furious voice. "I blame both of you. Georgette sleeps with married men when she is desperate for the money she spends like water to support her lifestyle. You overtake an entire house in the hope of finding honor. Do either of you care that others might suffer for your selfishness?"

He shook his head. "I never realized until I came here that my obsession would put other innocent people at risk. But don't be angry at Georgette. Forgive her." He lifted his hand to catch the tear that slipped down her face. "Forgive me."

"I'm weary of whores," she said in a flat voice.

He nodded. "I understand."

She tossed her head. "And I'm even wearier of the men who create them and the helpless children they create in their sin. And I have nothing but contempt for men who lead women to believe they are loved when all they want is a whore."

"Are you weary of love?"

"How would I know? It has never come to me."

"Perhaps it will. Kate, perhaps it has and you don't realize it."

"Either way, it is not your business."

"I've already made it my business. You can't leave Georgette because I forced her to explain your past to me. I needed to understand you."

"Why? So you can make me fall in love with you and then abandon me?"

"That wasn't what I had in mind."

"Go visit your widow."

"I don't want her. I want you."

"Well, you can't—"

"And you want me."

He wrapped his arm around her waist, bent his head, and silenced her with a deep kiss. She gave a moan, her body limp against his. He slid his hand down her neck to her bottom, caressing her until her breathing slowed and he knew that she would give him another chance.

She turned her head to the side. "One of us has to find the strength to stop this."

He buried his face in her neck. "It isn't going to be me."

It wouldn't be Kate, either. His kiss laid open the deepest layer of her inhibitions and exposed the desires she had convinced herself did not exist. It was dangerous, yes, to give him the power to dominate her. Had he promised her anything? But did it really matter anymore? Ten years of not allowing a man to touch her. Ten years of believing she did not deserve anything but abuse.

Just once, then, she would know.

He breathed a sigh in her hair. "Do you hear voices in the hallway? Please tell me you don't."

She turned to the door. "Oh, no. It's Georgette with the squire and his wife. She *never* uses the library."

"Then why is she coming here tonight?" Colin asked tersely.

"She wants to open a literary salon when she retires," Kate whispered, her eyes wistful. "I think it's a lovely ambition. I promised to help."

"Is there no place in this house where a man can woo a woman in private?" he asked in a disgruntled voice.

"Hush. Don't breathe a word." Kate took his hand and drew him into the stuffy stairwell, squeezing around him to close the secret panel moments before Georgette and her company entered the library.

"What do we do now?" he said, gazing up the stairs to the partially opened door at the top.

"I suppose we sit and wait."

But that was easier said than done. The stairs were so narrow that she couldn't sit comfortably unless she moved above or below him. Instead, she settled down at his side. She was tired and tempted to rest her head against his shoulder, close her eyes for a moment.

"You're built like a pillar," she murmured.

"Where does that door lead to at the top of the stairs?"

"My bedchamber."

"Does Mason know?"

"Yes. He bought the house because it was riddled with hidden escape routes that he can use in an emergency."

"Who does he need to escape from?"

She hesitated. "You. He's scared to death that you're going to hunt him down like you did his father."

He didn't deny it as she hoped he would. But he was considerate enough to change the subject. "I'm sorry I didn't reach Troy before the walls collapsed."

"Did you enjoy the play?" she asked, slipping her hand inside his jacket.

"All I watched was you."

They subsided into silence as laughter and the clinking of glasses drifted from the library. "How long do you think they'll keep this up?" he whispered. "We can't sit here forever."

She lifted her head from his shoulder. "Georgette can entertain until breakfast. It's not as if she has anything else to do."

"Breakfast? Good heavens. You'd better go to bed."

"That's a good idea," she whispered, easing out of his lap. "Come with me."

"What did you say?" His voice held an edge that stirred her nerves.

"You could escape through my bedroom door and not be seen. Nan and the children won't awake again tonight."

He stood; even in the dark his sensual intensity quickened her breathing. "If you take me to your room, I might not be able to leave. I've made it clear that I desire you."

She allowed her body to brush against his. Her night rail and robe provided little protection from the heat he radiated. He ran his hand down her back in a caress that electrified her senses. She had believed for years she would never experience a passion that wouldn't shame her.

She wanted to feel such passion now. To know pleasure in his arms. She wanted this man to show her what she had missed. She would grieve when he left. But it would be worth it. She would never meet anyone like him again. She could live on the memory of him for the rest of her life.

She had second thoughts as soon as they reached her room. Perhaps she wasn't ready to take a risk, although for all practical purposes the world viewed her as an impure. Keeping her virtue intact mattered only to herself. Perhaps she ought to wait. But for whom?

Perhaps she shouldn't have encouraged him in the lodge, or in the library.

Perhaps—she stole a look at him. He didn't appear to be in any hurry to leave.

He glanced around the room as she hurried about to tidy the stacks of books and papers heaped on her desk and bed and chairs. He came forward and wrestled a box of letters from her arms.

"Love letters?" he asked, turning his head to read the note that sat on top.

"Yes. To Georgette. Not to me."

"Has anyone ever sent you a love letter?"

She smiled. "I didn't say that."

"And you haven't saved yours?"

"Why would I? I've no intention of writing my memoirs based on a half dozen indecent offers."

"Good for you." He placed the box on the floor beside her desk. "I've never understood why a woman hangs on to old letters."

"Perhaps it's because when she grows old she can read them as proof that once she was desirable."

"Isn't that what her husband should do?"

She looked down at the floor, only now spotting the kettle lid she had brandished as a shield during the play and beneath it the ivory silk dress that Etta had worn as the goddess Eris. "Look at that," she said in reproach. "The children must have sneaked in here after the performance." She bent in resignation to stow both items behind her dressing screen.

"The children love you," he said.

She laughed, rising slowly. "It may not always show, but I love them, too."

"I think everyone in this house loves you," he said. "And your love for them does show."

His implacable stare quickened her heart. "My room is usually not in such a shambles. I expect we'll be finding props around the house for the next month."

"I don't think you'll be here that long," he said, his mouth tightening at the corners.

"Don't say that. We have nowhere else to go, and Georgette hasn't saved enough to even afford—"

The muffled sounds of movement in the library below diverted her attention. "Oh, dear."

"What is that?" he asked, staring down at the floor.

"Madam and her company have set up the card table. It's going to be a long night, I'm afraid. What does she care? She can sleep all day if she likes."

"Well, I won't be able to sleep worrying that Hay might return to the house." An unfathomable expression settled on his face. "In fact, I don't feel at all tired. Do you?"

She nodded absently. "I've cleared a path to the door.

You should be able to escape without tripping and alerting Georgette or her guests."

"I know that my presence in your room is unnerving you." He sat down in a chair by the fire. "But unless you insist that I leave, I'm going to stay. And not fall asleep."

She shivered. The deep resonance of his voice proved irresistible to ignore. But then, he had not waited for an answer before he took off his jacket and vest and loosened his neckcloth in a leisurely manner. She swallowed, uncertain what she should do next. She had never entertained a man in her bedchamber. Perhaps she should have paid closer attention to how Georgette conducted her affairs. It was easier for Kate to write about an intimate act than to initiate one. Did he expect her to give him an invitation? He had never hesitated to admit his desires before.

"Did you enjoy the play?" she said to fill the silence between them.

He replied without a moment's hesitation. "I hated it."

"You what?" she said, this disclosure enough to put all the other concerns from her mind.

"Yes. I could not take my eyes from you. Nor could every other male sitting in the audience."

She frowned to cover the flustered pleasure she felt at this confession. "That isn't true at all. Georgette was the attraction. No one noticed me for one moment onstage."

"Well, I did." He twirled his neckcloth in his hands, the movement fascinating her. "Is the door to the hall locked?"

She glanced up into his face, not calmed at all by his forbidding smile.

"Yes."

"Then remove your robe."

"Why should I?" she asked softly.

He sat back in the chair, his gaze dark, expectant.

"Don't make me wait too long or I'll take it off you my-self. It looks too pretty on you to risk it being torn. I am struggling to hold back my instincts, which I suspect you already know."

"I can't," she whispered, her throat tight.

"Why not?"

"The coals are too bright."

"You invited me here," he said quietly. "What does it matter how bright the fire burns?"

"I just can't. It isn't dark enough."

"Come here," he said, the stern gentleness in his voice her undoing. "Stand in front of my chair and un-dress for me."

She fought back panic, shame, temptation.

He beckoned her with his hand. "It gives a man plea-sure to look at what he possesses."

She lowered her gaze. "Then you don't understand."

"Do you desire me?"

"You know that I do."

"Well, then, show me. Would you prefer that I go first?"

He unbuttoned his shirt. She glanced up, intrigued, at his solid chest and the steel-hard plane of his stomach. He made as if to rise, his hand lifting to his waistband.

"It's different for a man," she said, forcing her eyes to his. "I can't even bear to look at myself in the mirror."

"I can't bear to think that you have so little trust in me. But perhaps that is my fault. Can you give me the chance to prove that you have changed me?"

She untied the sash at her waist and let the robe slither to her feet. Georgette's voice whispered in her mind, "Do what pleases him, and then do a little more."

She reached up, one shoulder at a time, and untied the laces of her night rail. His eyes widened as the garment slipped slowly to the floor. The rasp of silk felt decadent against her bare skin. She had become unbearably sensitive, aware, under his intense scrutiny. Her heart raced in anticipation. Did her body displease him? She lifted her arms to cover her breasts, to hide the scars—

"Don't," he said sharply. "You are the most perfect woman I have ever seen. Do you think me so shallow that those marks on your skin would matter to me? Or to most men, if you want the truth."

"It isn't the marks," she said. "It's the memory of how I came by them. I doubt I would care if I'd been injured saving one of the children. I had done nothing to encourage him. I worked hard. And yet it was his word against mine, and no one would come to my defense. No one would believe me except Georgette. He threatened to send me to prison. He accused me of trying to seduce him."

His face hardened into a grim mask of resolve. "Then take my word. After tonight, no other man will debase you or make you doubt your worth without answering to me."

"I still wish she hadn't told you."

"Why should you carry the shame for what a monster did? Why should you deprive yourself of passion because of one man's perversion?"

She lowered her arms. He couldn't know how he affected her. She barely felt the fire burning at her back. But she could feel herself enshrouded in the sexual heat he exuded.

Steam. Smoke. It rose like incense between them. She took a breath and let his warmth enfold her.

"Colin," she whispered, averting her eyes.

She heard his boots hit the floor and looked up as he pulled off his shirt and finished unfastening his trousers. Her heart ached at the beauty of his body, his sculpted perfection. From his wide shoulders and narrow waist to the heavy organ between his thighs, he was a dominant male, and unabashedly determined to make her aware of the fact.

His virility overpowered her in the most pleasant way. Never had she dreamed that she could revel in feeling defenseless, or so delicate that if he touched her she might dissolve. In fact, she thought she was melting by the moment.

"Kate," he said, moving toward her.

He clasped her face in his hand and captured her mouth in a kiss that promised that his claim on her would be irrevocable. She shivered at the contact of his tall, muscular body against hers. He trailed his fingertips down the curve of her spine to her bottom.

"I want all of you," he whispered, his erection jutting against her belly. "I wanted you before I even knew how strong and giving you are. I was sure you were a temporary obsession, and I had to wait for it to pass."

"And?" she asked, enthralled by his admission as he led her by the hand to the bed.

He pulled her down on top of him, his eyes heavy lidded and dark with unfettered desire. "And the more time I spent in your company and watched you fight for my son, the less I could deny that what I feel went far deeper than lust. By the way," he added, tumbling her to her back, "your body is bliss. I apologize now for the pain you'll feel tonight and perhaps in the days that follow."

"I might not break as easily as you seem to think."

"You will if I don't restrain myself the first few times."

"I want you, anyway," she whispered. "I've decided, and don't try to change my mind."

"Do you think I'm mad?"

"I need you, Colin."

A devilish smile darkened his face. "Your body is begging for a master."

*   *   *

Her warmth had penetrated his blood, his bones, his heart. It would be impossible to exorcise her. The only way he could survive was to bind her to him. She needed his protection. He needed her at his side to light the darkness he had made of his life.

He rose up on his arm and deep-kissed her into a delirium. He took pleasure in her response — a quick intake of breath, the nipples of her full breasts darkening as she arched in helpless surrender. She wanted him to take her. Instead, he took his time.

He brushed a kiss of possession against the blue-veined pulse that throbbed at the base of her throat. Her lips parted. He closed his eyes for a moment, his stones tightening at the thought of her sweet mouth sucking his cock. The demons of his desire fought to make him forget this was her initiation.

How tempting to possess her all at once and sate his needs instead of allowing her a gentle deflowering. Slowly he drew his fingertips across the slopes of her breasts, circling each engorged nipple but not touching. He wanted to entice. Excite. Make her desperate one caress at a time.

She stirred, her breathing unsteady. "Is this the pain that you warned me to expect?"

"I have been in pain since the night you let me touch you in the lodge."

"That's what you get for luring me there under false pretenses."

"I should be ashamed of myself."

She regarded his saturnine face in rue. "You might try to look repentant."

"Well, you've heard the saying 'Passion cometh before penance.'"

"I must have missed that pearl of wisdom."

"Don't worry," he said with a dark smile. "I've taken it as my duty to further that lapse in your education."

"How kind of you," she whispered. "Perhaps in the course of our lessons, I might regather my wits and remember the insight Madam has shared with me over the years."

The devil on his shoulder could not let a virgin's taunt go so unchallenged. "Theory is one thing, sweetheart. But it takes practice to perfect a skill. Unless one is gifted at birth with a talent."

She drew her fingers down his chest to the tip of his turgid erection. His penis thickened, pulsing with the blood her featherlight touch sent rushing through his body. The temptress in the garden. "It would seem," he conceded, "that you are not without a natural skill."

"Have I overstepped my bounds, sir?"

"I'm afraid you have," he said in a hoarse voice.

"There's no going back, is there?"

He shook his head.

He resumed stroking her breasts, finally pinching in turns the delicate tips until she moaned. Her hand fell away from the knob of his cock, and he gritted his teeth, tempted to beg her not to stop.

"Colin," she murmured.

He slid down the bed. "Hmmm?"

"I was wrong."

He pushed her knees apart and inhaled sharply as he spread open the folds of pink flesh. Her cleft glistened with the creamy fluid that would make his penetration easier. Her vulnerability was unveiled for his taking. He battled to subdue the primal impatience that urged him to sate his needs in her. Another wave of blood surged through his veins, into his head, his loins, until he felt like a cauldron. He knew she had said something. He looked up briefly, his gaze unfocused. "What did you say?"

"I was wrong. I am going to break."

He didn't answer. He was lost to reason, more intent on licking and suckling the bud of her sex than to pretend he gave a damn about anything except taking her to the edge. She was close, wet with excitement, under his control for the moment.

But he wouldn't last. He'd wagered either too much on the benefit of his experience or too little on the impact of her innocence on his libido. It seemed like ages before he felt her belly contract, her body suspended on the cusp of climax. Black heat burned through what remained of his restraint.

Forgive me.

I need you.

I need you tonight and tomorrow and as far into the future as I can see.

He raised himself up and guided the head of his penis to her cleft. He pressed inside until he felt the barrier of her maidenhead. She gave a ragged gasp, her hips rising in either encouragement or the aftermath of her orgasm, it didn't matter. His body could not change course.

"Now," he said. *"Now."*

Wet. Tight. His to possess. He withdrew slowly and thrust deep, her helpless cries intensifying his pleasure. She writhed her hips, clearly seeking a reprieve from the slow forceful strokes he couldn't control. "Lock your legs around my ass," he whispered through the harsh breaths he drew into his throat. "Anchor yourself to me or we will end up on the floor."

"It . . . hurts."

"I'm sorry. It won't always feel like this." He lowered his head to kiss her, his mouth muting her broken sigh as he embedded his cock inside her with a desperation he had never known before.

"Colin—"

"I need more. I need you." He wanted to fill her. The muscles of his back strained. He set his teeth, gripped by a tension so intense he thought his heart had stopped. But his body did not stop until at last he bucked his hips and impaled her in a powerful thrust of possession. Only then did he close his eyes and come inside her, lost in sensation and satisfaction, lost to the woman he had finally made his own.

Chapter 31

She woke up hours later to hear Colin asking if she would be all right. She managed to answer, "Mmm," before he said, "Are you sure?"

"Yes. Why shouldn't I be? I'm—" She forced through a languorous fog to open her eyes. He was standing at her bedside, tucking his long shirt into his trousers. Except for the stubble that outlined his cheeks, he looked nothing like a man who'd spent the night indulging his sexual appetite. Or satisfying hers. But beneath the dark possession in his eyes burned a tenderness that allayed her fear. He was hers now, she thought.

"It's still dark," she whispered, rising up on the pillow before she realized that she was lying nude in her bed.

He bent over her, his gaze traveling from her face to the breast that the bedsheet didn't quite cover. She reached down without thinking, but Colin caught her hand. "You are never to hide yourself from me again. I will take it as a sign of mistrust if you do."

He kissed her breast, then the back of her hand, and before he straightened he kissed her softly on the mouth. "I know you'll never forget what he did to you. But do you think I can make the memories less painful?"

"I think you could make me forget my own name."

"Or take a new one," he said with a pensive look that made her think she had missed something in their conversation. He reached back for the vest he had slung across the chair.

"What are you trying to say?" she whispered, slowly aware that her body felt tender, sweetly bruised from the intimacies they had shared.

"The head groom and the governess are getting married. I don't have time to make a proper proposal."

"Well, you had enough time to be improper when it suited you."

"Yes," he agreed wryly. "But improper acts come easily to me. Marriage proposals don't." He pulled a clean handkerchief from his vest pocket. "Let me wipe off the evidence of our lovemaking. There are bloodstains on the bed that you might not wish the maids to see. I would have done this sooner, but I decided you needed to rest."

She blushed fiercely, biding her time before she could comment on his knowledge of after-coital affairs. "Where are you going now?" she murmured, closing her eyes in a swelter of emotions as he erased most of the dampness from her inner thighs.

"Down to the library to explore the hidden room."

Her eyes opened slowly once more. "Let me get dressed. I'll help."

He frowned. "If we are caught, we'll be in the same predicament as we were last night. Not that it will greatly matter now that we are engaged."

"Maybe not to you, but I'll be teased from now until the wedding." The words felt so sweet on her tongue, she was tempted to repeat them.

"If I don't show up before breakfast, you might come to the library to make sure I haven't trapped myself inside the wall. In the meantime, I'd rather you stay here."

"But I think I could help you, and if we are discov-

ered, at least we shall be fully clothed and can claim that
we arose early to tidy up downstairs."

"Except that I'm not a housemaid, and no one will
believe us for a minute." He regarded her with a reflec-
tive smile. "I have not known pleasure like last night's. I
hope you feel the same."

"I feel ravished," she said simply.

"I feel immensely relieved."

And then he left through the door to the library stairwell.

Pleasure? It was more than that. Yes, she had felt passion, relief, a release from the bondage of her past. He
had breached her secrets, and it had been a beautiful
liberation, all the more powerful because it came from a
part of her that she had learned to associate with shame.

She huddled in bed, images of their indecency flood-
ing her mind. She must have been overcome by the enor-
mity of what they had done, because she had a sense she
hadn't completely grasped their last conversation. He
had asked, or rather *told* her, that they were engaged.
How would she explain this to Georgette, the children?
When would the marriage take place? And where? Did
it change his plans?

For now she knew only that she was a fallen woman
who had fallen in love with the one man she should have
resisted. Yet she could not pretend regret. She couldn't
deny how *right* it felt.

Colin frowned as he discovered a few faded papers
wedged between the drawers of Mason's desk. Hay must
not have seen them. From what Colin could determine
in the light of his dying candle, the documents were old
accountings of the trading firm's business, indicating
healthy profits.

The rustle of silk outside the hidden recess jarred his

concentration. He turned, hoping that Kate had disobeyed him. It would take considerable willpower to keep his hands off her now that they were to be man and wife. He grinned. Or groom and governess.

He blinked. The figure peering in on him was a female, but it wasn't Kate; it was Georgette—or Aphrodite, looking a little worse for wear after a night of drinking, gambling at cards, and entertaining company. The cushion she brandished over his head did not invoke the impression of the goddess of love, her disheveled charms notwithstanding.

"What the devil?" he said, reaching up to wrest the useless weapon from her hand. "You could have knocked over the candle, woman."

"I was about to knock off your block!" she explained. "What are you doing? What is this place?"

"One of Mason's secret passages. Haven't you ever seen him use it?"

"He and *I* only came in here for an occasional drink."

"Which could have been poisoned."

"Don't try to mislead me." She examined him in suspicion. "Where did you vanish to after the performance? You weren't in *here* or we'd have heard you. Kate went to bed, and you—you—you didn't go after her?"

"Everything will work out," he said, gathering up the few documents before he extinguished his sputtering candle and stepped into the library. She looked upset enough to entomb him in the wall. He threw the cushion back onto the sofa.

"You immoral man. You disgraced my governess while I sat in the room below, innocently toasting her demise with champagne. You didn't even wait a day after I betrayed her."

"I did not disgrace your governess," he said in irritation, turning to the bookshelf to close the panel. "I seduced the woman who will become my wife."

"What?" She turned bone white and dropped onto the couch where she had entertained her friends last night while the aforementioned seduction and marriage proposal had taken place.

"How dare you?" she sputtered.

"I explained my feelings to you about her. I thought you understood."

"You didn't explain that you intended to take her away from me."

He looked up at the ceiling, wondering if he'd committed too many sins to ask for divine intervention. He would promise to stop, but that would be a lie. It seemed pointless to add another transgression to the list that had likely begun the day he took his first step.

"Georgette, it has been a long night for all of us. I haven't discussed any details with Kate yet. Perhaps we shall all live close to one another. There is no reason you won't be allowed to see each other."

She gazed at him in mounting anger. "And what about Brian? He loves Kate. So do the other two children. What do you think he'll do if he loses her?"

"I intend—"

"He'll run away again, and he won't come back. He's so like you. He wants adventure. You ran away, too. It's in the blood."

"He needs a stable home and a university education."

"Well, he certainly won't get either from you."

"Yes, he will. And I would never keep you from your son. It would be unnatural. If Brian is part of my family, then so are you as his mother. He may stay with you whenever he likes."

"What will happen to me?" she asked, her eyes dark with tears.

"I will make provisions for you and the children, no matter what."

"What about Nan? You can't put her out in the gutter."

"I'll take care of Nan, too," he promised.

"And Bledridge?"

He hesitated. "Yes. Why not?"

"Have you considered Griswold? The forgetful old dear is fading from this world. He can't possibly live, let alone work, in another household. It would be morally wrong to discard him when I haven't paid his wages in ages."

Good night. The peaceful future he had envisioned was to be populated by a cast of players that rivaled the characters in one of Kate's amateur theatricals. "Fine. Everyone is included."

"How?" she demanded.

Colin half wished he could disappear back into the wall. Even then she would probably find a way to pursue her unmerciful line of questioning. "How what, my dear?"

"Don't 'my dear' me, you ruthless scoundrel." She stood, her goddesslike bosom quivering with injustice. "How are you going to support me? It will take time for my memoirs to be published. I shall have no reliable income until then, and I am accustomed to certain comforts."

He paused. Perhaps he should have watched the end of last night's play. Had Paris survived in Kate's world or had the wretch received his due? "Calm yourself. If necessary we will have to live under the same roof."

She gasped as if a spear had struck her in the heart. "Are you asking me to depend on your charity, to be shunted into a back parlor as if I were your grandmother?"

"God forbid."

The door to the hall swung open. Colin and Georgette

turned like a pair of guilty siblings arguing over who deserved the last treat on the table.

"I can hear the both of you from my room," Kate said with a decorum that she hadn't shown a few hours ago. In contrast to her undignified self, now she looked so fresh and wholesome that Colin realized he needed a bath and shave before he could present himself to the house again, even as a stable groom.

"She knows," he said quietly.

"I can tell."

Kate walked up to Georgette and crossed her arms. "You broke your promise to me."

Georgette glanced at Colin. "He made me do it."

"I didn't *make* you," he said. "I asked."

"It amounts to the same thing," Kate said, suddenly on Georgette's side. "You have a talent for getting your way."

Colin stared at both women in vexation. "Why do I deserve all the fault? Some of it, I accept. But—"

Georgette cut him off to speak with Kate. "Please believe me. I did it because I thought it was best for you."

"It's fine, madam. It has turned out well."

"I hope my teachings helped you a little last night."

"They did, indeed," she replied, and she gave Colin a personal smile that could have started another epic battle for him to fight.

"Well, then," Georgette said, looking from Colin to her companion. "In that case, there is nothing left for me to do but offer my congratulations. I'm sorry we drank all the champagne after the party and have none on hand to toast your engagement."

Kate brought the children outside to the paddock after their morning lessons. She wasn't quite sure how to explain her engagement to them, or whether they needed to know how it had come about. But by the grins they kept exchanging she decided they understood more than was necessary for the moment. Perhaps Colin or Georgette had let the secret slip. Neither of them had a great regard for discretion. As far as she knew, however, they still had not told Brian the truth about his relationship to Colin.

She sighed in pleasure as Colin backed up his horse to the fence, offering her his hand. "Come inside the gate. Don't ask questions. Children, stay *outside*. We're about to give you a demonstration."

"Of what?" Kate whispered, as dubious of the mischief in his eyes as she was drawn to it.

"This is *The Abduction of a Governess*. You inspired me last night in more ways than one."

"Have you written a play in my honor?"

"Some men prefer to express their sentiments in physical action. Reach up your hand," he said with a supercilious flick of his gloved fingers.

Kate shook her head. "For what—? I'm not dressed for riding. I'm not *good* with horses."

He shook his head in disagreement. "You were very good with me last night."

She was at a temporary loss for words. When she recovered her voice, it emerged with her recognizable authority. "I am not getting up on that horse."

Clearly a man who did not recognize authority, he said, "Speak up, would you?"

"Bless my boots, you cannot have your way all the time."

He leaned down and without ceremony lifted her in front of him onto the saddle. She settled uncomfortably between his thighs while her own tender muscles tightened in opposition.

"This is not acceptable, Colin. Some acts are to be carried out only behind closed doors."

"Voice is everything to a horse, Kate. Why don't you

enjoy yourself? You are being abducted." His mouth grazed her ear. "There isn't much you can do about it."

His arm encircled her midsection. The horse eased into a canter toward the meadow, the steady movement lodging her backside in Colin's lap. His deep laughter soon relaxed her mood, and yet her entire body tensed, preparing for what, she wasn't sure. "What am I going to tell the children?"

"I have taken care of that. I explained that I'm abducting you."

The horse surged with her exclamation. "You did what?"

She felt a moment of unfettered freedom, of hope, of chains broken. She should have known better than to believe him. She wasn't a young girl who gave her heart away at the first promise. She was also not a woman to be thrown across a horse in abandon and appreciate it. "You colossal fool. You—" She was falling. She didn't trust the horse, and the horse did not trust her. She was certain it wanted to throw her, despite Colin's bone-crushing hold.

"I'm falling!"

"Sit straight. Lift up your rump."

"I'm losing my—" She was sliding off the saddle, unbalanced, gripping the pommel for dear life, when a blast exploded across the glade. Kate pulled herself upright and noticed two men crouching in the tall meadow grass. One sprang up, a gun in hand. She felt Colin's body tighten in reaction for only an instant.

Another shot rang out, and the horse balked. Kate pitched forward only to fall back against Colin's chest. A moment later his entire weight pressed her down against his thigh. Had he been shot? He had forced her so far to the side that all she could see were the horse's hooves churning through the meadow grass. She angled her head to look up his at his face.

"Colin?"

He glanced down at her once. His arm encircled her in a hold so tight that her ribs ached; the fury in his eyes would have frightened her at any other time; for now it gave her solace. Whoever had shot at them had missed.

"Colin, the children—"

"Put your head down, for God's sake, and be ready to run like hell for cover the instant your feet touch the ground. Hang on."

The animal went into a gallop that made Kate feel like a performer at an amphitheatre. Shaken to her skeleton, she had no choice but to do as Colin demanded. No sooner had they reached the gate than she slid limply to her feet. He wheeled the horse around, leaving her with a curt but unnecessary word of advice.

"Run."

Colin's last instinct was to turn and retreat in the face of hostile fire. The warrior in him rose up, ready to charge, take control. But he had neither a sword to swing nor a brigade at his back.

He had fought and won battles on horseback. The thirst for action still lingered in his blood. But he could hardly gallop down his attackers with Kate slung over his thigh and three children watching what he hoped they would misinterpret as part of Kate's abduction.

This wasn't a military campaign.

His mount had not been trained for war, and it took effort to keep her focused on his commands. He nudged the mare with his knee and then outside leg, hoping she would take the cue to turn. She did, and he abandoned Kate with faith in her common sense, which she displayed by bolting for the stables without a backward glance. No sooner had she disappeared inside, presumably to join the children, than Lovitt came flying around the paddock on the young gelding he had been training. "I've two guns, sir!" he shouted.

Colin searched the tall grass that rose into the hillock of brushwood and farther up to the copse. The two attackers had escaped; he assumed they knew the poachers' paths and hiding places that Colin had not explored.

"Split up," he said as Lovitt jogged alongside him, passing him one of the pistols he had instructed him to leave in the stables when the children took their lessons.

"There's only one route of escape from here, sir. It's over the knoll and down the lane. Unless they have their own mounts waiting, we can catch them easily."

"Are the children and the stable boys safe?"

"Tom took everyone who was outside into the stables." Lovitt bent to catch his breath. "Griswold had been getting water from the pump a few minutes earlier. I don't think they were shooting at anyone in particular."

"I don't give a damn if they were shooting at dandelions." He nudged the horse up the path strewn with old chestnuts and moldy leaves. "I want them found."

It was so easy a task that Colin had to swallow in disgust when he discovered the two culprits cowering behind the thick vines of honeysuckle that grew atop the low stone wall.

Boys, he thought. Seventeen at most. They might be farm laborers to judge by their leather breeches and long smocks. One wore a battered round hat.

"A child would have caught you," he said, yanking one about by his waistband and leaving Lovitt to flush out the other. "Where are your weapons?"

The older of the two shrank at Colin's savage growl. "We threw 'em in the grass when you came after us. No human rides a horse like that."

"You could have killed the other rider on my mount," Colin said, forcing the miserable excuse for manhood to the wall. "You fired a gun in the presence of children. I could happily strangle you right now."

The man shook his head in violent denial. He might have been full of bravado while hiding in the grass with a firearm. But flattened to the wall with his arms and legs spread and his deep-sunken eyes wide with terror, he looked more like a ginger man facing a fox than he did an assassin. "We only wanted to give you a scare. We fired into the air."

"Why?" Colin demanded, forcing him by the shoulder to his knees. The man whimpered.

"We were supposed to aim at you, but I couldn't shoot when you had that governess on your lap and little children watching. He didn't pay us enough."

"Shut up," his friend said, dirt and perspiration gathered on his upper lip. "We don't know nothing about—"

He didn't utter another word. He couldn't very well converse with Colin's hand around his throat and Lovitt's pistol poised to fire.

"Who paid you?" Colin said, searching the young man's worn jacket with his free hand and finding a knife concealed in his pocket. He handed it to Lovitt and picked up the gun they had dropped. "Lovitt, search the other one."

"I've got nothing to lose now," the older youth said. "It was Ramsey Hay, Mr. Earling's lawyer. He wanted the whore out of the house, and he wanted her old footman dead. He was convinced you were an imposter."

Colin frowned. The old footman? That had to be Griswold. Why kill a footman? Unless Hay knew that Griswold had witnessed the crime. "How many more attacks are planned?"

The youngest offender started to lift his head, only to

see the look on Colin's face and drop to his knees. "Three, sir," he said, cringing with his shoulders hunched.

"And the next?"

"Tonight."

"So if I take you to Mr. Hay's office and confront him with what you have told me, what do you suppose he'll say?"

The older boy snorted. "He won't say a word. He's gone. He left in the middle of the night. I visited his office this morning, but it was closed. His house is all shuttered up, too."

Colin expelled a harsh breath. Hay had been the key all along. He had managed Nathan Earling's affairs while he lived in Ireland, and he managed—or mismanaged— Mason's now. How could Earling not realize his solicitor was bleeding him dry? He had signed the invoices, took out insurance for his shipments. Or had his signature been forged?

"Where did he go?"

"I overheard his clerk say that he would be in London for some time," the eldest muttered.

Colin looked back at the house. Why should Mason return? He hadn't paid his lease, his paramour's pocket money, the upkeep of the servants and animals. Hay must have warned him to stay away. Had they made plans to meet in London? Would Mason leave the country on one of his own ships if he knew Colin had returned?

"I beg you, mister," said the youth in the round hat. "We didn't mean no harm—"

"Firing a gun into a paddock? Stay down on the ground."

He glanced back again at the manor, distracted by the flutter of white from the kitchen yard. What in the name of hell-foolery was that? It couldn't be. The laundress was hanging up the wash. Hadn't she been warned? Was the rest of the house vulnerable to attack? Were the gardeners pruning roses unaware?

"How many of you are there?" he demanded.

"How many—how many...how many what?" the boy in the round hat asked in confusion.

"How many of us attacked the house today, you jingle-brains," his partner said.

"It was just us two. Today."

A maid joined the laundress in the garden. It took all of Colin's willpower not to allow the little bastards to scuttle off to be squashed another time. "Lovitt," he said quietly, "do you think they deserve any mercy at all? Should we haul them before the magistrate?"

"The magistrate." The eldest youth spat in the grass. "I'm not trying to stir up more trouble here, but you're wasting your time. I've lived in this village all my life. What makes you think that the justice will take the word of a shit mucker to a doxy over one of East Crowleigh's own citizens?"

Colin lifted his brow. "When you argue your case with that eloquence, I'm almost tempted to agree."

The man elbowed his companion. "Take a lesson from—"

"But I don't," Colin said, turning his head to call his horse.

The man's smug grin vanished. "You don't what?"

Colin waved his pistol over their petrified faces. "I don't agree."

Chapter 32

$\mathscr{A}$ half hour crawled by before Kate decided it was safer to chance hiding the children in the house than to wait another minute crouched together in an empty stall. The silence from outside strained her nerves. She listened intently, but there was nothing—not a shot, a hoofbeat, a sparrow's chirp.

"I'm hungry," Charlie said, slumped across her lap with his face buried in the straw.

Etta had fallen asleep, and Brian was keeping watch through the loft window above with one of the two stable boys. "Charlie," he whispered down, "if you're really hungry, I'll give you some horse feed."

Charlie sat up, stretching his short arms in Kate's face. "Does it taste good?"

"It's delicious." Brian hung his head and arms down from the rafters like a bat.

"Don't tease him like that," Kate snapped in a voice that startled Etta from her nap. "It isn't fit to eat and you know it."

"Oats and apples, miss," Brian said, tossing a handful of hay into the air. "Why couldn't I have gone with Castle? Why did he pick you to ride instead of me? I weigh less. I don't bounce in the saddle like a sack of grain."

"But Mr. Castle doesn't want to marry you, Brian," Etta said. "He's asked Kate to be his wife, and she's going to leave us for the underhanded scoundrel."

"Etta!" Kate exclaimed. "Who on earth told you such a thing?"

Etta pulled a silk rosette from her skirt. "My mother did at breakfast. She said that you're leaving us without a care after all she's done for you."

"That isn't true." Kate felt suddenly desperate for a breath of air. "We can't stay in here for—"

"Hush!" Tom, the stable boy in the loft with Brian, cut off the conversation with an excited whisper. "I think I hear voices from outside. There's someone in the back garden. Oh, God. It's the girls hanging out the laundry. Are they daft?"

"The laundry?" Alarmed, Kate set Charlie aside, unlatched the stall door, and started to climb the ladder to see for herself. "What is it? What are you looking at, Tom?"

Brian fell back against the blankets laid over a thick matting of hay. "He's gawking at the disgusting garments that girls have to wear underneath their dresses."

"They can't have any idea what happened," Kate said as she peered over Tom's shoulder. "They wouldn't be in the garden doing chores if they knew." She returned to the ladder and slid down to the lowest rung. "Tom, put your eyeballs back in your skull and come down here. Henry, you stay at the window and keep watch."

"Yes, miss," Tom said, dropping down beside her into the main stable block.

Kate moistened her bottom lip. "We're going to make a run for the house."

"What if we get shot?" Etta asked, staring at the unraveled flounce on her skirt.

Charlie rubbed his eyes. "Then we'll die."

"Those men are gone," Kate said firmly. "No one is going to die. But I am thirsty."

Brian looked down from the loft. "I'll stay here with the horses. There's a bottle of wine up here, by the way."

"Thank you, Brian. I do not need Dutch courage, but I insist you come inside."

"But I want to help," Brian said.

"You protect the children and Miss Kate. As soon as you're inside the kitchen, signal me from the hall window." Tom grinned down at Etta and Charlie. "You little runts are going to run like hell."

Etta's mouth dropped open. "Ooh. Miss—"

Tom shook his head. "Who's man enough to watch your mother and old Nan? Not Bledridge. Not Griswold, God love him. You need to rally the other footmen together."

Brian, disgruntled and disappointed, slid down the ladder and turned his back to Kate the moment she reached for his shoulder. "One day," he said, "I might really run away, and no one will find me."

"What'll you do for food?" Charlie asked in concern.

Kate herded them to the door. She'd worry later about Brian's threats. For now all she wanted was to see Colin and Lovitt riding back across the meadow, bringing word that the siege was over and that they could feel secure again in the house.

Kate took a deep breath. "Let's do this before I lose my nerve. I can't stand waiting another minute."

"I'm unlocking the doors," Tom called up over his shoulder to Henry. "Now, all of you start to run, and don't stop for anything until you're inside the house."

They made a dash through the wash drying on the clothesline, bringing down a few wet sheets in their rush.

"Hey!" Cora said indignantly, one hand on her hip. "Do you have to play chase through the clean laundry?

Joan and I just finished hanging up Madam's French drawers and stockings. They don't wash themselves! I have raw knuckles from all that cold water and soap."

"French drawers, indeed!" Kate exclaimed, snatching a stocking from the ground. "This isn't a game. Two men shot at us from the meadow."

"Where is Castle?" Cora asked, eyes growing wide.

"Somewhere safe, I pray. Please, grab Joan and get inside. Hurry!"

Kate grasped Etta and Charlie by the hand, glancing back to make sure Brian had followed. Although she couldn't risk the time to make sure, she thought she spotted Colin in the horse chestnut trees.

Moments later the six of them burst as one through the kitchen door, Kate pushing the children to the fore. Charlie and Etta grabbed two chairs and dragged them to the window. Brian charged up the stairs and into the hall for sentry duty. Bledridge emerged from the pantry, took one look at the muddy footprints on the floor, and threw up his hands in disgust.

"Miss," he said through his nostrils, as Kate plucked first Etta and then Charlie off their chairs. "I understand that your engagement is foremost on your mind, but—"

"Make sure all the doors are locked and that everyone is brought to the library."

He paled. "Whatever for?"

"We've been attacked again, Bledridge," she answered distractedly. "I apologize for the mud. And to Cora and Joan for bringing down the washing. It couldn't be helped."

"Attacked, miss?" he said in horror. "How did it happen?"

"We were shot at in the paddock," Charlie blurted out.

Bledridge looked over the boy's head to Kate. "Is this true, miss?"

Etta nodded vigorously. "Ten times."

"We were shot at once," Kate said hastily. "That was enough. Castle made us hide in the stables while he and Lovitt gave chase. They are still outside."

"Dear God," Bledridge said, staring at the dogs snoozing around the hearth. "Not a bark to warn us." He swung around to withdraw into the pantry for his blunderbuss. "Bolt all the doors," he said when he reappeared. "Close the curtains. I fought against the colonies under Farmer George, and I will not surrender again."

Cook bustled down the stairs from the hall, stopping in breathless agitation when she saw the blunderbuss in the butler's hand. "I do not think that will help Madam in her current state."

"What's wrong with Mrs. Lawson?" Kate asked, dreading the answer. A governess could only do what she could do.

"Griswold brought her the morning post and she lost her head over a letter that he helped her read. She's been flinging things about all morning. She was furious that you couldn't be found."

Kate propelled the children toward the stairs. "I wonder whether this letter has anything to do with the men who shot at us."

"Bless me," Cook gasped, standing aside to let Bledridge up the steps. "Not again. What are we to do?"

Bledridge straightened his tall frame. "Everyone to the library. There's supposed to be a secret passage inside the wall. I don't know if it's big enough to fit anyone, but we might squeeze in the children and Madam, if she can manage to stop her shrieking long enough to hide."

"What's wrong with my mother?" Charlie asked. "Was she shot? Do you think Mr. Castle has been killed?"

"I—"

Brian shouted from the hall above the kitchen. "He's riding home now! Lovitt's with him."

"How do you know?" Kate asked, her heart thumping in her throat.

"I saw them from the window when I signaled to Tom and Henry that we were safe. They're coming home!"

Kate could have collapsed with relief. "And they looked unharmed? At least from what you could tell?"

"Of course they do," Brian replied rather proudly. "But I don't know about the two men they rode down. I think Castle might have killed them. They're lying in the grass."

Colin and Lovitt entered the kitchen fifteen minutes later to a round of applause. Cook wept and said that Colin was more heroic than Wellington at Waterloo. The maids gathered around him in awe, and Bledridge brought out his best port and glasses.

Kate hung back, letting Colin take in this tribute, which he only laughed off. "Put away that bottle, Bledridge. I would prefer a beer. Lovitt?"

"Yes, please, sir."

"And let's take some grub and drink out to the stable boys."

"Are we safe, sir?" Cook asked, drying her eyes.

"I believe so. But we won't let down our guard again." His gaze lifted to Kate. "I'm sorry about the gallop. Were you hurt?"

She was more afraid of horses than ever before; her knees still felt shaky, but she wouldn't admit it. "All I need is a good soak in hot water."

And him.

She needed him more than anything.

Chapter 33

Colin couldn't sleep that night. No one in the house could. He lay fully clothed on Kate's bed, his arms encircling her, his thumb idly caressing the curves of her breasts through her shift. It was the first time she hadn't complained about his boots or the fact that the children had been allowed to stay up with Cook to bake scones for breakfast.

Everyone in the house had praised Colin for his heroics, with the exception of Georgette, who had taken her nightly laudanum before Kate understood why she had gone into hysterics over a letter. There had been such an uproar over the day's incident that it was universally decided to let the mistress of the manor sleep off her distress.

Colin didn't feel like a hero. He couldn't protect the house alone. Perhaps it was time to reach out to his family, pride be buggered, and ask for help. He had not kept his promise to his father's memory, but he had tried.

"What are you thinking?" Kate whispered, staring at the assortment of pistols that had replaced the books and papers on her whatnot table. "Will they come back?"

"I doubt it." He released her from his arms, dropping his legs to the floor. "But I'm not about to take another chance. We're leaving here the day after tomorrow. If it were possible, we'd be gone tonight."

She sat up, her hair cascading over her shoulders. "To where? Where in the world can we take refuge on such short notice and not attract attention as we go?"

"My cousin Grayson has his country seat in Kent," he said, rubbing his face. "I'll send Lovitt ahead to alert the caretaker."

"He must have a palace if he's able to take our brood under his wing. Are you sure he won't object?"

"One never needed an excuse or an invitation in our family to stay out a storm in past days. I haven't any reason to believe a basic Boscastle tenet is no longer respected."

"Yes, but this is more than a storm."

"Grayson is the Marquess of Sedgecroft. From what Georgette has said, he has weathered quite a few storms and scandals since his father's death."

"A man that important won't mind sheltering three children, Nan, and the servants?"

"Don't forget the horses, dogs, and a cat," he said with a droll smile.

She shook her head in doubt. "How big is this house?"

"It's a vast estate with a lake and wooded hills covered with apple trees and caves where the children can play and forget what happened here."

She slipped to the floor and knelt before him. "You look tired."

"You look like the woman I dreamed about last night. I don't think you should put your hand that high on my leg."

"How do you know the marquess is there?"

"He might not be. But there will be a caretaker, gamekeeper, and gardeners to greet us before we enter the gates. Our families met every Christmas and on various occasions through the years. The grown-ups would dance and hold parties and play cards. The boy cousins took the girls captive in the treasure cave."

"We can't simply show up on the doorstep like refugees and expect a warm reception."

"I'm wagering that we can. While we wait for Lovitt and Tom to return, you must help Georgette pack what can fit into one carriage. You should start tonight."

"One carriage? Georgette would need a wagon for her perfumes and powders alone."

"We'll send the footmen back for anything we've forgotten."

"What about the horses and dogs?"

"I haven't decided how we'll take them. We aren't leaving the animals here unprotected." He leaned down and looked into her eyes. "Courage, Kate. You have a Visigoth now as your guardian. If anyone attacks us on the road, they will be in for an unpleasant surprise."

"I don't want another surprise," she whispered. "What about Mason? What about the years you've lost and your honor?"

"I'll have to live with that. The world won't end." He curled his hands around her face. "But it would if anything happened to your or your makeshift family."

She swallowed. "Family—what will yours think of us? You dropping in with your former mistress in one hand, and me in the other."

"Don't give it a moment's thought. Decadence runs in the blood."

"It's not going to run in Brian's blood if I have any say in his future. When are you going to tell him?"

"Before we leave." His fingers tightened possessively around her face. "Neither Brian nor I intend to lose you. I had, however, wanted us to be married before I unleashed the family on you."

"Unleashed?"

"I just asked you to marry me. Lovitt will arrive at Kent with a request for someone in the family to obtain a special license. Will you?"

She smiled slowly.

"Shall I get on my knees?"

"I'd like that, but grant me a favor first—hide all those guns while you propose. I don't want anything to mar my memory of this moment."

He lowered his hands and slid beside her to the floor. She stared up at him expectantly. "Kate—"

"What if Mason *does* return? All you have is the word of two hooligans. What will Georgette say?"

"Darling," he said, "it might help if you sat in the chair."

She looked at the chair behind him and laughed, rising to seat herself above him. "There."

"Do you find my wish to make a proper proposal amusing?" he asked.

"Not at all."

"Then why are you laughing?"

"I'm not used to all this attention."

He bent on one knee. "Beloved—"

She stared over his shoulder, clearly not as impressed as she should be.

"What is it now?"

"I can still see one of the guns."

"Dear God." He rose, wrested a sheet from the bed, and threw it over the table. "Is that better?"

She bit the inside of her cheek. "Yes."

He bent on one knee again. "Katherine, will you do me the honor of being my wife?"

She slid from the chair and flung her arms around his neck, kissing him with the passionate instincts he had taught her to trust. "I love you, Colin. I love you so much it terrifies me. Honor. Dishonor. Right now it doesn't matter."

He kissed her even as he gently disentangled himself from her stranglehold. "And you'll do anything I ask?"

"Almost—yes, I will. Do you want me to prove it?"

She undressed him on the floor, peeling off his jacket between hot, hard kisses, unbuttoning his vest and pulling his shirt from his waistband. Breathless, still on her knees, she stared up at him as he stood to take off his trousers and lift his shirt to uncover the body whose shadow contours and strength she craved to touch, pleasure, and explore.

She caught his wrists and pulled him back down to his knees. His erection rose stiff against her as he unlaced her shift. His arms encircled her, fusing her bare flesh to his. His hard chest felt like heaven. She kissed his neck, indulged her senses in the scent of his warm skin.

He opened his thighs, lowering his hands to grasp the globes of her bottom. "You've got me on the floor now," he whispered. "You know what that means?"

He leaned back slowly until his shoulders touched the carpet. She fell against him as he stretched his legs out, trapping her between his thighs.

His phallus looked like polished wood, and before she realized what he wanted her to do, he lifted her by the waist and lowered her onto the entire length of his erection. She shuddered, not breathing, as he raised his hips. He reached up to caress her swollen breasts. Brazenly she rubbed her nipples across his palms, tempting him as he tempted her. "Is this what you had in mind?" he asked.

She arched her back, felt his hand tighten to hold her still. "You can't expect me to carry on a conversation in this position," she whispered, the words broken by the shallow breaths she managed to steal.

He felt larger than she could possibly take inside her. But when she lifted herself slightly from his impalement, he locked both his hands around her hips and drew her down with a force she felt to the back of her throat.

"Why don't we talk later?" he whispered, his voice deep with unabashed pleasure. "Relax, kneel astride me."

She shook her head, her hair spilling over his neck. "You're rather big. Give me a little time."

"Don't make me wait."

"Why not?" She raised herself until his cock almost slid from her sheath. His body trembled. His face darkened.

She lowered herself down hard, gloving his prick to the root. A stab of pain momentarily slowed her, but the sensual urgency in his eyes reminded her that she would endure anything to please him. She felt the fullness of his cock to the tip of her womb, the pit of her belly.

He groaned, one hand still teasing her nipples, the other grasping her bottom. It seemed to Kate that her body's moisture eased her discomfort enough that she could concentrate on him. His breathing became erratic. He lowered his hand from her breast to the bud of her sex and played her until she was half-wild, raising herself up and down on his shaft without volition.

She undulated her hips, lifted again, and bore down on his cock with a wanton instinct she could not control.

He exhaled through his teeth. "When did you learn to move your ass like that?"

"Do you like it?"

"Sweetheart, the only thing I'd like better is for you to take me deeper."

"Deeper? I—"

He tightened his lower back and drove upward before she could finish explaining that she thought he would tear her apart. But her body stretched, sliding up and down on his with an unbridled eroticism that he acknowledged with a deep groan. It was easier now to take pleasure in his sexuality, and in her own. The stark desire on his face as he watched her encouraged her efforts, promised a reward.

"Perfect," he whispered. "Don't stop."

How could she stop when she shared his passion? She moved to an instinctive beat, pressure building, her muscles trembling to hold him inside. He stroked steadily at the nub of her sex. She felt her spine flex as the friction became too intense to bear.

"Not yet," he said, his eyes locked with hers.

"When?" Her eyes slowly closed; his image was seared in her mind. She writhed as he took control, quickened the pace, heightened her need until she broke in a beautiful climax that rendered her helpless, his to use at will.

"Now," he said in a low voice that intensified every emotion, every feeling that flooded her. "Let me show you my love."

He drew his hands down to her bottom to keep her steady as he surged, his breathing harsh, his hips bucking. She opened her eyes, the spasms still rippling through her belly when he growled and pumped one last time inside her.

She watched the elemental darkness on his face ease. She felt his warm semen seep out of her body and slide down her thighs. His eyes held hers in uninhibited possession. The moment spun into an eternity. She had learned many things from Georgette's life as well as from her memoirs. But it was only now that she understood how sacred was the aftermath of intimacy.

"Was it too rough?" he asked, caressing her shoulder.

"Yes," she replied, trying to hide a smile.

"And you liked it?" he inquired.

She released a sigh. "I refuse to flatter your conceit with an answer. Are the scattered remnants of my composure not enough to satisfy you?"

He sat up, still embedded in her, and hooked one arm around her neck to kiss her in grateful contentment. "I told you that I would make a rider of you yet."

She nestled her head against his shoulder. She soaked in the feel of him. Strong, unrestrained, to be her husband. Hers to spoil at her leisure. She shivered in pleasure at the thought of the years ahead. "Let's get you into bed again," he said at length. "I have to leave."

"Already?"

He withdrew from her body, rising to lift and gently drop her on the bed. "You said all night," she whispered.

"I'll be back. The other men and I are sharing watch."

She stared at his profile, afraid he was trying to bolster her courage. "Do you think anything will happen?"

He turned to the washstand and moistened two towels. He brought one back to the bed to gently bathe her, lingering on the scars that marred her skin. With the other he briskly cleaned his body and dressed before she could reach for the robe at the end of the bed.

"Sleep," he said, placing his hands on her shoulders. "I don't think they'll ever return. But I'm not taking another chance." He hesitated. "Should I tell Georgette the plans or will you?"

"I will."

"Thank God. The best of luck."

She sat up to slip on her robe. Goodness knew where her night rail was. Perhaps in the day's ill-fated washing. "Be careful, Colin. I won't rest until I see you again."

Chapter 34

*S*he should have known better; there was no rest for the wicked or for fallen women. She sat up guiltily as the door clattered open and a round figure in aquamarine silk flew to her bedside.

"Are they here again?" she asked, slowly recognizing Georgette in the dark. "Should I wake the children? Do I have time to dress properly?"

"I don't know," Georgette said wryly, dragging a chair to the bedside. "Do you? You don't appear to have time for the person who has gainfully employed you for over a decade."

"I—oh, madam. I'm sorry. It was a wretched day. I had to feed the children and stay with them until they slept. Then the other servants and I went about locking—"

Georgette's eyes gleamed. "You didn't lock your door against a certain gentleman."

Kate took Georgette's hand. "No. I didn't."

Georgette sighed deeply. "What did I tell you? It was fate."

"I suppose it was."

Georgette rose, taking the taper in its brass holder from the night table to light the wick from the dying embers of the fire. After she returned the burning taper to its place, she went back to the chair and drew from her bodice a crumpled letter.

"Do you know what this is?" she asked, charging on before Kate had a chance to read a single line. "It is a notice to terminate my contract with Mason as well as to evict me from his house."

Kate rescued the letter from Georgette's fist. "Well, we knew we couldn't stay here, and we knew what sort of man he—"

"I was wrong again. It only proves what my father always said. I'm stupid, Kate. I thought Mason cared for me. I could believe anything except that his feelings for me were false."

"Madam," Kate said, staring at the signature scrawled across the bottom of the letter. "I believed, too, that Mr. Earling loved you. He must have been upset when he wrote this. His signature is slightly different from what I've seen of it before."

"You mean when he *used* to write me love letters? Obviously he doesn't love me enough now to return or answer to Colin once and for all."

"Loving you may not have made him brave."

"Everyone knows better than a whore. I had to have Griswold read this humiliation to me because the words made my head spin."

"Are you still angry at me, madam?" Kate asked in hesitation.

Georgette gave her a vacant look. "For what?"

Kate shook her head, laughing helplessly even as she held back tears. "I do love you."

"Good," Georgette snatched the letter from Kate's hands and tossed it over her shoulder into the fire.

"Wait! I wanted to look at it again in better light."

"It can burn in the brightest flames of hell for all I care," Georgette said. "We have much to do before Colin takes you from me. We shall finish my book even if we spend your honeymoon chained to your desk to write from morning until midnight."

"I can't imagine he would agree to that."

"You can't spend all your time in bed with him, can you?"

Kate blushed, rising to escape behind the dressing screen.

"I forgot," Georgette said. "Of course you can. We'll have to work every spare minute in the meantime. I'll publish the damned book if only for a pittance. It's the only revenge left for a woman forced to rely on her wiles."

Chapter 35

*M*ason Earling sat in glassy-eyed silence at the table of his private room in the riverfront tavern that lay between Southampton and East Crowleigh. His solicitor ate heartily of a thick slab of steak and kidney pie. But Mason thought he might be ill. He took a deep draught of his beer, his stomach sour as Hay crammed a huge portion of pie into his mouth.

"I warned you, Mason. I told you that taking Boscastle's old lover as your mistress would lure him to you. Stupid male pride."

"I have always cared for Mrs. Lawson."

Hay grunted. "This is why your accounts are depleted. You throw money at a harlot when you should be bolstering the investments the company has made."

Mason set down his mug in consternation. "The last I heard from London, the firm had started returning high profits again. Did I misread the recent statements?"

Hay scowled, regarding Mason as if he was too simple to understand the basic machinations of his own business. "Possibly. You've been so engrossed in your mistress that I doubt you are all there."

"How is she? Is everything well at the house?"

Hay stabbed a chunk of kidney with his knife. "She is as selfish and frivolous as a Covent Garden whore. Why you couldn't have found an heiress to enrich your coffers, I'll never understand. And why you keep paying for that incompetent staff of servants is beyond me. That old footman should be in the grave by now. That hag of a nursemaid belongs right beside him."

"I have loved Georgette for years," Mason said, flushing in resentment.

"Have you?" Hay eyed him in disdain. "What a pity she doesn't love you."

"I don't know what you mean."

"She is sleeping with the man who plans to kill you."

He shook his head in bewilderment. "You can't mean Boscastle? He's in—"

"—Georgette's bed, which I believe you purchased and had brought from London to please her fickle tastes."

Mason reached for his beer. The mug shook in his grasp. "It is impossible. How could he be that brazen? He must be insane. Haven't you done anything to stop him?"

Hay sat back, not a trace of sympathy on his thin face. "Do you realize how highly placed—how influential—his family is?"

"But it's mad. My father didn't murder Viscount Norwood."

"No," Hay said thoughtfully. "Your father admitted on his deathbed that you poisoned the man."

Mason let the mug drop to the table. "How do you know that?"

"There were other witnesses in the room besides Colin Boscastle and the priests. Two physicians, a blood letter, and three business associates. Your father condemned you with his dying words."

"But I was not even of age," Mason said, sweat soaking the back of his linen neckcloth. "What motive would I have to kill my father's partner?"

"I don't know, Mason. But it was you who poured the viscount's wine that night, wasn't it?"

"I never—I barely remember anything that happened before the viscount became ill. It was thirteen years ago."

"You went to the sideboard and fetched a bottle of wine. You filled the viscount's glass, didn't you?"

Mason's head began to pound. "Damn you, I don't remember!"

"Yes, you do," Hay said without emotion. "There were witnesses who saw what you did that night. Was I there? Do you remember?"

Mason put his hand over his eyes. "Not everything, but I know I never poisoned anyone. I don't believe there were witnesses at all. I don't believe my father accused me of murdering Joshua Boscastle, either."

"Think back. You felt important because you were invited to attend a dinner and the Boscastle brothers had to stay home."

Mason swore under his breath. "I—"

"You had a rivalry with Colin over the slut you couldn't have then. You don't even have a claim on her now. She has shifted her allegiance to him without a qualm."

"This isn't true—"

"It is."

"You weren't there that night!"

"But are you positive you didn't pour the viscount's wine?"

Mason stood, shutting his eyes until the throbbing in his head subsided. "I don't know. Maybe— I—"

Hay rose in undisguised disgust. "What a useless performance to put on in your own defense. You cannot even convince yourself of your innocence."

"But I'm not on trial. Do *you* believe I committed murder?"

"It doesn't matter what I believe."

"I want him out of my house. I refuse to live the rest of my life unable to sleep at night for fear he will destroy me."

"He is destroying you."

"Then what do I do?" Mason said raggedly. "Face him in a duel?"

"He would kill you," Hay said, putting his hand on Mason's shoulder. "And if by some miracle you survived, it would not end there."

"No," Mason agreed, his face pallid.

"Will you take my advice now?" Hay asked slowly. "I may have an answer, but it would require both of us meeting in London, and I have to plan for your escape."

"My escape?" Mason said, too stunned to do anything but agree.

"You will leave here tomorrow by public stage for London. You must not speak of your intentions to anyone, not even your footmen. Dismiss them today."

"Will you at least give Georgette a message from me?"

"Yes. I will pay her off and terminate your arrangement as is written in the contract for such an eventuality."

Mason breathed out a sigh. "I will have nothing, then."

"You'll have your life. Be grateful for that."

"You haven't sent her the letter of termination yet, have you?" Mason said, suddenly suspicious.

"That is an insult. Do you believe I would draw up a contract you hadn't read or forge your signature except in the event of an emergency? Why do you even ask? I am your oldest, perhaps your only friend."

Mason felt himself sink into a pit of despair. "I have sent her presents and letters—I promised I would. And she promised to write to me."

Hay gave him a humorless smile. "What more proof do you need of her betrayal?"

Chapter 36

On the morning of their departure, Kate discovered Georgette seated at her dressing table, drably clad in a gray silk gown she had last worn in half mourning for her husband. "Really, madam," she said. "Isn't that taking fashion to express one's sentiment a little far? I know how deeply you feel the loss of leaving this house and the hopes that you had for Mr. Earling, but that is rather morbid."

Georgette frowned at Kate's reflection in the mirror. "The only reason I'm wearing gray is because it travels well. I'd rather die than meet members of the aristocracy with the children's fingerprints on my gown. I intend to change the minute we arrive. Have you seen the processional outside?"

Kate walked to the window. It was a typical overcast misty morning and yet excitement enlivened the estate. Liveried footmen darted about loading luggage into four black traveling carriages, five wagons, and a crested coach drawn by six white horses. Even the dogs seemed to sense the air of excitement, barking and tripping up the servants scurrying across the lawn.

"You don't have to wear gray, madam. Besides, it's too

tight in the bosom. I'll travel in a separate coach with the children so that you will arrive looking as bedazzling as ever."

"It will be the last time," Georgette said with a wistful shrug.

Then suddenly they were in each other's arms, holding back tears, talking at the same time, saying anything but that they would soon be parted, perhaps each lost without the other.

Georgette composed herself first. "Undo my gown."

"Why?"

"You are right. The children won't be allowed to embrace me until after I've been introduced."

"But your belongings are packed."

"Kate, a woman can't change her past, but she can change her clothes—which will be the first thing that Brian's family will notice about me. We haven't left yet. Could you not ask the footmen prettily to help you find a more suitable gown for me?"

"I don't want to disturb all their work."

"I'll never ask anything of you again."

"We both know that isn't—"

A screech cut through the outer hall.

Georgette turned; Kate moved straight to the door. "What is this unearthly clatter on the stairs?" Georgette whispered. "Do you think they've come for us?"

"Hide in the dressing closet," Kate said quietly. "No one could have sneaked into the house with that cavalcade outside."

"Of course they could. What better time than when everyone is distracted?"

Packing up the house reminded Colin of moving camp for battle. Mason had not fulfilled his promises as a provider or protector. Therefore, Georgette had convinced the servants to remove from the walls the most valuable portraits, tapestries, and candle sconces that time allowed. "Where does she intend to put them?" Colin asked Bledridge in consternation.

"It isn't right for a butler to belittle his mistress, sir, but mark me, she'll find a place. She's never been on the market for more than six months at a time."

"Six months?" That was half a year of Colin and Kate living in cramped quarters with—well, he'd find a place, too. Maybe he would buy a farm. It was better they live under one crowded roof than to force anyone onto the streets. He searched from corner to corner of the music room. The morning light broke across the bare spaces on the parquetry floor.

"Wasn't there a piano in here?"

"Yes, sir, there was."

"Don't tell me—"

"Yes, it's in the last wagon. Lovingly wrapped in Mr. Earling's tapestries."

"My God," Colin said. "So much for a subtle escape."

A shriek from the main body of the house, followed by a series of bumps, drew Colin and Bledridge to the door in alarm. Colin ran out toward the staircase, from the top of which the chaos seemed to issue.

Another scream of unbridled emotion pierced his ears. Bledridge stationed himself behind the arm Colin rested on the balustrade. "I'll catch whoever lands first. You take the second."

"Yes, sir," Bledridge said, positioning himself, knees bent.

Colin raised his voice. "Don't hurt your sis— *Stop!*"

Too late. Charlie had already launched Etta down the stairs in a brass-hinged chest, the lid thudding, his behind bumping on a silver serving tray alongside her.

"Watch out below!" Charlie shouted, losing his cap as he, on his tray, and Etta, in the chest, gained speed.

Colin vaulted up three steps, swooping Etta into his left arm, halting the runaway chest with his right, and leaving Charlie for Bledridge to rescue.

"What'd you do that for, sir?" Charlie asked, arms and legs flailing in the air. "We were having a race, and I was about to overtake her."

"You could have cracked your heads open," he replied, setting down his squirming captive in the hall.

"You sound like Miss Kate," Charlie said dolefully.

Colin blinked. He'd just realized that Etta was wearing a corset over her traveling dress. "Is that what I think it is?" he demanded. He looked down at the trunk, whose contents had been tossed about the stairs: sleeves, gloves, stockings, fans. "Where did this all come from? Your mother's closet? We can't carry another piece of luggage on our parade. And Etta, take that thing off, or she will be furious."

Etta stepped out of the unlaced corset. "These are Nan's. They hold her together. She forgot to pack. She can't go without them."

"I should hope not," Bledridge said, shuddering. "Excuse me, sir," he said to Colin, putting Charlie on his feet. "Shall I gather up the disturbing evidence before anyone else sees it?"

"Please do." Colin gestured Charlie and Etta to sit on the bottom step. He paused as a door above groaned open in the sudden quiet.

"Now you're done for," he said quietly. "Kate's heard. Take this last piece of advice from me: When we arrive at my cousin's house, this conduct—these antics—must continue. I cannot abide perfectly behaved children. And don't make me tell you again."

*   *   *

Georgette took Brian into the garden for the last time. She had been afraid of this moment since he was born, but finally she had dredged up her courage and told him who he was. He accepted the truth with a maturity that stunned her.

"I loved my other father," he said, walking slowly beside her.

She smiled sadly. "He loved you, too. There's no reason we should not respect his memory."

"He was old," Brian said. "He never took us outside."

"Yes, but he was good to us when he was alive. He gave us a home."

Brian bent to pet one of the dogs sniffing at his feet. "Does that mean Etta and Charlie aren't my brother and sister?"

"Of course they are. I'm still your mother, too, but you and the two terrors have different fathers."

"Why didn't he come back to see me?" Brian asked, his brow furrowing.

"I didn't tell him about you," Georgette said softly, looking around to see Colin coming toward them. "Ask him yourself. I'll go for a stroll with the dogs. You can have a manly talk about it."

Brian looked at her in concern. "Will he take me away?"

"Not forever," she said. "I think he'll do what is best."

Colin looked up at the window for courage. He knew Kate was watching, and he thought he saw Nan's withered face between the curtains, too. What was he supposed to say to his son? It had been easier to behave normally when he hadn't known for certain that Brian was his.

Brian stared at him in curiosity.

"Your mother told you, I assume. What do you make of the situation?"

"It depends, sir."

Colin frowned. "On what?"

"Well, I don't mind being your son, except you're rather bossy, but I do mind if I can't be with the rest of my family."

"I'll never stop your family from seeing you," Colin said, hoping that was the proper response. "You'll have other family, too. Uncles and aunts and young relatives like you."

"Someone has to take care of my mother, sir. She doesn't know how to do much of anything except—"

"Yes," Colin said before Brian blurted out what they both understood. "We'll find a way to take care of her, if necessary. All of you. Is that acceptable to you?"

Brian shrugged. "It's not like I have a choice, is it?"

"Well, you're not exactly going to be hauled off with a ball and chain."

"Can I have a horse?"

"Absolutely. And we'll ride together all around town."

"Not with Kate or my mother. They're awful about horses."

Colin laughed. "But they have qualities that make up for that failing."

Brian glanced up at the window.

Colin wanted to put his arms around his son. He said, "I'm sorry I wasn't here to watch you grow up."

"I know why," Brian said. "I'd have gone with you if I had been allowed."

"I love you."

Brian grinned. "Go on."

"You don't have to say anything for now. We'll work it out together. Just swear to me you won't run away again. And, Brian, I'll never stop you from seeing your family. If you are unhappy living with me and Kate, I'll understand if you want to leave."

"But not run away?"

Colin grinned back at him. "You won't ride that fine horse I promised for months if you do such a stupid thing again."

Chapter 37

A small crowd of villagers stood at the side of the road to witness the courtesan's departure. Georgette waved from the window as if she had been crowned queen and now, to the regret of her subjects, must depart for the royal palace. Squire Billingsley's son stared at her in love-stricken sorrow. The rector bowed his head in an attitude of prayer, perhaps of thanksgiving to see her go, perhaps for her redemption.

Kate thought it might be a little of both.

"I told Nan I had admirers," Georgette said, heaving a sigh. "Did you notice the three men cursing outside the driveway? I never failed to give them a smile of gratitude for their services. It grieves them to lose the small light I brought into their lives."

"It grieves them to lose the money you owe them, madam," Kate retorted. "One is the haberdasher, the other the linen draper. The third, I believe, is—"

"Let Mason face his creditors," Colin said, smiling ruthlessly at the thought. "If there is anything left of him after he reviews his books."

Georgette's mood brightened. "Do you think your family will recover some lost funds?"

"If I do, I'll pay for the piano."

"And lessons?"

"Georgette, if any of those three children show the least aptitude for music—and shrieks don't count—I shall buy you a private concert hall."

"I suppose I have the marquess to thank for this escort," Colin said to the head groom of his cousin's household, who would supervise the journey.

"In part, sir. But it is Lieutenant Colonel Lord Heath Boscastle and his wife who are planning a party to welcome you this weekend. His lordship hopes that this guard will be sufficient for your travels."

Colin's mirthful gaze took in the caravan from its gilt-paneled coach to the pack wagon and pony at the end. Brian sat astride the gray that Colin had bought from the blacksmith the previous night. Lovitt sat mounted a few paces ahead at the gate.

"I'm humbled," Colin said to the groom. "I came here to do what I thought was right. I caused chaos, and now my family, who I abandoned, answers my call for help the first time I ask."

"Sir," the groom murmured, touching his forehead in respect.

"Do we have to sit in the driveway all day?" Charlie called out from the window of one of the smaller, black carriages.

Colin nodded to the groomsman. "Thank you. It's best to get on the road as soon as we can."

Tom, watching Colin's every move with pride, hastened forward to mount the mare he had been holding by the reins. Colin hadn't taken a step before he noticed Brian turn to look at him in distress.

"Sir," he mouthed. *"Sir."*

Colin glanced past his son and through the gates to the slightly built fair-haired man in a gray frock coat and buff trousers who was trying to slip into the hubbub unnoticed. He carried a bulging leather bag and stopped in uncertainty before he strode past Kate's carriage to where Colin stood.

A few of the maids waved shyly at the man from their windows. Etta started to shout at him that her cough was gone and that she had passed it to Nan, who had given it to her mother, and that they had the tomcat in the carriage.

"Hold still, child," Nan cried, and pulled Etta back into the coach, drawing the curtain to shield either the world from disobedient children or the children from the disgraceful world.

Colin straightened. He didn't reach for his gun. What he saw in young Stanley Wilkes' face could not be fought by physical force.

"Sir?" Stanley said, swallowing hard. "I've come to ask your permission to speak with Miss Kate alone for a few moments."

Colin felt a muscle quiver in his cheek. "She's in the head coach."

Stanley looked up, seeming to lose his nerve.

"She's traveling with Mrs. Lawson," Colin added. Wilkes was good-looking, now that Colin saw him in the daylight. Tall, lithe, but not a weakling. He had an unassuming face wreathed in red-gold hair, and he had gentle eyes. What else was he carrying besides his bag? How had he arrived, on foot or by horseback? Did he intend to leave by himself?

"I'd like a word with her in private, sir, if you don't mind," he said again.

Why wouldn't Colin mind? Was he a fool? Why should he give this unromantic Romeo another chance at Kate when he'd told her quite bluntly that she didn't pass his family's approval?

"You'll have to ask her yourself," Colin said, his tone grim. "Please be aware that we need to be safely away from here before long."

"I understand, sir." But Wilkes had already started to weave his way to her coach before he waited for Colin to respond.

What was Colin supposed to do? Act as if there was nothing unusual about leaving his fiancée alone with the man she had hoped to marry before he'd had the devil's fortune to find her? He paced to the end of the caval-cade. He was anxious to leave.

Kate had descended from the carriage. Wilkes was walking her slowly toward the wall where Colin had kissed her. The best mistake he'd ever made in his life. What were they talking about? Wilkes bent his head, obscuring Kate's face from Colin's sight.

Kate gazed down at the grass. She couldn't look into Stanley's earnest face and try to act as if she wasn't aware that Colin was waiting. She could hardly pay attention to a word of what Stanley was saying. And that bruise on his forehead from her slipper. She winced inwardly.

"I've thought about it," he said. "I've thought about nothing else since the last night I saw you."

"It?" she said faintly, noticing how many burdock weeds had sprung up in the grass. Would Mason ever return to notice, or would Colin find him first?

"Us," Stanley said, dropping the hand he'd extended so he could touch her shoulder.

"I wouldn't do that," she whispered. "He's acting as if he can't see us, but he can."

He glanced back at the carriages, where Colin stood, tall, wide shouldered, in the stance of a protective fiancé. "Do you want to run away from him? From this life?"

She started. "Now? Here?"

"Well, I'd heard you were leaving, but if I'd known you would be caught in this procession when I arrived, I'd have come to you last night to propose."

"To propose marriage? Are you out of your mind? Now? Do your parents know?"

He swallowed. "No. It won't be easy for us, starting out together with the little money I've saved—"

"It won't be a life at all," she interrupted before he could say anything to make the matter worse. "He'd kill you. And I don't know what he would do to me, but it's too late."

"Do you mean that you and he have already become lovers? And why is he dressed like a gentleman? Who sent all these servants and carriages?"

"I can't explain any of it now." She lowered her voice. "Do you really expect me to believe you love me?"

"I believe I might. I thought *you* loved me."

"So did I," she said gently. "Or I hoped I did. It doesn't matter now. I'm marrying him."

He frowned as if struggling to understand. "I heard a rumor at the smithy that he is of noble descent and that he's the reason Hay scurried off like a rat. Was Hay behind the attacks?"

She edged toward the coach. "It should be better now for everyone that he's gone."

"Take this bag. It's tonic for the children."

"Thank you." She smiled briefly, catching the dark look Colin sent her way. "It wouldn't have been right for us. You didn't know about my past."

"I know enough about you to realize my mistake," he said, stepping out of her path. "I wasn't brave enough. That's why I lost you."

She didn't look back. She didn't have the nerve. Colin was striding toward her.

*   *   *

She couldn't have changed her mind. She shook her head. Something Wilkes said had upset her.

Colin couldn't stand it. She belonged to him. Why should he let the man have even a moment with her?

"Damn him," he muttered, sensing the curious glances of servants, the maids, the footmen hanging on their straps. "She's mine." *She's mine.*

Etta's piping voice had dispelled the tension.

Somehow—Colin suspected that Charlie had played accomplice—the young girl had escaped Nan's carriage and tumbled out the other side into the gravel. "Miss Kate! Hurry up! It's awful sitting with Nan and not being allowed outside. We're like prisoners!" A moment later the nursemaid had reclaimed her errant charge.

Wilkes had followed Kate; she was clutching the bag he had given her. Colin looked the other way, but from the corner of his eye he watched Wilkes walk toward the gates and Kate climb into the coach.

He joined her and Georgette several moments later. "Ladies, are we ready to leave?"

Georgette held Kate's hand, her plaintive gaze riveted to the house. Kate looked at him, and he searched her face—for tears, for regret, for sadness. Then she smiled, and he knew it was all right.

"Any doubts?" he asked.

"Not on my part."

He glanced out through the doorway at her unfortunate suitor. "Then that's the last I hope to see of him."

She settled comfortably beside Georgette, who had apparently been watching the scene unfold from her window.

"That was a surprise," Georgette said. "I was afraid we would be delayed by a duel. I was impressed if a little disappointed at how civil you appeared, allowing them to talk alone. In your place I might have been tempted to intervene."

"What makes you think I wasn't?" he said, laughing.

"You appeared to be in complete control of your feelings," Kate agreed.

He grunted. "I was aware of the children's feelings. I've no desire to give them nightmares for the rest of their lives." Nor was he about to admit how close he'd come to throttling his competition.

Chapter 38

They arrived at the Marquess of Sedgecroft's Kentish estate an hour before midnight. Even in the dark, Kate was bespelled by the splendor of the sixteenth-century house. It was a place of magic. Moonlight gleamed upon a lake at the end of a park, reminding her of a bolt of water silk unraveled. Mist drifted from the encircling hills, like wraiths coming out to welcome them.

Elizabethan or Baroque, she was not expert enough to discern the architectural style, but she was impressed by the magnificence of the manor.

"Is that a tennis court?" she whispered to Colin as the coach rolled to a stop, servants in gold livery swarming to attend the arrivals.

He stirred. "Yes. One could live on this estate and never miss the rest of the world. My cousins and I warred against one another here in our youth. The brick wings were added on to the original house to accommodate the family's growth."

A footman opened the coach door and released the steps, extending his forearm to Kate. "His lordship awaits your pleasure, milady. We trust you had an uneventful journey."

"I wouldn't know." Georgette woke up at the footman's voice. "I was asleep almost the entire time. Sir Colin and his betrothed did not sleep much, however. Perhaps they can describe the scenery that I missed."

"Apple trees," Colin said instantly.

"Wooded hills and half-timbered cottages," Kate said innocently.

"In that case," Georgette said, "you can both sit alone together in the coach admiring the tennis courts while I peek around the house."

It was quiet outside, but inside the house servants flittered through the torchlit halls to escort the guests to their individual suites. Kate noticed Colin disappear into a room with a lean, impeccably dressed gentleman who she guessed was his cousin Heath Boscastle. Had he been waiting up to greet Colin?

Suddenly the splendor of the house, of Colin's background, gave her pause. She had traveled all day on only two cups of tea, anxiety, and Colin's reassurances. Could she manage to make a pleasing impression?

She felt a tug at her sleeve. Etta's tiny voice carried to the gilt eagles carved into the ceiling. "Charlie's right. We've seen more busts in this hall tonight than at a corset maker's."

Kate could have melted in mortification. "You have corsets on the mind, child. Where is that young devil?"

A white-sleeved arm encircled her waist. "I'm right here," Colin said. "Did you miss me that soon?"

"Where is that little monkey Charlie hiding?"

"Heath took him and Brian into the weapons room. Shall I introduce everyone tonight or at breakfast tomorrow before the wedding?"

She stood, afraid to move, afraid to ask him to explain. Etta, her ears as alert as a French agent's, was of an age when everything inappropriate enthralled her.

"Whose wedding? Are you marrying Miss Kate or my mother? Could you marry them both?"

He released Kate to lean down to Etta's height. "She'll explain everything to you in the morning. It's late now. We need to go to sleep."

A servant materialized at Kate's side. "Are you ready, miss?"

She stared at Colin. "How can we be married that quickly?"

"Heath brought a special license from London."

"Where am I sleeping?"

"In the tower."

"The tower!" Etta exclaimed. "That's where the queen is imprisoned before they cut off her head."

Colin straightened, smiling into Kate's eyes. "I intend to keep her, for the rest of our lives."

Etta stepped protectively against Kate. "You can't lock her in the tower for the rest of her life. It's evil."

He looked relieved as Georgette returned with two footmen carrying her luggage. "Mama, Sir Colin is locking Kate in a tower. May I go with her?"

"No," Colin and Georgette said together.

"Then may I go into the weapons room with the boys?"

"Of course you may," Colin said, motioning a servant from the corner. "Just don't take any swords off the wall."

"But it's so late," Kate said, frowning at Etta's quick escape down the hall. "They need to go to bed, and I need to—"

"There are plenty of chambermaids about who are practiced in pampering young guests."

"And you're the one who accused me of spoiling Brian. You're every bit as bad as I am."

He walked her to the spiral stone staircase, a servant following behind. "I hope you sleep well tonight."

"I should," she said, faintly embarrassed that she could hear her voice echo. "The house is so peaceful."

He laughed. "It won't be after tomorrow."

"I won't see you tonight?" she whispered.

He shook his head. "No. Heath and I need to discuss the future. Perhaps tonight you will have sweet dreams."

Chapter 39

*M*ason Earling detested traveling by public stage, squashed between the unwashed bodies of endlessly chattering passengers.

He had not yet in his mind assimilated all that Hay had revealed to him of his father's deathbed confession or of Georgette's betrayal. He had no one without her — a whore. But he had trusted her. He had wanted her ever since he could remember. He had watched her fall prey to Boscastle's unearthly magnetism. He had waited and waited through the years, through her marriage and affairs, until he possessed enough wealth, or so he'd thought, to buy her loyalty. They had met infrequently at parties. At first she had pretended not to recognize him.

His obsession for her had evolved into love. He'd courted the favor of her governess and of her children, for he believed that Georgette would soon conceive his son or daughter. He thought back to his last conversation with Hay.

"A private vehicle could carry me to London with far more speed and comfort," he said, his bitterness growing. "Why can't I travel with you?"

"Boscastle is pursuing you. It won't take him long to

discover you aren't returning to the house. Furthermore, I've no wish to be murdered for your crime."

Mason had stood in the bustle of the tavern courtyard. "I didn't commit a crime."

"That's neither here nor there when you're up against a power that seeks your destruction. Do as I say. I will arrive ahead of you in London and make all the arrangements for your protection before he realizes you have escaped him."

"My life, everything I thought was mine, is slipping through my fingers." He glanced up sharply at Hay. "I insist that I at least send Georgette a letter explaining to her—"

"Goddammit, *no*." Anger contorted Hay's narrow face. "You've ruined your father's company, your fortune; you've tainted my good name with bad practices. You will not contact that whore again, else I wash my hands of you and let Boscastle or the courts do as they must."

"I did not murder Viscount Norwood."

"Your father's dying words to witnesses swear that you did. And if you do not like the discomfort of a public coach, I doubt you will find a bullet to the heart on a dueling field or the rest of your life spent in a fetid gaol cell more to your liking."

Chapter 40

Colin sat alone in the drawing room with his cousin Lieutenant Colonel Lord Heath Boscastle. The light from Heath's cigar glowed red in the darkness. "You look no different to me than you did when we took our female guests hostage in the treasure cave decades ago."

"You took your time finding yours," Heath said, his brow raised. He and Colin shared the common Boscastle traits of black hair, blue eyes, and an intensity of character. Without question Heath was the most private of Colin's cousins, a man to be admired for his sacrifices during the war. A man one could trust with any secret.

"I am curious to meet your wife," Colin said with a grin. "Does she know about the cave?"

"Oh, yes." Heath laughed. "Colin, it's been thirteen years. I wished you'd asked sooner for my help."

"It was my pride, I suppose. I thought that I had finally found the man, only to realize how stupidly I had been misled."

"Your brothers will want to know."

"If they're still speaking to me."

Heath said nothing. It was a revealing silence of the sort that one did not question. Colin shook his head in regret. "I hope Grayson doesn't mind the inconvenience."

"You must be joking. Grayson lives to entertain. His wife thrives on taking family under her wing. They are a splendid couple, but their combined charm is not for the faint of spirit."

"I warn you now that I brought an entourage of scandalous characters to this house. My betrothed is companion to the courtesan Georgette Lawson."

"I *knew* I'd heard her name," Heath said, lowering his cigar. "She's not as famous as Audrey Watson, but few women are."

Colin cleared his throat. "You'll be hearing more about her soon if she and Kate have their way, which, between you and me, I doubt will happen."

"Your note did not provide enough information or time for me to launch a proper investigation into Earling or his company. But I began an inquiry on your behalf before I left London. I shall enjoy helping you, if you'll allow me."

"I would be grateful."

"Your father was my favorite uncle," Heath said, resting his head back on the chair. "He paid more attention to me and my brothers the few times I saw him on holidays than my father did."

"I don't think I knew that," Colin said.

"You wouldn't. My mother covered it well. I only tell you this because we are family."

"I have a son, the tall boy you took into the weapons room. For thirteen years the only 'fathers' he has known have been Georgette's protectors."

"We will change that," Heath said. "Julia and I have not been blessed with children yet."

Colin let a moment pass before resuming the conversation. "I'd like to leave for London as soon as it is possible. Will I offend Grayson if I do?"

"Not if you're leaving half your household behind until other arrangements are made. I doubt anyone will note your absence, to be truthful. A bevy of guests are due to arrive anytime."

Colin grinned. "I don't deserve this reception. But I knew my family would not let me down."

Kate felt alone and anxious again. A friendly chambermaid led her up the spiral staircase and through a torchlit hallway. She unlocked the arched door at its end.

"It's lovely," Kate said in surprise. Her gaze went first to the writing table and then to the mahogany four-poster hung with velvet bed curtains. A fire glowed in the pink-veined fireplace.

"Shall I bring you up anything to eat?"

She glanced at the tray of bread, cheeses, and fruits arranged temptingly on the dressing table. A bottle of white wine and two glasses sat beside it. "That will be more than enough."

"No, it won't," Georgette said, energetically forcing her way around the chambermaid to the door, a long object covered in a sheet slung over her arm. "Miss Walcott and I are starving and will need a little more sustenance to see us through the night."

The chambermaid curtsied, smiling good-naturedly. "But of course."

"This is to be my bridal chamber," Kate said in vexation as the door closed. "I should be allowed a few moments here by myself."

"You need a few moments to make a few entries in the memoirs and try on your wedding dress. Don't deny me that much. You'll never be mine after you're married."

Kate looked in curiosity at the garment Georgette had draped carefully across the bed, drawing the sheet away to reveal a gown of breathtaking elegance.

It was a blue silk, banded at the elbows with satin ribbons and a buttoned Valenciennes lace back that flared into darker skirts flounced with white ruffles.

"Where did this come from?" Kate wondered aloud. "I've never seen you in such an elegant dress."

"Perhaps you never will. Mason had it made for me from a French magazine. Just don't tell Colin. He won't know if you don't say anything."

Kate stared at the dress.

"Is something wrong? You can't wait until the morning to try it on. It might need a tuck here and there."

"I don't think I want to wear it," Kate said, torn between her husband's feelings and her attraction to the gown.

"Well, you're marrying the first man I ever loved. Wearing the dress his enemy made for me doesn't seem all that offensive in comparison."

"What is it you want me to jot down? I'm too tired to write much tonight."

Georgette walked to the dressing table and picked up a wedge of crumbly cheese. "The first thing is a chapter that I have reconsidered: I don't want to reveal that Baron Atwood attended the opera dressed as a woman."

"That couldn't wait, madam?"

"He was a nice enough man, but far more fun as a lady until he fought a duel over a gambling debt in his skirts. I don't wish to shame him."

"Fine."

"Oh, dear." Georgette's attention had been drawn to the painting mounted above the mantelpiece. "Have you seen what the shepherd and shepherdess are doing under the hay in this watercolor?"

"What else did you wish me to revise in your memoirs, madam?"

"Revise? Oh. I'd forgotten. There was a bishop who

propositioned me in a graveyard while his innocent wife sat nearby in their carriage. Should I reveal his name?"

Kate ran her fingers over the bodice of the blue gown. "Absolutely. But not tonight."

"Then in the morning."

"I have as much invested in seeing you successfully published as do you."

Georgette shook her head. "Will you wear the gown?"

"I don't know."

"Try it on first thing in the morning. I'll even make an attempt to rise early to see what it looks like."

"Thank you, madam."

"It's nothing. I'll never marry again. Why should it go to waste?"

Chapter 41

The wedding ceremony took place before breakfast the following day. Etta and Charles had made friends among the servants' children; Brian took his first tour of a proper paddock and stable yard. And Georgette, whose penchant for luxury might have been overstimulated by the grandeur of the estate, had kept Kate up again half the night with a spate of suddenly recalled amorous anecdotes and morsels of advice to be included in her memoirs. "I was born to be pampered," she said as her only excuse for taking advantage once again of Kate's devotion. "I have worked diligently at my profession. Where is my reward?"

At daylight a troop of chambermaids in frilly caps and starched aprons bustled into the room with buckets of hot water for a bath. Lady Julia arrived shortly thereafter with another maid to arrange Kate's hair and to approve the minor alterations that had been hastily made on the dress meant for Georgette, who had not yet left her room.

Kate turned to Lady Julia, curtsying deeply in the blue bridal gown, which rustled in the stillness of the breaking sunlight. "I don't know how I'll find the courage to do this."

Julia laughed, her red hair a stunning contrast to her ivory skin. "I don't know how I found the nerve to marry Heath, either, especially since I shot him in the backside when we first met. I thought he was a fox. Not only did he forgive me for that accident, but by some miracle, he fell in love with me." She gave Kate an impulsive hug. "You'll fit perfectly into the family. We are every one of us awful and awe-inspiring."

"But I have skeletons in my closet," Kate murmured.

"All the better. If there's one thing this family can't abide, it's a person who claims to have lived a perfect life. In fact, when we return to London, we'll have a ladies' cabal and confess all the sins we've committed in the name of love."

"London?" Somehow she had put the thought of that city from her mind. To return would be to awaken memories of the one incident she had prayed to forget.

"Speaking of sins," Julia continued, in a lower voice, "I would be grateful if you could arrange for Jane and me to meet Mrs. Lawson for a little tête-à-tête. She must have a few scandals of her own to share."

"Oh, she does," Kate said enthusiastically. She might not feel at ease boasting on her own behalf. But she wasn't shy when it came to dropping hints in high places to stir up publicity for Georgette's fame. "Scandals that I have sworn never to share aloud. Unsurpassed deeds of such indecency that my face burns at the mere thought of them."

Julia smiled at her in curiosity. "Now I'm dying to know."

"All will be revealed in due time," Kate murmured as if she were a fortune-teller at a country fair.

"You don't say."

"No," Kate said quickly. "I didn't. I won't. I—" Her eyes widened at the rap on the door.

"It's time, my lady," the chambermaid said.

"You'd better go," Kate whispered to Julia, taking one last look at herself in the cheval glass. That elegant creature wasn't Kate Walcott. "You've been too kind to me already."

"Well, I'm not kind enough to commit bigamy with my husband's cousin, or to stand in as your proxy. So yes, my dear. Go."

"But she said—"

"*Lady* Boscastle. She was using the title that will henceforth be yours, unless you miss your wedding."

"Oh." Kate stared at the door, her lips compressed to contain her laughter, while Julia made no effort at all to control hers.

Colin had never thought he would know happiness again. He'd made a mess of the past. The future was uncertain. But for this moment, as his cousin Heath walked Kate to the altar of the small chapel, he felt an overpowering sense of love for her that gave him hope that if he could change, then anything could.

After all, he had a family to protect. As he had promised Kate, he would never turn his back on those Brian loved or who loved his son. He looked at Nan, snoring in the bride's pew, then at Georgette, weeping her heart out as if this were a funeral instead of a wedding.

His wedding.

He smiled down at Kate and saw no one else—because in all of England there was no woman to compare. She looked too beautiful to touch in her shimmering blue dress with its deep ruffles of white satin. She had put her trust in him. Now he would endure the torture of a wedding reception and the hours before dark until he would have her to himself. Then he would touch and possess her whenever and wherever it pleased him. Or her.

*   *

"It was a beautiful wedding," she whispered as he carried her across the threshold of the tower room. "It would have been proper of us if we'd stayed for at least half of the reception."

He deposited her on the four-poster, leaning down to kiss her into breathless silence. "I took the idea from a play I recently saw. You may have heard of it, *The Abduction of a Governess*? The lead actress was so beautiful that a war was fought over her. I didn't think you'd want that to happen on our wedding night."

She rose from the bed, laughing, and locked her arms around his neck. "Did you see the look on Georgette's face when you picked me up in front of everyone in the reception hall? For an instant I thought she would order you to put her companion down."

His grin deepened the grooves in his cheeks. "Let her take care of herself. She has a dozen servants at her command. Better yet, let me take care of you."

"Are you offering to brush out my hair, tighten my corset, and fetch me my shawl when I complain of cold?"

"No, Lady Boscastle. But I'll be more than happy to unlace your stays, place you flat on your back, and warm you with my body before you have a chance to feel a hint of cold."

"Give me a chance to catch my breath."

He shook his head, walking her against the door and bolting it behind her back at the same time.

"Whyever not?" she asked weakly as he first removed her veiled cap and then untied the sleeves that fluttered like wings from her shoulders. There would be nothing angelic of her left after tonight.

"I want you to be breathless until morning."

His large hands skimmed her waist, slowing at her

hips to unfasten her overskirt. The tight bows unfurled at his urging. He unfastened the buttons that secured the back of her gown. Then off slid her petticoats, along with the rest of her undergarments.

He was right. When her bare shoulder met the cool surface of the oaken door, he slid one hand around her neck and warmed her skin with his gloved fingers. His other hand played with her breasts until he dipped his head to lash at each engorged tip in unhurried enjoyment.

She reached between them and pulled the glove from the hand that was caressing her breast. "I still think we should have made more of an attempt at a subtle escape," she whispered, dropping his gray glove to the floor in a flagrant act of enticement that Georgette would have applauded.

He glanced down, then up at her again, assessing her as he would a rival. "If my son's governess sees that, I'll be done for."

She stared back at him with a guileless smile, feeling behind her back for his other glove. She who was experienced in undressing wriggling children found a willing husband to be less of a challenge. The glove sailed through the air and hit the dressing screen. "Kiss me once," she whispered. "Then take off your clothes. And make this kiss count."

His hand glided up her nape and sank into her thick hair. His head lowered. He forced her against the door, let her body cushion the angular planes of his. His kiss ravished her, dominated, and demanded that she yield, left without a single defense or doubt that he could deliver whatever she needed.

She gasped into his mouth, felt his hand stealing down her belly to the slickness between her thighs. He pushed three fingers inside her at once, still kissing her into dark oblivion until he broke away, breathing hard, staring at her through heavy-lidded eyes.

"There's champagne on the night table," he said, pulling off his white neckcloth. "Pour a glass."

She smiled. "For you or for me?"

"For you." He removed his long-tailed coat, lifting his damp fingers to his lips. "I'll drink what's left."

She poured two glasses, leaving hers untouched, and retreated to the bed, so desperate for him that she did not trust herself to hold the champagne flute in her hands. She sat and examined his God-given attributes through the half-open bed curtains. He undressed in front of the fire, treating her to such an uninhibited display of his body that she felt hot and faint.

His shoulders. Was that the part of his body that she loved best? Or his arms, the muscles so deeply defined. But nothing compared to his eyes. He could entice her to her last breath with those blue eyes.

"I hope you aren't falling asleep in there," he said casually, unfastening the fly of his pantaloons to release his hard erection. His clothes cast off, he walked, comfortable in his devastating nudity, to push open the curtains behind which she waited. "Lady Boscastle?"

"Sir Colin."

She rolled onto her stomach, undulating to the edge of the bed, where he stood, thighs apart, his rampant manhood so close she could kiss its engorged crown. Which she did.

"Kate," he said hoarsely. "Oh, please."

Her tongue traveled the length of the pulsing-veined flesh to the root of his dark, crisp hair. She inhaled his scent.

He stared down at her through half-closed eyes. She pushed up on her elbows, emboldened by the groan of pure animal pleasure that escaped him. He was hers to tease, to please. She lapped her tongue around the head of his prick, encouraging him to thrust into her mouth.

"Is it too much?"

"Is it too much for you?" She settled into a more comfortable position, taking more of him into her mouth. Just as his hips jerked, she let him slide out between her swollen lips. He was shaking. When his breathing grew calmer, she began again to stroke her tongue in a spiral around the core of him.

"Enough," he whispered, not moving.

She couldn't stop. She wanted the taste of him in her throat. She wanted to seduce and enslave him as he had her. She levered herself closer still and settled her hands on his steel-hard hips, all the better to concentrate on her job.

He was hers. He was close to climax. She felt the tension in his body, in her own. But just when she thought she had turned the tables on him, she found herself lifted from her advantageous position and redeposited on her posterior at the edge of the bed.

He stood over her, his face hard and hungry, his large hands sliding under her bottom.

"What are you—"

He pushed her thighs wide apart. Her legs dangled. Her feet just reached the floor. "You tear my heart into pieces, Kate. I thought I had lived in darkness for so long, I wouldn't be able to recognize the daylight again if I saw it. But I have a fever for you in my blood that at times I feel will consume me."

And as he covered her with his body, she was aware only of the love that filled her heart and the desperate heat he kindled in her body.

Chapter 42

On Wednesday afternoon it rained. Colin informed the rest of the house that his wife was indisposed, and that was the end of that. The only persons wicked enough to listen outside the tower door to the odd noises within were Etta and Charlie. When discovered by Georgette, they only made matters worse by asking her whether Kate had contracted the same malady that plagued their mother.

"Whatever do you mean?" Georgette asked crossly, dragging each by the hand down the stairs.

"Well," Charlie said. "Those are the noises that you make when you've taken a new lover."

"Lover?" Georgette said in shock. "How many times do I have to explain that your mother takes protectors?"

Etta looked at Charlie. "That must be what they mean by being lovesick. I don't want to catch it, do you?"

"Bend over, both of you," Georgette said, dropping their hands to raise hers.

"Run for it!" Charlie said to Etta, and at the foot of the stairs he charged off to the right, and Etta to the left, their mutiny synchronized for maximum confusion.

Lord Heath came sauntering down the hall from the library. "Is anything wrong, Mrs. Lawson?"

"Yes." She sniffed back a tear of pride and self-pity. Wasn't there an ugly man in the entire Boscastle family? Was her son destined to turn women into puddles of hopeless admiration?

"What is it?" he asked with such concern that she was almost ashamed of her thoughts.

"I've lost my companion, the one person who took care of me with unfailing devotion, who saw me at my worst and still loved me—and who even loved the monsters that will no doubt be the death of me."

He smiled, a man who apparently was not flustered by monstrous children or emotional women. In fact, she had a feeling that nothing upset him. "It may seem difficult to accept today, but—"

"It is your cousin's fault," she burst out. "He wasn't content to ruin my life once. He had to come back and do it again."

Heath blinked. "Surely you cannot blame my cousin for wanting to protect you and your family from a murderer? I know you have been inconvenienced, displaced, left in an uncertain condition, but you have to agree that it is at least a safer one."

"Murderer," she muttered.

"Colin understands that you still feel an attachment to this man, that you are not entirely convinced of his guilt." He hesitated. "A woman of your passionate reputation will find a guardian the moment she makes it known she is back on the market for one."

"Is that right?"

"Unless you aren't on the market, in which case I apologize profusely—"

"What I'm in the market for is a companion and governess like the one your cousin stole from me. I don't want another protector. The life of a courtesan exhausts one after a time."

"I can imagine," he said politely, taking a pause. "What do you want, then?"

"I can't tell you," she said, sighing deeply.

"Why not?"

"The success of my dream demands the utmost secrecy."

Heath studied her as if he were decoding an encrypted message. "Solving problems, puzzles, is *my* passion, Mrs. Lawson. I don't know why, but I sense that I could be of help to you. But, of course, you would have to trust me and know that I have never broken a confidence. Do you wish to speak at length about your situation? If so, we can talk in the library."

On Thursday evening Grayson Boscastle, Marquess of Sedgecroft, his wife, his son, and a phalanx of personal attendants swept into the driveway and disappeared into the house before Kate could hasten to the staircase. To her disappointment she could not get a decent look at anyone except a tall footman snapping out orders. She returned to her room and went to the window, while her husband slept fitfully in their marriage bed. The momentous occasion of Sedgecroft's arrival was marked only by the joyful barking of his keen-scenting wolfhounds and a flash of gold across the skies—a white-orange burst so bright that Kate opened the window to stare outside and wonder what natural phenomenon she had witnessed.

A meteor shower? Lightning? She felt a chill of excitement like a child on Christmas morning. She hopped back to bed, knocking her knee into her husband's head as he awakened to question what she was doing. In a blur of movement he had a pistol pointed at the window. "What's the matter?" he said gruffly.

"It's like Cinderella's coach. It's a fairy tale. I've never seen anything so beautiful—good grief, put down that gun. It's off-putting, I tell you. What if I brandished a pistol every time the children barged into the room?"

"They'd likely have learned to knock by now."

"Or you'd have shot one of them."

"Take off that night rail."

She crawled into bed beside him. "I can't believe I have the shivers. Feel my arms."

"It's our honeymoon. You should be shivering and I should be feeling more than your arms."

She turned her head on the pillow. "Not those kind of shivers. What if the rest of your family disapproves of me?"

He leaned over her, peeling the covers from her shoulders. His gaze traveled over her shapely curves. "Why wouldn't my family like you? You brought me to my senses after all of these years."

"That doesn't seem fair. After all, you made me lose mine." She stared down from his face to his nude body. "Don't you think you should at least wear a robe to bed in your cousin's house in case of a fire? I would die a thousand deaths of shame on your behalf."

"I wonder if my brothers traveled with him," he said absently.

She started laughing. "They at least must have seen you naked before."

His eyes warmed; he was fully awake now. "Why are we wasting breath on them when we could be making love instead?"

"If you're going to proposition me, you could at least put your pistol away."

He reached his arm back, placed the gun on the dresser, then leaned forward and pulled her atop his fully aroused body. "Better?"

"Let me unlace—"

"There's no need," he said, his voice deep pitched. He pushed her night rail up around her waist and eased his swollen cock inside her, giving her a moment to adjust before he grasped her hips, lifted his ass from the bed and thrust into her as hard as he could.

She arched her back, her breath catching. "Thank you for the advance notice. I hope that I will be able to walk in the morning."

"Should I stop?"

She shook her head and bore down before he thrust again. "Can you?"

"I could, but it would kill me," he said and gripped her harder as he set up a rhythm of penetration and withdrawal that she instinctively began to follow.

"Colin—"

She felt her body tighten, felt him watch her face, waiting for the moment when she unraveled and belonged completely to him. He cupped her breasts in his hands, squeezing her nipples between his fingers. Her heart beat wildly. She closed her eyes, the friction of his thrusting against the hood of her sex stealing her control.

He grunted, pumping harder. She did indeed die a little death, convulsing as moments later he came inside her. Neither of them stirred for long moments afterward. The night air shivered over her bare skin. Her lips stung, as did the hollow of her cleft, where their bodies remained joined.

He pulled her down against his chest and wrapped his arms around her, whispering, "Do you want anything? Champagne? A castle? All the diamonds in the world?"

"No. Just hold me until I fall asleep."

"Kiss me once, then," he said. "And I might let you rest through the night."

"What did you mean about your brothers?" she murmured. "Is there some estrangement between you?"

He kissed her lightly on the lips. "We'll find out tomorrow. It has nothing to do with you. I've been away from home a long time. It would be naïve to expect that they haven't changed as much as I have, or to hope that they will help me when I haven't played any part in their lives."

Chapter 43

$\mathcal{K}$ate promised she would guide Georgette through the evening of their official introduction to the marquess and his wife, although she was unbearably anxious herself about meeting the patriarch of Colin's family. Despite her husband's assurance that he would not abandon her, Colin walked the two women into the formal gold drawing room, stood for their introductions, and was promptly lured away by some male friends from his boyhood who demanded drinks all around in his honor.

"Don't drag your tail," Georgette whispered. "You're one of them. And remember what you told me. I'm the mother of one of them."

Kate burst into giggles.

"That's better. Levity always helps."

Except that she couldn't stop.

"Now you're making an ass of yourself," Georgette said, edging several steps to the right to place distance between her and the spectacle Kate was creating. "She's had a few too many; it will soon pass," Georgette said to the footman who gave Kate a quizzical look. "She doesn't get out much these days, I'm afraid." She turned to Kate in reproach. "And no wonder. Kindly keep those snorts under control. You're at a party, not in a pigsty."

"A p-p-pig—" It was her nerves. She clapped her gloved hand to her mouth to smother a fresh episode of giggles, aware at this point that people had begun to stare and that, oh, goodness—the marchioness was cutting through the crowd to either expel her from society or demand an explanation for this breach of etiquette.

Everyone stood aside for Lady Jane's passage. When she reached Kate, she lifted her hand in the air and asked in sympathy, "Choking? Would you like a good thump between the shoulders?"

Tears of mirth filled Kate's eyes. She managed to shake her head in apology. Georgette, the traitor, had wandered off and attached herself to a rakish young gentleman who had taken out his quizzing glass to admire either her bosom or her emerald choker.

"Bridal nerves," Kate sputtered at last. "I'm all right now. I apologize from the bottom of my heart."

The honey-haired marchioness regarded her in amusement. "I wanted us to meet alone. I am Jane, Colin's cousin-in-law."

Kate curtsied. "I'm honored, ma'am."

"First of all, congratulations on your marriage to Colin. I wish the entire family could have been here to witness it. A wedding of a black sheep returned to the fold is a double reason to rejoice."

"Thank you," Kate said, glancing around the room. She thought she saw Colin walking out onto the terrace with two other men.

"Those are his brothers, Sebastien and Gabriel," Jane said quietly. "I suppose we should give them time alone before I introduce you."

Kate glanced back at her. She had not imagined the note

of concern in Jane's voice. "They don't appear to be celebrating their reunion."

"As I understand it, they have a common enemy to be caught. Oh, listen to me. That is a dark subject we can discuss another day. Tonight I want to welcome you to the family."

Jane chattered on. Now Kate didn't feel like laughing at all. What were Colin and his brothers planning to do? She shook herself as she realized Jane had just asked her a question and was expecting a reply.

She stared blankly, trying to discern from Jane's face what she had said. Something about a courtesan— merciful heavens, did the family assume that *Kate* was a courtesan? It wouldn't be a surprising leap in logic. Colin had mistaken her for a harlot the night they met. Why wouldn't a person assume Kate had padded her purse with a paid liaison here and there? Birds of a feather did flock together.

"Will you?" Jane whispered, winking at Kate in some unspoken conspiracy.

Kate blinked when she suspected she should have winked back. "Will I what?"

"Urge Mrs. Lawson to accept an invitation to my suite later on tonight for a private chat with Julia and me about her experience as a courtesan. You're invited, too, of course. Her profession isn't a secret, is it?"

"Oh. *Oh.*" Kate was too relieved to take offense. "No. On the contrary. I'm sure she would be honored to accept, except that it looks as if she might be making plans for another after-midnight rendezvous."

Jane stared across the room at the gentleman whose company Georgette was obviously making an effort to escape. "It's that vile Viscount Portland. Why Grayson invites him to our house parties I don't understand. He's a hopeless philanderer with too much money and not a moral bone in his body."

"The marquess?"

Jane laughed in delight. "Oh, heavens, no. I wouldn't put up with that a moment. Ah, Mrs. Lawson has given the vile viscount the shoulder. Shall I take you out onto the terrace to meet Colin's brothers? I understand there is an older one who is in some exotic country and has been away from England longer than your husband."

"I don't want to intrude on their reunion."

"Nonsense. This is your honeymoon. If they don't desire our company, we shall leave."

Colin shook his head, afraid he would express too much emotion. "Dear God," he said with a laugh to his youngest brother, Gabriel, Colonel Sir Gabriel Boscastle. "Do you know what I remember about you the last Christmas Eve we spent together as a family? You riding a mare bare-arsed backward and Mother dropping her favorite plate on the floor when she saw you from the window."

Heath smiled. "He hasn't changed much, according to his wife."

Colin shook his head again. "You married the village lady who scorned you, and I did not marry the girl that I promised I would." He turned to his brother Sebastien, who behind Colin's back had become Lord Sebastien Michael Boscastle, First Baron Boscastle of Wycliffe. "I am glad to see you well. I regret that I wasted two years of your life. I know it seemed cruel when we went our separate ways."

Sebastien shrugged. "Cruel? We made a blood pact to find Earling."

"I couldn't justify forcing you to starve and sleep in fields because of my vendetta."

"I thought he was my father, too," Sebastien said, staring out across the garden.

"No one ever said otherwise."

"Do you remember what you said to me that night in the barn?"

Colin caught Heath's eye. *Careful.* This was not a boy's anger, but a man's. It had festered for too long to be lanced and healed in a few moments. "Not exactly, no."

" 'It's time to grow up. I don't want you at my side for the rest of my life. Find your own way.' "

"I did it for you. There was a war. We both enlisted—"

Sebastien straightened. "The war is over. But you still need to be the family hero. It's your game. You're in charge."

Colin felt heat rush to his face. "What game are you talking about?"

"You misled me. You planned to resume the chase for Earling the entire time. You denied me that honor."

"That is partially true," Colin said. "But if I had decided to waste the rest of my life hunting him down, I wasn't prepared to sacrifice yours."

For an instant he thought Sebastien would strike him. A physical confrontation to clear the air would have been preferable to the pain that flared in his brother's eyes and was quickly extinguished. "I could have made the decision for myself."

"Then help me now—"

Sebastien turned on his heel and descended the steps into the garden, leaving the three men behind him in absolute silence, his tall figure soon engulfed in darkness.

It took Kate and the marchioness a full twenty minutes to reach the other side of the room. Jane paused every so often to introduce Kate to one of the guests; they broke free just as Heath entered through the French doors and headed for a door to an antechamber. Colin and a swarthy gentleman who greatly resembled him followed behind. Kate assumed he was one of Colin's brothers.

Her husband's grim expression discouraged her from making her presence known. She understood instinctively that this was not the time to demand his notice.

Instead, she stood immobile, as did Lady Jane, who patted her arm in distracted comfort and said, "I shall get to the heart of this. It has nothing to do with you."

"If it hurts my husband, it does involve me. Isn't there a brother missing?"

"Yes. Have a glass of champagne. Drink one for me. I believe I might be expecting."

"How wonderful."

Jane smiled. "I think so. Now, be strong. Mingle with the other guests while I investigate."

Despite Jane's advice, Kate walked toward the French doors and then out onto the terrace, the room suddenly stifling, too many voices buzzing in her ears. In the moonlight she discerned a familiar figure darting behind one of the neatly clipped yews. "Come out, Brian. I know you're there."

He stepped out to face her. "I didn't mean to eavesdrop this time. But I was hoping to meet my uncles, and then I heard the arguing, and I knew my father would be furious."

"It's all right."

He came up the steps. "Is it because of my mother?"

"No. Not at all."

They stood together for an interlude, listening to the laughter and music from within the house. At length he said, "What do you think will happen?"

"I can't imagine."

He looked at her. "Maybe you ought to go back inside. My mother's talking to another man. This time it appears serious."

She swung around. He was right. "Maybe you—"

"I've been given permission to sleep in the stable tonight. It's ever so grand."

"Go, then, Brian. Whatever is amiss might be better in the morning."

Chapter 44

Georgette was bubbling over like a fountain of champagne when Kate finally reached her. "The most wonderful thing in the world has just happened to me," Georgette whispered. She drew Kate around a cluster of older gentlemen, none of whom were the white-bearded guest, who had made a timely escape before Kate could give him the evil eye. He'd looked rather distinguished, actually, a little on the heavy side, but impeccably dressed, and well liked to judge by the crowd that thronged around him as he left Georgette's side.

She looked at Georgette and felt the usual tug of fondness and chagrin. Georgette's ebullience could only mean she had stumbled upon another besotted man who had vowed to cherish her until the end of time or the end of the year, whichever came first.

"The most wonderful thing has happened to me, too," Kate said wryly. "I just got married."

"Yes, yes," Georgette said impatiently. "But now I've finally met the man of my dreams. Don't give me that look. I vow on my soul that it is true. There has never been a more perfect man for me in the world."

Kate stared across the room at the gentleman in question. "That man?"

"Lord Aramis Philbert," Georgette said in wonder.

Kate gasped. "The *publisher*?"

"The one and only," Georgette replied, although Kate doubted Georgette had ever heard of him before tonight.

"The *happily* married publisher with children? And grandchildren, from what I understand. I can't believe my ears. What are you telling me?"

Georgette gave one of the shrugs she had perfected in front of her looking glass. "I won't have to burden you and Colin like an old dowager. I shall have my own lodgings in London."

Kate's eyes widened. The old devil was standing beside a silver-haired lady who could only be his wife. "And . . . and he wants you to be his mistress, in London, behind Lady Philbert's back? With her permission?"

Georgette looked appalled. "What on earth gave you that idea? For your edification, this is a business deal, not a dalliance. Why does your mind leap to the most unsavory conclusion?"

Kate folded her arms. "I haven't a clue. It wouldn't have anything to do with your career, would it?"

"My past career, you mean. I am soon to be a writer, bought by the same wonderful man who publishes some of *your* favorite books."

"*The Wickbury Tales* by Lord Anonymous?" Kate asked, disbelieving.

Georgette broke into a grin. "Yes!"

"But those are fiction, madam. Yours are factual."

"Precisely," Georgette said, nodding at Kate as if she were a dog who had learned a new trick. "That's why Aramis is certain I shall become a best-selling author."

"Why you?" Kate asked bluntly, miffed that she had been excluded from Georgette's moment of glory.

"Why not me?" Georgette asked. "Aramis only confirmed what you've said all along—memoirs of famous personalities are the rage, and the populace can never read enough of our naughty secrets."

Now that the shock had begun to wear off, Kate allowed herself to share in Georgette's elation. It was indeed a dream come true—as long as Georgette had not misunderstood.

"How did he know you were writing a memoir?" she wondered aloud.

"He didn't. His wife suggested it—I appear to be more well-known than I realized—and after three glasses of champagne I asked if I could trust her with a confidence, and she said on her honor, yes, I could. It never would have happened without you, Kate." She paused to draw a quivering breath. "I suspect Lord Heath had a hand in this. I told him about my memoirs. Isn't this the most incredible night of our lives?"

"Yes," Kate said, afraid both of them might dissolve into tears. "Congratulations!"

Georgette lifted her head. "I forbid you to make me cry. Wherever did your husband get off to? It's time for him to realize that I'm not as empty-headed as I look."

Kate counted her blessings as she burrowed against Colin in bed later that night. She hadn't told him about Georgette's triumph. Nor had he mentioned his falling out with Sebastien. She waited, uncertain whether she should admit that she knew. No. Best not to interfere. He'd talk about it when he was ready. Her thoughts drifted. Look how long it had taken her to admit what had happened in her past, and even then it hadn't been a voluntary confession. Still, she wished to offer comfort—

"Are you asleep?" he asked.

She stirred, her cheek pressed to his shoulder. "No."

"You were."

"I wasn't." She raised her head. The raw pain in his eyes disconcerted her. "What is it?"

"You've heard?"

She couldn't lie even to save his pride. "Yes."

"Well, then. You are the rock on which we all stand. What should I do? If I go ahead with what I have planned, Sebastien will despise me forever."

"And if you don't?"

"I don't know that I could live with myself."

She breathed out a sigh, subsiding back against his chest. "You've already made up your mind. When are we leaving for London?"

"You don't have to come with me," he said quickly. "You can stay here as long as you like."

"Brian and I will go wherever you go."

"Then we'll be on the road early Sunday morning with Heath and Julia. They have offered to let us stay in their town house until we put down roots."

She thought of her dream, of her own home, of brothers and sisters for Brian. She had not been back to London since leaving there in shame. What if Earling and Hay escaped? Worse, what if they proved more dangerous when cornered than during the years they had eluded Colin? She wished that this night would never end. Everyone she loved was gathered around her in one place. London had come to mean loss to her. Yet she had to believe it would be different now. She wasn't returning as a servant, but as Colin's wife. *Please,* she prayed. *Let the past not repeat itself. Let London offer solace and not pain.*

Sunday morning began in chaos. Kate met Colin's brothers during a rushed breakfast, and both treated her with touching respect. She had said her private farewells the night before to Georgette and to the servants who had been her family. The two women promised to take tea once a week together in London, to outshine each other at the opera, and to start a literary salon in the town house Georgette would purchase from her publishing success.

But at the last minute, Etta and Charlie vanished and no one on the estate could remember seeing them at breakfast. Heath and Julia, waiting in their carriage, disembarked to join the hunt. Soon the Marquess of Sedgecroft's senior footman arranged a search, lords, ladies, and servants splitting into innumerable parties to find the missing children.

"Might they have fallen in the lake?"

"Are they hiding in the house?"

"I don't want to even *think* it, but could they have been snatched?"

"From Sedgecroft's estate?"

It was Sebastien, accompanied by Brian and four wolfhounds, who found the two miscreants playing in unholy glee a half mile from the house at the ditch that had been built as a defense and for decades had posed a bog-filled menace.

Etta and Charlie had been racing across the rickety footbridge in the hope it would collapse just as they crossed to the other side. It had not, and they'd scrambled up the muddy incline in complete disregard for safety or hygiene.

Kate stared at the filthy twosome in a grateful fury. It was a disgrace. The dogs, the children dripping bog mud in the courtyard, the senior footman's glance branding her a derelict governess, for who else could take the blame if not the person who had raised the little heathens? To underscore her indignity, it seemed as if every guest at the house party had gathered behind her in the courtyard. "How embarrassing," she whispered, choking not only on the words but on the pungent stench of Lord Philbert's cigar. "What if the bridge had collapsed? Where do these fiendish ideas come from? Are you possessed of wrathful spirits?"

Charlie wrinkled his nose. "Sir Colin said last night that he and his brothers and all the cousins did it."

"Did *it*?"

"Dared the bridge to break."

Kate looked at Colin, who only shook his head in mute rebuttal. "Well, I must thank you," she said in heartfelt gratitude to Sebastien.

He expelled a sigh. "It was nothing," he said in a subdued voice. "There are times, I suppose, when the sins of the past work to our benefit. At least I knew where to look."

Chapter 45

$\mathcal{M}$ason had gone numb with shock as he read the announcement in the *Morning Chronicle*. The news could not be true. Sir Colin Boscastle had married Miss Katherine Walcott in Kent at the Marquess of Sedgecroft's country estate. The recently wed couple were temporarily staying here in London with relatives before setting up a permanent residence.

He couldn't breathe. His breakfast toast rose in his throat. He pictured Georgette's comely governess, who had been unfailingly polite and kind to him. Had Hay known of this? What did it mean? Hay had already eaten and left for the wharves.

He read the announcement again. There was no mention of Georgette. What had become of her? The children? He closed his eyes. Why hadn't he defied Hay and written to her again? He almost wished Boscastle would walk into this room and kill him. Death was preferable to the fear that had become an invisible noose around his neck.

Even after he hid aboard the ship bound for India tonight, he would not feel safe. He might survive a storm at sea only to be murdered by pirates or one of the mercenaries sailing on the same vessel. If he reached India alive, he would be alone in a foreign land. He had no friends, no connections there.

What did Georgette think of him? Would she ever truly understand that he had loved her since they were children?

Heath Boscastle and his wife resided in a modest town house on St. James' Street. It was a quiet place, a little too quiet for Kate's liking. She missed Georgette and the children. Of course, she had Brian, and they had Colin to themselves.

Well, not entirely. Her husband spent their first day closed up in the study with Lord Heath and various gentlemen. Many of Heath's friends, Julia confided, worked for the Home Office to prevent subversive activities against the government.

"I should have remembered my history," Kate said as the two ladies shopped on Bond Street the next afternoon. "There are always plots and intrigues hatching to overthrow the Crown."

"Not to mention the spies employed by a famous duchess—one of whom is Sebastien's wife."

Kate hurried toward their parked carriage. "A duchess—spying?"

"Not the type of spying you'd imagine. Her Grace employs ladies of the court, servants, and street vendors to spy for her."

"Who are they spying on? Criminals and jewel thieves?"

"They've snared a few, but not on purpose. They spy on other women in society. Who is sleeping with whose husband? What color gown is a countess planning to wear at a ball to steal the show, and how much did she pay to have it made?"

"Intrigues of the highest importance," Kate said with a laugh.

"Do not underestimate the intensity of female rivalry in the beau monde. I believe Sebastien's wife has a dear friend in the duchess."

"You aren't speaking of the Duchess of Wellington?" Kate asked, stopping for the footman to release the carriage steps.

"I might be." Julia climbed up with a laugh. "What secret passions do you bring to the family?"

She was about to say, "Writing and putting on amateur plays," when Colin's low voice from inside the carriage answered for her, "Her passion is me. It's really because of her that I'm rejoining the pack."

He half rose, drawing her down beside him. His eyes flickered over her with the possessive heat that had become familiar, even if it still unbalanced her. But she sensed a wariness behind the warmth; in fact, the moment she turned to talk to him, he stared past her to the street, frowning as if he expected another passenger to join them.

She glanced around and saw a gentleman strolling by, doffing his hat casually to the occupants of the carriage. "That was Sir Daniel Mallory," Julia said in surprise. "Is that coincidence, Colin, or has Heath asked him for help?"

He took Kate's hand; his firm clasp felt protective. "Sir Daniel Mallory is a former Runner who works primarily for private individuals," he said to Kate. "Yes, Heath thought it wouldn't hurt for him to act as a guard until Mason is found."

Julia frowned. "Wouldn't it be wiser to put his experience to use helping with the search?"

Colin blew out a sigh. "Perhaps. If we had not been dealing with men who believe shooting at innocent woman and children is justified." He drew the crumpled edition of the *Morning Chronicle* out from his long-tailed coat. "And if this announcement had not been published for all of London's social enlightenment."

"Your wedding announcement?" Julia guessed.

"I'm afraid so." He squeezed Kate's hand. "Under normal circumstances I would not have wished to keep our marriage secret for a single hour. But of course news travels."

"Perhaps I should take Brian elsewhere," Kate said thoughtfully.

"I hope that won't be necessary," Colin said, and although Kate knew he meant to reassure her, she felt only a foreboding. "But I would feel better if you both stayed close to the house until we are sure there is no danger to you."

Chapter 46

$\mathcal{K}$ate wanted to go for a walk. Everyone in Lord Heath's house that night betrayed some sign of restless tension. No one had exchanged more than a polite word or two at supper. Even Heath's massively built footman, Hamm, so cheerful the day Kate had met him, stood now by the window of the drawing room like a gigantic shadow of gloom.

Kate lost at cards against Julia so many times that they quit by silent accord in the middle of the last game.

Sir Gabriel had arrived after supper with two of Colin's Boscastle cousins, Lords Devon and Drake. The three men promised to take Brian riding in the park the following day.

Kate knew why.

It was because Colin, Lord Heath, and Sir Daniel Mallory were sequestered in Heath's study, plotting what they meant to do tonight.

Kate glanced up and saw Brian standing in the doorway. "Do you want to play a hand?"

"With you two?" He grimaced, glancing at the footman, who, Kate guessed, had sent him a sympathetic look. "I'd rather go out to the garden."

"Is it all right, do you think?" she whispered to Julia.

"I'd imagine," Julia said in an undertone. "You can peek out at him from the kitchen window if it makes you feel better. But I wouldn't let him catch you."

Kate nodded as if she agreed, but when Julia picked up a magazine, she looked at the clock on the mantel and decided he could have five minutes alone before she checked. It would give her another excuse to walk by Lord Heath's study. She and Julia had surmised that the three men had agreed to take action tonight, which could only mean they had located Mason and his solicitor. Kate knew that blood would be spilled before morning. Whose she would not dare to speculate.

Kate lasted three minutes before she eased out of her chair and edged to the door. The behemoth footman didn't say a word. Julia merely smiled, continuing to look through her magazine. "I'll only peek once from the kitchen window," Kate promised. "Brian won't even see me."

Colin turned his head, his concentration disturbed by light footsteps in the hall. His wife, he thought, forcing her tempting image from his mind. After tonight, God willing, he would have no greater aim in life than to indulge her and train up his son. Perhaps even the breach between him and Sebastien could be mended.

Heath's voice drew him back to the present. "So you are confident that Hay's plan is to leave England in the next day or two?"

Sir Daniel frowned. He had not removed his coat, nor had he taken his hand once from the walking stick that rested against his armchair. "Hay has leased cheap lodgings under an assumed name in Piccadilly. He withdrew all his funds from the bank yesterday morning. Quite a tidy sum, although most of the firm's creditors have gone unpaid for months."

"May I review the invoices and account books that you have acquired?" Heath asked, his brow drawn.

"By all means," Sir Daniel said. "I don't have them with me. I can send my assistant to bring them to you within the hour."

Heath shook his head. "I won't have time for reading tonight."

"There is an answer in those accounts," Colin said, closing his eyes for a moment. "But I don't know what it is."

Heath stared at him. "What do you mean?"

"Why are there creditors Hay feels comfortable dismissing while others he keeps current?" He stood. The flame of the single candle danced to and fro across the maps of Egypt that covered the wall. "Where is Earling at this moment?"

Sir Daniel's hand closed around the handle of his cane. "Hidden inside Hay's rooms, one assumes. The housekeeper next door said she has seen him peering like a prisoner through the window on several occasions."

Heath looked across his desk at Colin. "If we wait until the morning, there is a chance he will elude you again. I suggest that we act shortly after the lights are extinguished in his lodgings. Agreed, gentlemen?"

Sir Daniel nodded.

Colin answered, "Yes, although I have to confess that I would go there now if you had not tempered my urgency."

Heath smiled gravely. "I'd feel more at ease if our wives and Brian were staying at Grayson's Park Lane house. If I am not out of place, I suggest that we inform your brothers of our plan and allow them to participate. And, I think, the police should know that there might be a spot of trouble in Piccadilly tonight."

Chapter 47

$\mathcal{M}$ ason had taken a hackney to St. James' Street and hidden in a public house until it was dark. If Hay realized Mason had escaped his "protective" captivity, thus jeopardizing their plans to flee, he would desert Mason in an instant.

But if Colin Boscastle spotted Mason loitering on the street behind his cousin's garden, Mason would be dead before he could utter a word in his defense.

He gripped the small package in his hand. He could have sent it to Georgette, but she and her younger children appeared to have fallen off the earth. She had to be inside the town house. Where else could she have found enough funds when to all appearances he had left her without the support he promised?

Now he waited, debating whether he had the courage to knock at Lord Heath's door and put an end to it all. He doubted anyone in the Boscastle family would believe him, but in the end it was only Georgette's opinion that mattered.

He drew behind a parked carriage at the clanking of keys, a woman's voice calling out softly. She was a house-maid, to judge by her cap and apron, and she darted across the street to be caught up in the arms of a burly night watchman.

In dread Mason approached the gate, which she'd propped open with a broomstick. And then he saw the boy's face staring through the opening, into the street, directly at him.

"No, Brian. No. I'm not here to hurt you. I have something for your mother. Just take it and run inside. If you can summon any mercy for me, do not tell anyone but her that you saw me tonight. I did not kill Sir Colin's father. On my honor. Please take this to your mother and you will never hear from me again."

Kate took one look through the kitchen window and went flying to the door. The scullery maid dropped a plate in the small tub and called after her in alarm. "Lady Boscastle, are you all right?"

"There's someone at the gate!" Kate said hurriedly over her shoulder.

The scullery maid ran after her to the door. "It's only the housemaid, my lady, meeting that night watchman again. She'll lose her post for this. She's been cautioned. Shall I fetch a footman or Lord Heath?"

Kate didn't answer, although she'd absorbed the maid's explanation. Heaven knew she couldn't blame Brian for adolescent curiosity. She slowed to a walk. But when she saw him open the gate, the broomstick as a stopper, as he stepped out into the street, she went into a panic. What could he be thinking?

"Brian," she said, breathless, staring up and down the gaslit street and noting nothing out of the ordinary except a small carriage on the corner, the door open. "Brian?"

"I'm right here, Kate," he said in a faint voice she had

to strain to hear. "I was stupid again. I only meant to look outside."

She turned, looking into Mason Earling's anguished face.

"I didn't mean any harm. I just came here to leave something for Georgette. Hay is holding Brian in the carriage with a gun to his chest. I've no doubt he's corrupt enough to use it. You'll have to come with us. I'm more sorry than I can tell you."

Chapter 48

The small carriage sped through the gaslit streets, nearly all unfamiliar to Kate. Her first experience in London should have taught her never to return. She stared at Brian, glancing only once at the gun Hay held in his hand.

"It's my fault," Brian said, his blue eyes awash in self-recrimination.

"It is not," Kate said, swallowing painfully. "I would have been tempted to step outside the gate, too, at your age."

Mason's face twisted into a mask of agony. "He wouldn't have left the garden if I hadn't been followed here by my gaoler. I would have killed myself before threatening a child's life. I only—"

Hay's voice cut him off like a knife. "I would deposit all three of you at the closest church if I hadn't already made other arrangements."

Arrangements.

Kate fought to keep her voice steady as she regarded Hay. "Why? You paid those villagers to harass us—they could have burned down the house or shot one of the children. Did you want Georgette dead so desperately that it didn't matter that you might kill others instead?"

He stared at her in contempt. "I don't give a damn if the whore lives or dies as long as she isn't spending my money."

"*Your* money?" Mason said.

Hay did not acknowledge him. "It was the elderly footman who stood to ruin me. He knew that Mason had poured the wine that killed Joshua Boscastle. I was never sure if he remembered seeing me bring the bottle to Nathan's house the night before."

"You did it," Mason said in disgust. "Yet for years you let my father and then me take the blame."

"Your father knew what I had put in the wine."

"And he asked me to pour it?" Mason said incredulously. "He used me as an instrument of evil and made it appear to be a privilege. Why?"

"Do you think either of us wanted a murder on our hands?"

"My father will stop you," Brian said.

Kate glanced at him in warning.

"Your father," Hay said, "cannot stop a crew of sailors who will do anything for a price."

Mason shook his head. "You said there was no money."

"I said that *you* had no money. According to your legal documents, two shipments have been ruined."

"But we had insurance."

"Not on smuggled goods."

"Why resort to smuggling?"

Hay sighed. "To avoid the revenues that the Crown demands. It costs enough to bribe foreign clerks and pay the salary of the irregular soldiers who protect our overland shipments."

"I *never* agreed to bribery," Mason said.

"It is your signature on the invoices."

"Forgeries," Kate whispered. "He stole the original documents from the house."

Mason looked at her. "I had no idea. I am sorrier than you will ever know."

She didn't answer.

Someone had to have noticed by now that Kate and Brian had not come in from the garden. The scullery maid had seen her leave. Julia must have wondered why she had taken so long to return. She would have notified Heath immediately. The night watchman might have noticed the carriage. But how would Colin know where to find her and Brian? She had no idea of their destination. As the carriage sped onward, all she could do was conceal her apprehension from Brian and hope he would remain as calm as she appeared.

The three men rose, the atmosphere heavy, their intention decided. Lord Heath had just rung for a footman when his wife opened the door. Colin stared at her and knew. Her red hair contrasted vividly against her bloodless face. His mind followed her explanation in horror.

"Hamm has searched the street from corner to corner. Kate and Brian did not come back in the house, but the scullery maid thought she heard carriage wheels when she went outside. They had only gone to the garden for air. The night watchman did not notice anything unusual, but then, he had our housemaid in his arms."

"Go," Heath said to Sir Daniel, who was already on his way to the door. "I want Hay's lodgings searched. Colin, have three horses saddled. It will be faster if we separate. Julia, send Hamm to Park Lane to notify the family."

She stepped aside to allow the men to pass. Colin swore under his breath. "Brian has run away several times," he said tersely. "I pray to God that's all this is."

But for the life of him he could not envision Kate running after Brian without crying to the watchman that she needed help.

The carriage had stopped at the waterfront in what appeared to be the most deserted wharf on the river. She realized then what Hay intended to do. She glanced through the fog down the wharf to the fully rigged ship that sat at anchor. Lights shone in the great cabin, but before she could discern any movement on deck, Hay pushed her down the carriage steps toward a dilapidated warehouse.

She turned, meeting Brian's stare. Whatever he felt did not show. She took a breath and almost gagged on the stench of the Thames, ripe with rotting ordure and an anonymous corpse or two. Then Hay prodded her to move.

Mason watched, helpless and horrified, as two sailors bound Kate and Brian and locked them in a dark, filthy stairwell that led from the warehouse to the waterfront. From its depths he discerned the lap of water against the stairs, a scratching of what he dared not imagine.

Kate had only whispered once to Brian to be brave, that he was practically a man. But the look of defiance on Brian's face took Mason aback. It smacked of the same Boscastle arrogance that Colin and his brothers had boasted years ago when the young blackguards ruled the village.

At least now Mason understood the reason Colin had sought revenge against Mason and his father.

He'd never stood up to anyone in his life, but the time had come.

He swung around, picking out Hay's stooped figure in the lamplight. "I won't allow you to harm either of them. He's still a child, and that woman has done nothing to deserve your misuse. Moreover, I am not leaving England to escape what you have done."

Hay turned from the small desk, on which sat an open valise. His face looked distorted in the lamplight, or perhaps Mason saw what he'd been afraid to see all these years. "Do you think you have a choice? Do you believe for one moment—"

The dull splintering of wood vibrated from the foundations of the warehouse. Hay's features froze in uncertainty. But for the first time in Mason's memory, a deeper instinct broke through his fears. He knew now what to fight for and whom to fight against. He would not be ruled by lies again.

Another muted crash shook the floor. Mason dove for the gun that Hay had placed on the top of his valise. Hay reached out, ripped at the neck of Mason's coat. But Mason had a firm grasp of the gun, and he cocked it, oblivious to everything but the injustice he would finally end.

Kate thought that the river's tidal waters had begun to seep through the door at the bottom of the steps, that she and Brian would drown. It didn't matter that by now Colin must have realized she and Brian were missing. It wouldn't even matter if he knew where to find them. He couldn't arrive soon enough to free them. The tide would not stop for any man. Was there a waterline on the stairs?

Brian, his back to hers, their hands bound together, started at the splinter of wood below. "My father has come to save us," he said with certainty. "I knew he would. It's him, isn't it, Kate? Is it him?"

Two men climbed over the wreckage of the wharf door; another loomed in the background. The first held a lantern that cast his scarred face into strange relief. In one moment he appeared to be young, attractive, a man who would appeal to a woman's sympathy. In the next, his cruel expression extinguished the last spark of hope in her heart. Then he spoke, and his voice scratched like a nail down her spine.

"Listen one more time. I ain't repeatin' myself over and over. Never mind the spices or the damned carpets. Can't drag 'em down the docks and expect the good citizens of London to buy damaged merchandise."

"Not to mention stolen," his companion said over his shoulder.

"What we're goin' for is them shawls. I know they look like useless bits of cloth, but the ladies of Mayfair can't buy enough of 'em."

"My sister 'as one," said the looming hulk in the background. "She calls 'em paisley."

"It's cashmere," the man holding the lantern said, ascending the first step. "It's made of goat 'air, and each one sells for two 'undred pounds."

"For goat 'air? Why?"

"Who the 'ell knows? But put 'em all in the bags, careful like. You're not stuffin' a mattress. They gotta look new, not wrinkled like your ugly mug. When we're finished—"

He lifted the lantern and stared up into Kate's face. For the rest of her life she would wonder which of them received the greatest shock. She made an unintelligible sound in her throat. The man reared back, knocking against his two companions.

"What is it, Nick? The police? Damn it all. You should never 'ave promised Millie you'd fetch 'er a shawl to make up for what you did."

"God bless," the man named Nick said, evidently recovered enough from his shock to climb another step. "What do we 'ave blocking our way? A pair of lovers? Ain't that a sight to warm your bowels?"

Kate rushed to explain before he could enact any of

the grim acts of which he looked capable. "We have been abducted from my cousin's home by a man who is going to kill us, and he's liable to kill you, too, if he realizes you've broken into the warehouse." She drew a breath. "You are thieves, I assume? Not that I have anything but compassion for the lower classes who are reduced to criminal deeds in order to put bread on the table for their children—"

"Are we thieves, she asks?" the hulk in the background said with a guffaw that echoed through the stairwell. "You 'appen to be addressing the Arch Rogue of St. Giles—"

"Will you shut your trap?" the leader, who held the lantern, said in disgust. "The next thing I know you'll be 'anding out our reward posters and offering to sign your X for posterior's sake." He crept up the remaining steps. His gaze pensive, he examined Kate's silk dress, the ring Colin had recently placed on her finger, the ropes that bound her hands and feet. "I've 'ad considerable experience with the ladies," he mused, "and I gotta admit you don't strike me as a female who'd cause a man enough grief to wrap you up for Christmas."

"Oh, thank—"

"On the other 'and, I perceive you're a few chapters short of a story."

"Of course there's more to it than what I've told you," Kate said, blinking from the glare of the lantern he held to her face. She felt Brian shift, straining to see over his shoulder. She dug her nails into his knuckles to discourage him from saying anything that would worsen the situation. "But we—we don't have all night. Can you please set us free? We'll never tell anyone we saw you."

He shook his head. "Do I look like a charity worker? I set you free, and the next thing I know, you'll be screamin' your 'ead off, and what will I get for my trouble? A nice room at Newgate, rats and manacles compliments of the 'ouse."

"My husband will reward you for your bravery," she whispered, drawing back from the alcohol fumes he breathed down into her face.

His focus sharpened. He glanced again at her wedding ring. "A reward?"

"I swear that you will not be sorry. Set us loose and your reward will be greater than all the shawls your lady loves could wear in a lifetime."

"If you or that boy utters one solitary word that I set you loose as a kindness, I ain't gonna be pleased."

"I won't. We won't. But don't go in the warehouse. In fact, run from these docks as soon as you untie us. There is going to be a murder in that office tonight. You do not wish to be involved."

He shrugged. "It ain't as if it'd be the first time. Still, I never liked seein' anyone trussed up or chained," he said, pulling a knife from his boot. "I'll take you up on that offer of a reward. You just tell his nibs that Nick Rydell came to the rescue. Remember my name because I ain't waitin' around to shake the constable's 'and."

Kate squeezed her eyes shut as he sawed expertly through the rope. "Bless you. I'll never forget you."

"You better not. And what did you say your name was, my little treasure chest?"

"It's Kate—I'm Lady Boscastle. My husband is Sir—"

"Oh, my God." She flinched at the sneer that crossed his face. "What? Am I under a curse? Please don't tell me you keep a diary, too."

Her eyes lit with hope. "I am writing my mistress's memoirs. How could you possibly know?"

The report of a pistol from inside the warehouse startled both of them into silence. Before she could shake the blood back into her wrists and reach for Brian, their three uncouth rescuers had clambered over the wreckage of the door below and escaped through the water to the wharf.

Brian shot to his feet, bringing Kate with him. "What are we going to do?" he asked, staring at the water rising to their knees.

"Go as quickly as you can down the steps, and then run. Run in the direction of those men and do not wait for me if I can't keep up."

The three horsemen dismounted in the fog that drifted from the river. Colin detected footsteps thudding into the warren of alleys that led from the waterfront. *An escape,* he thought. He had arrived too late.

Gabriel glanced up, his voice grave. "Do I give chase or stay with you?"

Colin felt Sebastien brush past him. He stared at the anchored ship.

"There's a light coming from the warehouse," Sebastien said, breaking into a run. "I guarantee that was not your wife or son we heard running."

Sebastien was right. Neither Kate nor Brian knew the waterfront well enough to navigate it by instinct. He turned briefly. "Take the ship."

But as he started after Sebastien, he saw two figures darting through the fog. Two beloved faces materialized that he hadn't been certain he would ever see again.

He caught Kate in a hard embrace. Her hair hung down her back in snarls. Water stains reached to the waist of her off-white dress. "You and Brian stay here with Gabriel," he said, his voice hoarse with relief.

"It isn't what you think," she said brokenly as he released her into his brother's care. "Mason didn't kill your father. But I think he might be dead. I heard a gunshot. Hay threatened to kill all of us."

He pivoted and broke into a run, using Sebastien's figure as a guidepost. Sebastien, who like Heath had suffered and sacrificed during the war. It was only right that he should be the family hero. It was only fair that Sebastien claim whatever justice there was to be found inside that warehouse.

But his brother needed a defender at his back. He drew his gun as Sebastien threw open the main door to the warehouse. And there stood before them the man whose life Colin had ruined and would have taken in his misguided quest for honor. Mason held a gun loosely in his hand. Blood trickled from his mouth. Hay lay unmoving on the floor, a valise and its contents scattered around his body. Sebastien moved without hesitation to Hay's body and knelt to take his pulse.

Mason handed Colin the gun. "I killed him. Do what you want now to me. I did not poison your father, but Hay and my father used me for years, and now I have broken the cycle. Whatever punishment I will have to face is worth it. Whatever money the company has made is not mine. I have nothing, but I am not afraid at least."

Chapter 49

London

Colin rode his mare alongside Sebastien's stallion on Hyde Park's crowded track. Gabriel and Brian had trotted ahead, nodding to friends who greeted Gabriel on the row.

At length Sebastien said, "Sir Daniel confirmed to Heath this morning that the hero at the waterfront is indeed a criminal named Nick Rydell."

"I don't care if he has a tail and horns," Colin said. "I cannot bear to think what would have happened without him."

"His followers call him the Arch Rogue of St. Giles, leader of dark wiles."

"What reward has he demanded?"

Sebastien glanced at him in amusement. "He's asked for a night at Audrey Watson's House of Venus, all accommodations provided."

"And nothing else?"

"You haven't been in London very long," Sebastien said. "A night with Audrey would bankrupt the ordinary citizen."

"At least he didn't ask for Georgette's services."

They rode together in silence until Sebastien said, "Are you at peace with the past now?"

"Not exactly," Colin said. "I set out to be a hero and might have killed an innocent man to satisfy my honor. It does not give me peace to realize that I could have been a murderer."

"But at least you learned the truth," Sebastien said, staring across the park. "And you have the chance to begin again."

"With you?"

A smile crept across Sebastien's face. "Only if you swear that you will never charge off on another crusade without asking me to join you."

Colin slowed his mare, allowing two other riders to pass. "What crusades are left for me to fight? The war is over. I have come back home to stay."

"It was high time, too."

"Then I am forgiven?"

Sebastien started to laugh. "How could I hold a grudge against the brother who corrupted me? I don't know if I would have survived the war without the lessons you taught me when we ran away."

Colin grinned. "Perhaps you can give me a few lessons in return. Kate and I are visiting Georgette and Mason early this evening, and tomorrow night we're all attending the opera. I don't know how I'll be able to pay attention to anything but my wife."

"I'm afraid I have the same problem. The inability to think straight is what happens to a Boscastle in love."

The quill moved quickly across the foolscap, the writer struggling to put down the words dictated by the woman sitting at her dressing table.

> *I have a waiting list of lovers whose names I shall not reveal until I publish the second installment of my sinful life.*

The writer glanced up from the desk. "I will definitely revise this page. It should read: 'I have a waiting list of lovers whose names I shall forget, as I have entered the second installment of my life—marriage to the man I adore and maternal devotion to the children I will give him.'"

"That makes me sound like a schoolmistress, Mason," Georgette said, a perfume stopper in her hand. "I am not publishing a book on housekeeping. I have no experience in domestic affairs."

Mason glanced down at the clothes overflowing the three trunks on the floor. "I can't disagree with you on that."

"I have more appealing knowledge to impart."

He smiled. "Whatever knowledge you share will not leave this bedchamber, madam. I won't interfere with the publication of your first book. I will remind you, however, that you are still under obligation to me."

"You—"

"I did not draw up or sign a notice terminating our contract. That was a forgery."

Georgette turned, her eyes bright with challenge. "What are you trying to say?"

"I can either take you to court or take you as my wife. The choice is yours. I suggest that in the meantime you finish putting on some clothes. Our company is due to arrive within the hour."

Chapter 50

$\mathcal{B}$rian knocked at the door of his mother's town house, looking like such a young gentleman in his long black coat and pantaloons that Kate was overcome with pride. In fact, it took Bledridge a moment to recognize Brian, while Griswold, who had also come to answer the imperious knock, greeted the young master without any hesitation.

"Sir Colin, Lady Boscastle," Bledridge said with a bow, "allow me to take you into the drawing room. Griswold, please inform Mr. Earling and Mrs. Lawson that their guests have arrived for tea. And Master Brian—"

Bledridge looked around. Kate shook her head. Brian had already pounded up the stairs, presumably to find his mother and siblings, judging by the screams of joy that resounded through the house.

Colin laughed. "One would think they had been parted for a year and not a week."

"One would think they'd had an atrocious upbringing by the din they are making," Kate said.

Colin stared at her. "I like the sound of children's laughter."

Bledridge cleared his throat. "Would you prefer to

wait in the drawing room? Madam does take some time at her toilette."

"Don't I know it," Kate murmured.

Moments later Bledridge ushered them into a small room that overlooked the street. To Kate's pleased surprise, the furnishings reflected a simple but expensive taste. Of course, she hadn't seen Georgette's bedchamber yet.

"Well," she whispered to Colin, "what do you think?"

He looked at the white satin sofa. "I would hazard a guess that the children are forbidden to step one foot inside this room."

They sat down carefully together on the sofa. "This is rather awkward," he said under his breath. "What does one say to the man he has wrongly persecuted?"

Kate didn't have an opportunity to answer. Georgette came floating into the room in a pale yellow morning dress, Mason trailing closely in her cloud of perfume.

Colin drew Kate to her feet. She rushed forward to embrace Georgette. "You look ravishing, as to be expected, madam," she said. "I've missed you so much."

"I've missed you more," Georgette said with her usual frankness. "Mason is a thoughtful lover, but he's hopeless as a companion, and Nan has not approved of a single governess who has applied for your position. No one will ever compare to you, Kate."

Mason had wavered when he entered the room, hoping that Georgette or Kate would guide him through his conversation with Sir Colin. But the two women left him alone, and when he glanced up he realized that Colin had extended his hand to him in a gesture of conciliation.

"Sir," he said, "it is an honor to receive you in my house."

Colin looked him in the eye. "It's an honor to be invited. I expect that we'll meet quite often to discuss business matters. I am quite confident that the company will thrive under your management. Of course, the ultimate decision will be made by my eldest brother. I understand that he is returning to England."

"You would be willing to trust me?" Mason shook his head in disbelief. "After all the grief that my father and Hay caused your family?"

"You took care of my son when I was unaware that he existed."

Mason smiled. "I only caught a glimpse of him running through the hall to his mother, but I vow he has grown two feet taller since we lived in East Crowleigh. I am fond of him."

Colin laughed. "I became attached to his brother and sister myself."

"Oh, yes. They consider 'Castle' to be quite the hero."

"Then perhaps we can consider each other to be friends as well as business partners."

Epilogue

Colin watched his wife undress for bed later that night. "There was a moment tonight as we arrived at the opera that the crowd came between us. I felt sheer panic. I love you so much that at times I wish I *could* keep you to myself in a tower."

Kate reached for her night rail only to find herself naked in his arms, falling beneath him on the bed. His mouth covered hers, his kisses as essential to her as breathing.

"If it's any consolation," she whispered when he sat up to remove his shirt, "I think you might want to hide in a tower yourself when Georgette's memoirs are published."

He grimaced. "Then what she has revealed about me is truly that unflattering?"

She rose to pull his shirt from his shoulders, her eyes illumined with mischief. "On the contrary—what is written about you will make you the object of every woman's secret desire. I'm afraid that from the moment her book is published, I won't be able to let you out of my sight."

"Then don't. And I shall be forced to become the object of your secret desires alone. I believe between that duty and raising a family, I will have no incentive to care what other women think of me."

Continue reading for a special preview
of Jillian Hunter's next sensual and
exciting historical romance in the
Boscastle Affairs series,

The Countess Confessions

Coming from Signet Select in February 2014,
available wherever books and e-books
are sold!

$\mathcal{T}$he fortune-teller's tent was the scandal of the party. It huddled beyond the reach of the light shed by lanterns that twinkled in the trees. Even the footmen positioned in the garden wondered whether it had been pitched illegally or for entertainment. Judging by the chattering young ladies and gentlemen lined up on the footbridge to the dark hollow where the gypsy had encamped, no one cared why she was there as long as she predicted romance.

Here today. Gone tomorrow. A gypsy never stayed in one place for long. Few of the well-heeled guests would have found the courage to approach her if she had not appeared at the party. What an enchanting surprise.

"Lord Fowler must have paid her. She's reading for free, I heard."

"Well, I hope she doesn't run out of inspiration before my turn."

Inspiration? It was patience the fortune-teller needed. So far Miss Emily Selwick had predicted only happy outcomes for the lovelorn, and those had exhausted her talent for deception. The fifth person to seek her services happened to be a cad whom Emily disliked too much to hide her distaste. He whipped his horse to show off, treated his servants like lumps of dirt, and stared with vulgar fascination down Emily's bodice while she feigned interest in the palm of his left hand.

"I fear, Mr. Prickett, that your palm reveals a short lifeline." She drew her hand from his and slid back into her creaking chair.

"Nonsense," he said in an indolent voice. "Longevity runs in the family. Give me the name of the next lady fortunate enough to share my bed."

"Toad."

"I beg your pardon." His face portrayed the conceit of a man who refused to believe he had been dealt an insult. "Did you say 'Miss Todd'? I don't know anyone by that name. Is she here tonight? A lady I've yet to meet?"

"How should I—"

A loud cough from behind the tent reminded Emily that a fortune-teller told her clients what they wanted to hear, not the truth. But, honestly, what did she know of palm reading and tarot cards? Only what her half brother Michael had unwillingly crammed into her head.

She could not have been in her right mind when she had allowed her friend Lucy, Lord Fowler's daughter, to talk her into this scheme. Emily should have listened to Michael instead of letting Lucy's enthusiasm for matchmaking erode her judgment.

"You are desperate, Emily."

"I am desperately in love, yes."

"With a gentlemen who does not realize you exist."

"Perhaps it's for the best," Emily had suggested. "He notices other ladies. I've tried to make him notice me."

"You might have been too obvious."

"And wearing a curly black wig, tinting my skin, and telling omens is a subtle way to draw his attention?"

"You will not be Emily. You shall be a fortune-teller

who slips Emily's name into his thoughts. As soon as you're finished, you will disappear, remove your disguise, and become Emily again."

Mr. Prickett's voice startled her back into her role. "Where am I to meet this lady?" he asked, apparently unaware that his plans for a lustful evening were of no concern to Emily.

Her brother bumped up against the tent, another warning to her. Michael was invigorated by his mystical Romany blood, which came from the secret affair their mother had carried on a month before she married the man who had believed himself to be Michael's father and *was* Emily's. When the young baroness was dying she had revealed the truth to her husband, cleansing her conscience and creating hostility between the baron and Michael that continued to this day. Only after Michael returned from war had he and the baron made a tenuous peace. It would be a humiliation for the baron to admit he had been cuckolded, that his only son and heir was not his own.

Mr. Prickett's voice jarred her again. "What else do you see for me and this woman?"

"Separation. Woe. Perhaps even a lawsuit."

He frowned. "Why don't you give the cards a try?"

"The reading is over," she said. "I have lost contact with the other side."

"What other side?" he demanded with a doubtful look.

The other side of the tent. The side of her that claimed some link to sanity. "Go," she said, rising from the noisy chair.

"But—"

"Next!"

He started to protest until a masked lady entered, forcing him to either make a scene or an exit. Fortunately he chose to leave. The lady who hurried around him perched on the stool in front of Emily's table. "Well?" she asked, biting her lip as she lowered her Venetian half mask. "Is our little fortune-teller ready to meet her fate?"

She stared across the table at Lucy's cheerful face. "Is he outside?" she whispered.

"He certainly is."

"How does he look?"

"No different than usual. Are you going to read my cards?"

"Not again. We spent all last night reading them, and Michael has given me so many details about the deck that I'm afraid I don't remember what all the inverted positions mean."

"Make them up. None of us at the party know. There's only one person who matters. Read the future in my palm." She held out her hand. "Practice for your next customer."

"I can predict your future if, against all odds, I manage to convince Cooper that he and I belong together. You will be a bridesmaid at our wedding."

"How lovely."

"But if by any chance he recognizes me, you and I will be found out and sent to our aunts for discipline. We shall spend the next season in disgrace."

A pleasant male voice called from the head of the line outside the tent's entrance. "Are you almost done in there? The band is tuning up in the ballroom, and champagne is being served. We don't want to miss the dance."

"That's him," Lucy said as if Emily would not recognize the voice that haunted her dreams. "I'll slip out the back and listen. Or do you prefer privacy?"

"Privacy? Michael has his ear to the tent so that I don't make an utter fool of myself. You might as well return to the party before your father finds out what we've done."

"Don't worry about him. He's too busy entertaining his important—"

A commotion of raised male voices, one of them Cooper's, diverted Lucy and Emily's attention. It sounded as if he and another man were exchanging words. But Cooper never quarreled. His even temper was one of the qualities Emily adored.

"Are they arguing?" Lucy whispered, her eyes wide with disbelief.

"Hush. I think so."

"Well," Cooper said, more placating than combative, "I *have* been standing in line a dashed long time, sir, but if you are in a hurry, I suppose I—"

Emily could not make out what else Cooper said. A deeper voice responded, and there followed a silence.

"I shall investigate," Lucy said before Emily, prompted by instinct, could ask her to stay.

She reached for the handle of the basket, in which several decks of tarot cards sat neatly tied in red silk ribbons. "Michael?" she said over her shoulder, but he gave no answer. Had he left his post to investigate the disturbance? She turned her head to glimpse Lucy escaping the tent. No sooner had her friend disappeared than the seventh person stepped inside.

Seven. It was a mystical number from ancient times. Michael might not believe in their mother's superstitions, but he did not disbelieve, either. When he'd suggested that assigning Cooper a number in line would give Emily time to prepare herself for his reading, she hadn't realized that she would become such a popular attraction at the party.

But Michael was gone. And the stranger standing before her in all his charismatic arrogance did not resemble the man she had expected, in demeanor or appearance. His hard face might not have disconcerted Emily if she had met the man before and had developed some immunity to his impact.

Seven.

Seven was a lucky number.

There were the Seven Hills of Rome. Seven sisters of the Pleiades. Seven days in the week. Seven archangels. Seventh heaven. Shakespeare's seven ages of man.

The number did, however, possess some dark connotations. An English gentlewoman visiting London would never want to explore the stews of Seven Dials. And wasn't there a fairy-tale giant who wore seven-league boots?

Emily leaned all the way back in her chair and stared at her seventh customer as he sat down casually on the stool. He cast an enormous shadow in the candlelit tent. He was wearing boots, too, with a long black evening jacket over a white shirt, and a pair of black pantaloons. She had *never* seen him before. She would not have forgotten those impious blue eyes and the smile that said he fully expected to be forgiven for ruining her scheme.

"I hope you don't mind my switching places with the other young man in line," he said, his gaze taking in her appearance as if he sensed there was something odd about it but he wasn't sure what. "I ran into a spot of embarrassment at the party. I noticed a person I wasn't ready to encounter quite yet. I needed a place to hide out to collect my thoughts."

"What happened to the man who was next in line?" Emily asked, taken back by his aplomb.

"Who? Oh, *him*. He was kind enough to give me his place."

"But . . . did he leave?"

"I've no idea. Does it matter?"

She realized then that there were seven deadly sins, and that the man who stared back at her with false guile looked prepared to commit at least one of them before the night came to an end.

Also available from
New York Times bestselling author

Jillian Hunter

THE DUCHESS DIARIES
The Bridal Pleasures Series

As headmistress of the Scarfield Academy for
Young Ladies, Miss Charlotte Boscastle is tasked with
keeping her charges free from notoriety. But when
Charlotte's diary goes missing, she can't imagine
having her most intimate secrets fall into the
wrong hands.

Although the confessions in the diary he found spark
his interest, the Duke of Wynfield has every intention
of returning the journal. But when Gideon's encounter
with Charlotte takes on an unexpectedly passionate
nature, his indiscretion causes a scandal that only
marriage can cure...

**Available wherever books are sold or at
penguin.com**

facebook.com/LoveAlwaysBooks

Also available from
New York Times bestselling author

Jillian Hunter

A DUKE'S TEMPTATION
The Bridal Pleasures Series

The Duke of Gravenhurst, a notorious author of
scandalous romances, is accused of corrupting the
morals of the public. But among his most
devoted fans is the well-born Lily Boscastle,
who seeks employment as the duke's personal
housekeeper. Only then does she discover dark
secrets about the man that she never
could have imagined.

**Available wherever books are sold or at
penguin.com**

facebook.com/LoveAlwaysBooks

S0205

Also available from
New York Times bestselling author

Jillian Hunter

A BRIDE UNVEILED
The Bridal Pleasures Series

Violet Knowlton is betrothed to the sensible, if
tedious, Sir Godfrey Maitland. When Godfrey escorts
her to a fencing demonstration, she looks forward to
the adventurous diversion, but everything changes
when she realizes the swordsman displaying his skill—
and dashing good looks—is none other than her
childhood friend Kit.

Soon the flames of their forbidden past ignite into a
passion neither can refuse. Although Violet has been
promised to another, Kit remains her first and only
love. He vows he will possess her, no matter what
stands in his way...

**Available wherever books are sold or at
penguin.com**

facebook.com/LoveAlwaysBooks

S0325